V.C. DEATH

When Major Falconi's signal sounded, Archie took a step back from the window, raised his silenced pistol in both hands and slowly, calmly squeezed the trigger. The window shattered, and Mr. Ngoc's bodyguard bounced off the wall. Still standing, his body rebounded forward. His hips collided with a chair, and he sprawled onto the table in the middle of three V.C. agents. They were taken completely by surprise.

Major Falconi crashed into the room and shouted, first in Vietnamese and then in English, "Don't anybody move!"

But one man refused to heed Falconi's order.

The Falcon lashed out with a twisting punch from his hip, directing the first knuckles of his index and middle finger into the agent's soft gut. The punch penetrated the untensed, yielding muscles, and his fist rammed home against the front of the man's spinal cord. Then Falconi hit him on the bridge of the nose, breaking the cartilage. He used the heel of his hand in a swift, upward stroke to drive the sharp fragments up into the agent's brain.

Falconi received no more resistance from the others. . . .

THE BLACK EAGLES
by John Lansing

#1: HANOI HELLGROUND (1249, $2.95)
They're the best jungle fighters the United States has to offer, and
no matter where Charlie is hiding, they'll find him. They're the
greatest unsung heroes of the dirtiest, most challenging war of all
time. They're THE BLACK EAGLES.

#2: MEKONG MASSACRE (1294, $2.50)
Falconi and his Black Eagle combat team are about to stake a
claim on Colonel Nguyen Chi Roi — and give the Commie his due.
But American intelligence wants the colonel alive, making this
the Black Eagles' toughest assignment ever!

#4: PUNGI PATROL (1389, $2.50)
A team of specially trained East German agents — disguised as
U.S. soldiers — is slaughtering helpless Vietnamese villagers to
discredit America. The Black Eagles, the elite jungle fighters,
have been ordered to stop the butchers before our own allies turn
against us!

#5: SAIGON SLAUGHTER (1476, $2.50)
Pulled off active operations after having been decimated by the
NVA, the Eagles fight their own private war of survival in the
streets of Saigon — battling the enemy assassins who've been sent
to finish them off!

#6: AK-47 FIREFIGHT (1542, $2.50)
Sent to stop the deadly flow of AK-47s and ammunition down
the Ho Chi Minh trail, the Black Eagles find the North Vietnamese convoys so heavily guarded it seems a suicide mission. But the
men believe in their leader Falconi, and if he says they can do it,
by God they'll do it!

*Available wherever paperbacks are sold, or order direct from the
Publisher. Send cover price plus 50¢ per copy for mailing and
handling to Zebra Books, Dept. 1677, 475 Park Avenue South,
New York, N.Y. 10016. DO NOT SEND CASH.*

#8
BOOCOO DEATH

BY JOHN LANSING

ZEBRA BOOKS
KENSINGTON PUBLISHING CORP.

ZEBRA BOOKS

are published by

Kensington Publishing Corp.
475 Park Avenue South
New York, NY 10016

First printing: October 1985

Printed in the United States of America

Dedicated to
Susan Cheney

Special Acknowledgement to
David Cheney
and
W. L. Fieldhouse

Chapter One

Seven days had passed since the tiger began his itinerant journey from Cambodia into South Vietnam. His bed of grass, which lay within the sanctuary of the shadows, was tossed and shaken by the pattern of bombs dropped from the flight of United States Air Force B-fifty-two bombers passing overhead.

The detonation of the bombs, one half mile from the tiger's nest, was equal to an earthquake of six on the Richter scale.

The incident disturbed the tiger's sense of territory. He followed the spore of game which had fled radially from the area of the airstrike. It was during this trek that he found the first bodies of the Viet Cong.

The bombing woke the tiger from his three day long after-dinner slumber and did little to quiet the churning of his empty stomach. In the natural course of events a hunt that evening would have followed his awakening. But the recently mangled flesh of the V.C. aroused his senses and feeding behavior.

The tiger's instincts told him there was no sense in letting fresh meat go to waste. Although a predator, he was not above scavenging.

He did, however, forego his natural practice of camping out by the kill and eating and sleeping in alternating shifts until nothing was left of his victim but the stomach and the bones. The disturbance of his psyche prevented him from staying in one place that long.

The feline continued his westward journey. A new entrée had been added to his menu of proper prey, an entrée normally sampled only by the aged, diseased, or crippled among tigers. His fall from grace had been prompted more by opportunity than by necessity. But that made no difference in the scheme of things.

The tiger was not yet aware of it, but his status had changed. He was now a man-eater.

He migrated West through the increasingly disturbed swampland of the Mekong Delta. His natural prey were spooked by the unnatural rhythms of human warfare. They became more difficult to capture, and his feeding periods became farther apart.

Thus the tiger's memory drifted back and focused on his meal of Viet Cong and his perception generalized from the dead to the living. In his feline fashion he was terribly efficient at creating carrion where there was none before.

The lord of the big cats padded silently forward under the shadow of the mangrove swamp. Thus far he had crossed one major river and two irrigation canals. Crossing water channels posed no problem for the ponderous beast.

The primordial origin of his species was the tundra of Ice-Age Siberia. Hence his design was long on overcoat and short on cooling capability. Water usually came as a relief rather than a hindrance. But he shared with all the other creatures of the swamp the hazards peculiar to marine passages.

Although the tiger is superior in most respects to the lion, the reputed King of Beasts, the jungle can still pose threats to his existence: He can be mashed flat by elephants; trampled and gored by water buffalo; or even worried to death by packs of wild dogs.

Therefore, in a more normal setting he would hunt only in the darkest hours, striking his victim swiftly, and melting into the night scarcely having been seen or heard.

But the tiger's search for new territory found him coursing the trails of the delta in daylight, exposed and unaccustomed to the bright sun. As he prepared to cross the next river he chanced upon one of the local fauna with sufficient prowess and strength to challenge him.

When necessary, the tiger is an excellent swimmer, but, he is not, in the last analysis, an aquatic creature.

The crocodile became aware of the presence of the big cat when the tiger plopped his paw into the shallows of the river. The croc waited until the unknown prey waded into deeper water a few feet closer, then made an exploratory sweep with his tail.

To the tiger it seemed that a moss-covered, floating green log suddenly swept swiftly sideways, dislodging his feet from beneath him. Reflexively the tiger continued his roll and, having regained his feet, sought his attacker.

The crocodile's head came out of the water as he started another sweep of his tail. This time the tiger was prepared. His paws cleared the sweeping tail beneath him in a coordinated hop, and he pounced onto the neck of the croc using his traditional mode of attack. He expected his fangs to meet the soft, nonresisting flesh of a warm-blooded animal followed by the satisfying crunch of the vertebrae.

But the crocodile's hide was the product of the action of the symbiotic commensal organisms on his skin and the weathering of wind, water, and sun.

The big cat was startled when his fangs barely dented the frozen, salt water taffy consistency of the croc's hide. He relaxed the grip of his fangs to get better purchase. The croc used the opportunity to roll free and set up his

9

tail for another strike.

Then the tiger lunged at the croc's exposed throat to attempt his second favorite technique of death: suffocation. At the same time his rear paws beat a tattoo rhythm on the croc's abdomen, unsheathing his claws for an attempt at disembowlment.

But the damage to the croc's belly was minor, creating only a pink, frothy fringe of cutaneous confetti. The momentum of the crocodile's swinging tail rolled them both over into deeper water, and the tiger released his grip a second time, shaking the water from his whiskers.

The crocodile was finally in a position to snap his jaws on the striped nemesis. He was known to have the capability to leap six feet out of the water in order to take prey from the bank of a river.

However, at that moment the tiger chose to bound the length of his ten foot long body to regain his natural position on land. The soaking hadn't bothered him enough to break off the battle, but he found his inability to breath under water a disturbing disadvantage.

The tiger vented his rage and frustration in a tremendous reverberating roar and watched the crocodile scull downriver. He seemed to have completely regained his former confidence and dignity. But he walked parallel to the shoreline for a long time before finally crossing the river.

Trang Mei waved good-bye to her fifteen-year-old brother as she departed the rice fields for the short walk back to her village in the western province of Dinh Tuong. Today she had brought him rice balls and *nuoc mam*, the pungent fish sauce that was the daily staple of the Vietnam diet.

This was her last year in school. Her people were poor rural villagers of meager means, unable to afford to pay her expenses for the private school that would be necessary so far from the larger cities.

Thus far in school she had been taught the Vietnamese language, national history, as well as geography and civics. Mei was proud to have advanced beyond the minimum three years required by the government. She regretted being so close to, yet not receiving the *certificat d'etudes primaries*, the certificate of primary studies. She felt certain she would have passed the examination.

Next year, at the age of twelve, she would begin to assume some of her adult responsibilities at home and in the rice fields. As she walked the dirt pathway her satin black shorts and shirt accentuated the long flowing jet-black hair which trailed behind her. It bounced with every movement of her head.

Mei was also proud that her mother Trang Cam trusted her to make the journey alone. Many of the boys her age from the village would have used the opportunity to disappear until evening mealtime. Unlike them, she was a well-trained, obedient daughter who venerated her elders, living and dead, as decreed by custom.

Every holiday she repeated the names of her ancestors going back seven generations, as they were recited by her father, Trang Van, head of the Trang toc in her village. Long ago she had learned which flowers her mother favored to be displayed on the hardwood family altar in their home.

The Trang family practiced ancestor worship more as a custom than a religion. It was part of their Confucian heritage. They were Catholics who had fled the north after the partition in 1954.

The tiger heard Mei before he saw the girl or caught her scent. The sound of her wooden sandals scuffing against the hard-packed dirt pathway was a percussive

11

punctuation to the rustling leaves stirred by the wind and the scurrying of small animals in the bush.

He positioned himself off the pathway in heavy foliage and crouched, motionless, his muscles tense and ready. The tiger's instinctive preparation was thorough and well disciplined. Not a leaf was left drifting in the air, nor a puff of dust floating above the ground as he padded forward swinging behind the passing girl.

His enormous paw appeared suddenly in front of her, the claws biting into her solar plexus, her balance point, and knocking the wind from her. The movement of his paw snatched her bodily from the surface of the path, leaving her sandals positioned for her next step. Where Mei's tracks ended only the tiger's continued.

The tiger had only to take a few short hops on three legs, grasping her tightly against his body with his paw, to be completely enveloped by jungle growth. In the shadows, the last sight she saw was a huge whiskered head. Then he grasped her throat with his mouth and robbed her of her breath.

The tongue of a tiger has a texture somewhere between coarse sandpaper and a wood rasp file. With one paw on her torso he pinned the body of the small girl to the earth and licked the flesh from her still reflexively wriggling lower abdomen.

"Mrs. Cam, Mrs. Cam!" the man spoke urgently. "A tiger has been sighted to the east, near the rice fields."

Trang Cam was worried about her daughter Mei, who had not returned from the rice fields. But as the wife of the number one son, Trang Van, head of the Trang toc in this area, she would be expected to organize an effort to deal with the beast.

Trang Van was in Saigon, forty miles away, meeting with government officials. Cam was well aware of the high mortality rate of adolescents and infants in her environment. But she could have better accepted the shock of losing Mei to a poisonous insect or snake bite or to one of the many diseases due to marginal sanitation.

Tigers were another matter. Their very image evoked portents of vengeful spirits and the grim reaper, as though to be slain by a tiger was a curse on the family and village of the victim.

Cam had heard of instances where the more primitive, superstitious peasants abandoned their village site after a tiger attack. She would not permit such a calamitous consequence for her clan and the other people of the village who trusted and depended on her.

"We must ask the Viet Cong to kill the tiger or drive it away," said the man, with certainty in his voice. But his certainty was short-lived. Soon he began to fidget and glance nervously at the jungle.

Cam was reluctant to ask the Viet Cong for help because she remembered a recent incident when the V.C., who normally only roamed free at night, had made a rare appearance in the daylight to punish a busload of second year students whose parents disobeyed the guerrilla's directive to stay away from the government school.

One of the children was chosen at random, and a sharp splinter of bamboo was driven into his ear, puncturing the eardrum.

None the less, Cam concluded, the Viet Cong were the nearest men available with guns.

Finally, a group of V.C. was found liberating rice supplies from an outlying member of the village. When told of the tiger attack, the leader unconsciously held his ancient, French, bolt-action rifle closer to his body. He urged the men under his command to load the rice faster and make ready to move out. In a gesture of bravado he replied to her request for assistance. "Woman, you have more to fear from us than from a tiger. Make sure there are more rice balls and dried fish for us when we come back later this week."

Upon her return to the village Cam's worst fears were realized. Mei's sandals were found near the trail to the rice fields. The remains of the young girl were found close by.

Cam had managed to retain her composure to bolster the confidence of the others but now broke down and wept bitterly.

"How have I offended God so terribly that my Mei has been taken from me!"

She was angry at the Viet Cong, angry at the bearer of the bad news and angry that, at this point in mid-life, her role as mother to such an excellent daughter was robbed from her so cruelly.

She couldn't bear to accompany the other villagers to bring back the body of her beloved Mei. Except for the well-to-do, bodies were not embalmed in Vietnam and must be put to rest quickly.

Cam sent word to the next village, where they had a radio, to notify her husband near Saigon. But she feared he would not return quickly enough to oversee the beginning of the funeral. A candlelight rosary was planned that night near the center of the village. She found and laid out Mei's best dress which had been received as a gift during the last Tet celebration.

The villagers were returning with Mei's body draped in a clean linen sheet. Cam tentatively pulled it back, released it, and patted it tenderly.

"The bruising is not too bad around her neck," consoled Cam's nearest neighbor and nonrelated confidant. "A little tinted lime powder should take care of it."

A pug mark pattern of claw punctures covered the girl's entire diaphragm. The raw redness that began

14

below that point was farther than her mother could bear to look.

Mei's face reflected peaceful repose, no longer vulnerable to the ravages of nature and chance. The shock of finding herself in the tiger's grasp had caused the release of Mei's natural endorphins, pain-killing hormones, in response to the horror. She now possessed the peace of a small sparrow in the grasp of a hawk's talons. It was evident that her mind had been spared any further suffering.

The false dawn was ending. The rain-dampened surfaces of Saigon reflected the golden sunlight which burned away the mists and low lying clouds. A windowpane, a galvanized roof, a standing pool of water in a parking lot massaged and transformed the hints of dawn which poked gently through the lace curtains of the second-story apartment in the east of the city. With their last influence they illuminated a complementary patch of bronze skin on the bed, giving it a gray cast.

The light was still too dim to resolve the shape into anything recognizable. It was too round for a chin, too sharp for a shoulder.

Maj. Robert Falconi leaned forward on his elbows and blew softly on the quiescent nipple, still embedded in the center of the areola. The woman moaned softly, rolled onto one shoulder and turned her face away from him.

He couldn't be sure that she was not still asleep. Increasing his precarious inclination he blew again and watched the nipple grow until it protruded erotically from the pear-shaped golden breast.

A smile stretched the lips of the lovely Eurasian face. Major Falconi discovered that a part of his body, already aroused by the situation, was abruptly and firmly in Andrea's grasp. He hadn't sensed the movement of her hand beneath the satin sheets.

"Robert," she addressed him sleepily. "You've left me lopsided. I demand you rectify the situation immediately."

"More than a mouthful is a waste," he replied and did his best to engulf the remaining orb in his mouth, maintaining a light suction while he massaged the nipple with the tip of his tongue.

Andrea arched her back, digging in her shoulder blades, and moaned in response. Then she reached lower and tickled his scrotum. His attempt at symmetry completed, he moved downward beneath her venus mound and teased her labia to swell and part. Then, raising his tongue, he kneaded the upper part of the passage, causing the engorgement of its surrounding cavern. The formerly relaxed and gently curving tunnel straightened into a turgid tube, trembling to trap and harvest its penile partner.

"Finally, there's a light at the end of the tunnel," he mumbled through laboring lips and slid his chest forward on her perspiring stomach. Their tongues met in a deep, devouring kiss. His prick, finally released from her milking massage, slid homeward repeatedly into its cyclically repositioned and eagerly awaiting scabbard. They moved together toward one purpose in a partnership of passion.

Later they rested against the double pillows and threw back the satin sheets which were hardly needed for warmth. They served rather as wicks in this climate to draw the moisture off their sleeping bodies.

"Did you like my sleight of hand?" Andrea asked.

"That's a switch," Robert answered, believing the woman was asking for a performance report.

"I was only wondering how tired you are," she rejoined. "Do you feel up to it again?" She grasped his relaxed organ, minutely examining it for signs of life.

"Well, darlin'," he said, lapsing into a cowboy drawl, "I feel like I've been rode hard and put away wet. If we don't do something about this lack of exercise we'll have to start watching our weight."

They were beginning to fall into a satisfied sleep when the phone rang.

"Major Falconi, sir? This is Sergeant Dudley at Air Force Base. We have a Vietnamese gentleman here by the name of Trang Van who requests to speak with you. I told him you were not here, but he says he will wait for you. I think we are going to have him camped on our doorstep until you get here. Shall I tell him how soon that might be, sir?"

"That's okay, Sergeant. Tell him to hang loose. I should be there inside an hour. Thanks for the call. Goodbye."

"This is not fair Robert," Andrea said and pouted. "It reminds me of the first time we made love. What is taking you away from me this morning?"

"I don't know, Andrea," he replied. "I can't tell, yet, how important it is. I'll try to get back as soon as possible."

"As you were, soldier," she said. "I have some paperwork to finish at the base anyway. I will accompany you."

Major Falconi stood, listening intently to the short Vietnamese standing in front of him, attired in peasant garb: black cotton shorts and shirt with a black conical hat.

"My name is Trang Van, Major Falconi. I have come to you because you were of great assistance to the Trang toc in their village when you directed the Special Forces unit that helped them set up their strategic hamlet last year."

"Are the Viet Cong threatening you again, Mr. Van?"

17

queried the tall, dark-haired, green-eyed American, dressed in sharply pressed but untailored fatigues and a black beret on his head. He carefully addressed the Vietnamese gentleman with the honorific, "mister," followed by his first name, Van as was the custom here in Vietnam.

"They threaten us no more than usual," replied Trang Van. "That is not the problem. I suspect it is too minor a thing to occupy the time of an important American advisor."

Trang Van's deference did not lead Major Falconi to immediately conclude that he was being patronized or set up. Trang was merely observing the correct and normal politeness of his people. He encouraged Trang to continue.

"Please explain the situation to me, Mr. Van. I'm sure we can find some way to be of assistance to you." Falconi deliberately left his alternatives open in case the problem could not be appropriately addressed by himself or his team and should be passed on to another level.

"My wife has sent me a message from our village that a tiger has wandered into our area and attacked and killed our daughter Mei, and it is threatening the lives of the other villagers. We are, for the most part, Catholics, who fled to the south in 1954 and who were assigned an area to farm in the Mekong Delta. But there are those among us who are not Christians but rather animists and spirit worshipers who in their terror see the tiger as the revenge of a witch. In the panic that is developing, they may influence the rest to leave and settle elsewhere."

Major Falconi understood the nature of the problem immediately. He expressed sympathy for the man's daughter but helped the conversation to return quickly to the unstable village population. He agreed with Trang that the situation threatened the security of the entire Hamlet program. Many Indian and African villages had

18

been abandoned in the face of a threat by a man-eating cat. Because he was the initial American advisor to deal with this toc or clan, the term for a closely related tribal group in Vietnam, Falconi felt it was only right that he should bird-dog the matter until the tiger was eliminated. The Black Eagles were now on R and R from their last mission.

Robert Falconi assured Trang Van that he would send a message firming up their plans to deal with the tiger. The village chieftain thanked him profusely and departed.

Robert Mikhailovich Falconi was born an army brat at Fort Meade, Maryland in the year 1934.

His father, 2nd Lt. Michael Falconi, was the son of Italian immigrants. The parents, Salvatore and Luciana Falconi, had wasted no time in instilling an appreciation of America and the opportunity offered by the nation into their youngest son as they had their other seven children. Mr. Falconi even went as far as to name his son Michael rather than the Italian Michele. The boy had been born an American, was going to live as an American, so—*per Dio e tutti i santi*—he was going to be named as an American!

Young Michael was certainly no disappointment to his parents or older brothers and sisters. He studied hard in school and excelled. He worked in the family's small shoe repair shop in New York City's Little Italy in the evenings, doing his homework late at night. When he graduated from high school, Michael was eligible for several scholarships to continue his education in college, but even with this help, it would have entailed great sacrifice on the part of his parents. Two older brothers, both working as lawyers, could have helped out a bit, but Michael didn't want to be any more of a burden on his family than was absolutely necessary.

He knew of an alternative to paying a university. The nation's service academies, West Point and Annapolis, offered free education to qualified young man. Michael, through the local ward boss, received a congressional appointment to take the examinations to attend the United States Military Academy.

He was successful in this endeavor and was appointed to the Corps of Cadets. West Point didn't give a damn about his humble origins. The Academy didn't care whether his parents were poor immigrants or not. The fact that his father was a struggling cobbler meant absolutely nothing. All that institution was concerned about was whether Cadet Michael Falconi could cut it or not. It was this measuring of a man by no standards other than his own abilities and talents that caused the young man to develop a sincere, lifelong love for the United States Army. He finished his career at the school in the upper third of his class, sporting the three chevrons and rockers of a brigade adjutant on his sleeves upon graduation.

Second Lieutenant Falconi was assigned to the Third Infantry Regiment at Fort Meade, Maryland. This unit was a ceremonial outfit that provided details for military funerals at Arlington National Cemetery, the guard for the Tomb of the Unknown Soldier, and other official functions in the Washington, D.C. area.

The young shavetail enjoyed the bachelor's life in the nation's capital, and his duties as protocol officer were not too demanding but interesting. He was required to be present during social occasions that were official affairs of state. He coordinated the affairs and saw to it that all the political bigwigs and other brass attending them had a good time. He was doing exactly those duties at such a function when he met a young Russian Jewish refugee named Miriam Ananova Silberman.

She was a pretty brunette of twenty-years years of age, who had the most striking eyes Michael Falconi had ever seen. He would always say all through his life that it was her eyes that captured his heart. When he met her, she was a member of the Jewish Refugees attending a congressional dinner. She and her father, Josef Silberman, had recently fled Josef Stalin's anti-Semitic terrorism in the Soviet Union. Her organization had been lobbying congress to enact legislation that would permit the American government to take action in saving European and Asian Jewry not only from the savagery of the Communists but also from the Nazis who had only begun their own program of intimidation and harassment of Germany's Jewish population.

When the lieutenant met the refugee beauty, he fell hopelessly in love. He spent that entire evening as close to her as he could possibly be while ignoring his other duties. He was absolutely determined he would get to know this beautiful Russian girl better. He begged her to dance with him at every opportunity, was solicitous about seeing to her refreshments and engaged her in conversation, doing his best to be witty and interesting.

He was successful.

Miriam Silberman was fascinated by this tall, dark, and most handsome young officer. She was so swept off her feet that she failed to play any coquettish little games or try to appear hard to get. His infectious smile and happy charm completely captivated the young woman.

The next day, Michael began a serious courtship, determined to win her heart and marry the girl.

Josef Silberman was a cantankerous elderly widower. He opposed the match from the beginning. As a Talmud scholar, he wanted his only daughter to marry a nice Jewish boy. But Miriam took pains to point out to him that this was America—a country that existed in direct opposition to any homogenous customs. The mixing of nationalities and religions was not that unusual in this part of the world. Josef argued, stormed, forbade and demanded—but all for naught. In the end, so he would not lose the affection of his daughter, he gave his blessing. The couple was married in the post chapel at Fort Meade.

A year later their only child, a son, was born. He was named Robert Mikhailovich.

The boy spent his youth on various army posts. The only time he lived in a town or civilian neighborhood was during the three years his father, by then a colonel, served overseas in the European Theater of Operations in the First Infantry Divison—the Big Red One. A family joke developed out of the colonel's service in that particular outfit. Robert would ask his dad, "How come you're serving in the First Division?"

The colonel always answered, "Because I figured if I was going to be one, I might as well be a Big Red One."

It was one of those private jokes that didn't go over too well outside the house.

The boy had a happy childhood. The only problem was his dislike of school. Too many genes of ancient Hebrew warriors and Roman legionnaires had been passed down to him. Robert was a kid who liked action, adventure, and plenty of it. The only serious studying he ever did was in the karate classes he took when the family was stationed in Japan. He was accepted in one of that nation's most prestigious martial arts academies where he excelled while evolving into a serious and skillful *karateka*.

His use of this fighting technique caused one of the ironies in his life. In the early 1950s, his father had been posted as commandant of high school ROTC in San Diego, California. Robert, an indifferent student in that city's Hoover High School, had a run-in with some young

Mexican-Americans. One of the Chicanos had never seen such devastation as that which Bobby Falconi dealt out with his hands. But he stuck in there, took his lumps, and finally went down from several lightning-quick *shuto* chops that slapped consciousness from his enraged mind. A dozen years later, this young gang member, named Manuel Rivera, once again met Robert Falconi. The former was in the Special Forces, a sergeant first class and the latter, a captain, in the same elite outfit.

Sergeant First Class Rivera, a Black Eagle, was killed in action during the raid on the prison camp in North Vietnam in 1964.

When Falconi graduated from high school in 1952, he immediately enlisted in the army. Although his father had wanted him to opt for West Point, the young man couldn't stand the thought of being stuck in any more classrooms. In fact, he didn't even want to be an officer. During his early days on army posts he had developed several friendships among career noncommissioned officers. He liked the attitudes of these rough-and-tumble professional soldiers who drank, brawled, and fornicated with wild abandon during their off-duty time. The sergeant's devil-may-care attitude seemed much more attractive to young Robert than the heavy responsibilities that seemed to make commissioned officers and their lives so serious and, at times, tedious.

After basic training and advanced infantry training, he was shipped straight into the middle of the Korean War where he was assigned to the tough Second Infantry Division.

He participated in two campaigns there. These were officially designated by the United States Army as the Third Korean Winter and Korean Summer-Fall 1953. Robert Falconi fought and froze in those turbulent months. His combat experience ranged from holding a hill during massive attacks by crazed Chinese Communist forces, to the deadly cat-and-mouse activities of night patrols in enemy territory.

Robert Falconi returned home with the rank of sergeant, the Combat Infantryman's Badge, the Purple Heart, the Silver Star, and the undeniable knowledge that he had been born and bred for just one life: that of a soldier.

His martial ambitions also had expanded. He now desired a commission but didn't want to sink himself into the curriculum of the United States Military Academy. His attitude toward schoolbooks remained the same: to hell with 'em!

At the end of his hitch in 1955, he reenlisted and applied for Infantry Officer's Candidate School at Fort Benning, Georgia.

Falconi's time in OCS registered another success in his life. He excelled in all phases of the rigorous course. He recognized the need for brain work in the classrooms and soaked up the lessons through long hours of study while burning the proverbial midnight oil in quarters. The field exercises were a piece of cake for this combat veteran, but he was surprised to find out that, even there, the instructors had plenty to teach him.

His only setback occurred during Fuck Your Buddy Week. That was a phase of the curriculum in which the candidates learned responsibility. Each man's conduct— or misconduct—was passed on to an individual designated as his buddy. If a cadet screwed up he wasn't punished. His buddy was. Thus, for the first time in many of these young men's lives, their personal conduct could bring joy or sorrow to others. Falconi's buddy was late to reveille one morning and Robert drew the demerit.

But this was the only setback in an otherwise spotless six months spent at OCS. He came out number one in his class and was offered a Regular Army commission. The brand new second lieutenant happily accepted the honor and set out to begin this new phase of his career in an army he had learned to love as much as his father did.

His graduation didn't result in an immediate assignment to an active duty unit. Falconi found himself once more in school—but these were not filled with hours over books. He attended jump school and earned the silver parachutist badge; next was Ranger school where he won the coveted orange-and-black tab; then he was shipped down to Panama for jungle warfare school where he garnered yet one more insignia.

Following that he suffered another disappointment. Again, his desire to sink himself into a regular unit was thwarted. Because he held a Regular Army commission rather than a reserve one like his other classmates, Falconi was returned to Fort Benning to attend the infantry school. The courses he took were designed to give him some thorough instruction in staff procedures. He came out on top here as well, but there was another thing that happened to him.

His intellectual side finally blossomed.

The theory of military science, rather than complete practical application, began to fascinate him. During his time in combat—and the later army schooling—he had begun to develop certain theories. With the exposure to infantry school, he decided to do something about these ideas of his. He wrote several articles for the *Infantry Journal* about these thoughts, particularly on his personal analysis of the proper conduct of jungle and mountain operations involving insurgency and counterinsurgency forces.

The army was more than a little impressed with this first lieutenant (he had been promoted) and sent him back to Panama to serve on a special committee that would develop and publish official U.S. Army policy on small unit combat in tropical conditions. He honed his skills and tactical expertise during this time.

From there he volunteered for Special Forces—The Green Berets—and was accepted. After completing the officer's course at Fort Bragg, North Carolina, Falconi finally was assigned to a unit. This was the Fifth Special Forces Group in the growing conflict in South Vietnam.

Now a captain, he worked closely with ARVN units and even helped to organize village militias to protect hamlets against the Viet Cong and North Vietnamese. Gradually, his duties expanded until he organized and led several dangerous missions that involved deep penetration into territory controlled by the Communist guerrillas.

This action brought him to the attention of a Central Intelligence Agency case officer named Clayton Andrews. Andrews had been doing his own bit of clandestine fighting which involved more than harassment in V.C. areas. His main job was the conduct of missions into North Vietnam itself. He arranged an interview with Captain Falconi to see if the officer would fit into his own sphere of activity. He found Falconi exactly the man he had been looking for. Pulling all the strings he had, Andrews saw to it that the Special Forces man was transferred to his own branch of SOG—the Special Operations Group—to begin work on a brand new project.

Capt. Robert Mikhailovich Falconi was tasked with organizing a new fighting unit to be known as the Black Eagles. This group's basic policy was to be primitive and simple: Kill or be killed!

Their mission was to penetrate deep into the heartland of the Communist enemy to disrupt, destroy, maim, and slay. The men who would belong to the Black Eagles would be volunteers from every branch of the armed forces. And that was to include all nationalities involved

26

in the struggle against the Red invasion of South Vietnam.

Each man was to be an absolute expert in his particular brand of military mayhem. He had to be an expert in not only his own nation's firearms but also those of the other friendly and enemy countries. But the required knowledge of weapons didn't stop at modern ones. This also included knives, bludgeons, garrotes, and even crossbows when the need to deal silent death had arisen.

There was also a requirement for the more sophisticated and peaceful skills, too. Foreign languages, land navigation, communications, medical, and even mountaineering and scuba diving were to be within the realm of knowledge of the Black Eagles.

They became the enforcement arm of SOG, drawing the missions which were the most dangerous and sensitive. In essence they were hit men, closely coordinated and completely dedicated, held together and directed through the forceful personality of their leader, now Major Falconi.

As unit integrity and morale built up, the detachment decided they wanted an insignia all their own. This wasn't at all unusual for units in Vietnam. Local manufacturers, acting on designs submitted to them by the troops involved, produced these emblems that were worn by the outfits while "in country." These adornments were strictly nonregulation and unauthorized for display outside of Vietnam.

Falconi's men came up with a unique beret badge manufactured as a cloth insignia. A larger version was used as a shoulder patch. The design consisted of a black eagle—naturally—with spread wings. Looking to its right, the big bird clutched a sword in one claw and a bolt of lightning in the other. Mounted on a khaki shield that was trimmed in black, the devise was an accurate portrayal of its wearers: somber and deadly.

They even had an unofficial motto, though it wasn't part of their insignia. The statement, in Latin, was simple and quite to the point: *calcitra clunis.* It is translated as kick ass.

Major Falconi passed through the second level of security at Tan Son Nhut Air Force Base that led to Special Operations Group Headquarters at Peterson Field. Inside the isolation barracks he spotted two members of the Black Eagles who had not yet joined their teammates on R and R: S. Sgt. Archie Dobbs, the point man and unit scout; and P O 3c., Blue Richards, a demolitions specialist from the U.S. Navy Seals.

In addition, a new face was present, sitting on a sea trunk with his duffle bag beside him. There was evidence before the major that they had been playing cards, but currently the new arrival, with hacked-off, sun-bleached blond hair was performing the time-honored game of guessing which of three twenty millimeter cannon shells was covering a small black plastic ball.

He addressed the two Black Eagles in a calm, sonorous stage voice.

"Here is a technique that is convenient to learn. You've probably seen a magician shifting a coin between the middle knuckles of his fingers. This exercise helps him to develop finger dexterity."

He removed a quarter from his pocket and began making it vanish and reappear between his fingers.

"It comes in handy when you want to make a coin disappear with only an imperceptible flick of a muscle."

He held up the back of his hand to Archie's face, turned his hand, and the coin was gone.

"Remember how all the magicians you've seen hold their hands, palm-wise, in a stiff stylized gesture? That's to make them pay more attention to the hand that is front

28

of their face while the other hand is doing something else. I can even illustrate this technique using only a pair of crumpled tissues."

He wadded the paper tissues into six balls and asked Blue Richards to sit at a right angle to Archie Dobbs. Then he held a tissue ball in one hand in front of Archie's face and made a pass-over movement with his other hand, snaring the ball with his second hand and flicking it onto the floor out of Archie's sight but in full view of Blue. Archie was still mesmerized with the first hand which now held nothing.

The magician now palmed another wad of tissue with his second hand and appeared to pull it out of Archie's ear.

"Here! Watch it again," he said, and repeated the trick.

Blue couldn't restrain himself. He began to giggle quietly. Archie looked at him and said, "What happened to the tissue?"

"It's all a matter of misdirection," the magician explained as he repeated the trick a third time and flicked another tissue onto the floor. He repeated the trick three more times. Each time Archie's eyes bulged out a little further. By the time the last ball disappeared Blue was convulsed in helpless laughter.

"You must be Sgt. Eddie Barthe," Falconi said, and extended his hand to the performer. "I'm Maj. Robert Falconi, your C.O. They call me Falcon, among other things."

S. Sgt. Eddie Barthe rose quickly from the sea trunk and took the major's hand.

"Yes sir!" he replied.

"Didn't you start out in the States as airborne with the Eighty-second?" Falconi asked.

"Yes sir," Eddie answered again. "Air Mobile Cavalry. I helped keep the big birds in the air as a crew chief until I

29

went to Special Forces school and got on a team over here in 'Nam. I spent the last three months setting up strategic hamlets in the highlands."

"I did a stint of that myself," the major commented. "Your specialty is small arms and your cross-training is in psy-ops. I'd say you arrived just in time."

"My purpose in coming to the base today is to round up these two reprobates," Falconi said, indicating Archie and Blue, "for an essential but unofficial mission. How would you three like to accompany me on a tiger hunt?"

"When do we leave?" replied Archie enthusiastically.

"All this and fun too?" added Blue.

Eddie Barthe hesitated for a moment. Hunting was his principle avocation and made up a large part of his life, but it was balanced with a healthy sense of ecology developed by a long-standing membership in the N.R.A.

Although he had been raised in an urban environment, his father had often taken him hunting using vermin, rabbits, and ground squirrels as targets. On one such trip Eddie's father sent him ahead to a ranch-style house in the high chaparral country within a mile of the Mexican border and instructed him. "Ask them if we can hunt ground squirrels on their property," he said. "Tell them that squirrels steal the feed left for livestock and that they are hosts for plague-carrying fleas."

To observe the habits of game, Eddie and his father roamed the back country, the mountain roads, and the desert canyons in a Volkswagen Beetle. Eddie recalled that his father would try to take that car anywhere and got stuck only once.

"Watch the rabbit," his father told him. "It will probably see you before you see it. Scan back and forth and let the edge of your vision catch their movement. When you see him, he will already be running, but don't shoot then, and don't give up. The rabbit will stop before he hops into his hole. That's the time to fire."

"Look to the rocky boulders for ground squirrels. They are very curious. If you can outwait them, one is sure to raise his head over the top of the rock to look at you. They also like to nest in hollow logs."

Eddie's father gave him his first rifle, a gallery style, pump-action .22 with a swing-up peep sight and a tube magazine under the barrel.

"What are you doing, Eddie?" his father asked. "You've been plinking at that same tin can for ten minutes and haven't knocked it over yet. A hundred yards away is the same thing as standing on top of it. I'm beginning to think that I should make an appointment for you at the optometrist's to have your eyes checked."

"I was becoming bored with knocking them over," Eddie explained, "so I'm trying to hit at the edge of the upper lid and chew the top off bite by bite."

His father took a closer look with the binoculars. Sure enough, the top of the can was carefully stitched with bullet holes, one following the other side by side. The next round Eddie fired flipped the lid off leaving the can gently rocking.

His father reflected for a moment and then said with a grin, "Look son, if you want to borrow the can opener, just ask."

Eddie's mother was a volunteer to the church schools in the area. To entertain the children she told Bible stories in addition to her magic tricks and often included Eddie in her act. He watched the eyes of the children open wider as his mother dramatized the high point of a story which she had illustrated with a miniature stage, cut-out paper figures, and a portable phonograph with background music of matching theme.

Thus, Eddie picked up the habit of reading aloud from the Bible. His rhythmic, soft, sonorous voice could relax and enthrall a group of fidgeting children.

At one time or another his mother had kept pigeons,

31

rabbits, geese, and turtles. His first pet house cat was an occasion for careful observation and deep reflection. He was fascinated by cats, large and small. He considered them the earliest evolved and most primitive of the predatory mammals.

When Major Falconi invited him on the tiger hunt, he answered, "Sir, I'd be proud to hunt with you guys, and I realize that this is one of the few areas of the world where the local species of tiger is not endangered, but, you mentioned that this is an essential mission. I'd like to know why."

"A point well taken, Sergeant Barthe," replied the major. "I should have mentioned initially that this cat is a man-eater."

Relief replaced the expression of consternation on Eddie's face.

"That puts it in a different light," he said with enthusiasm. "Turn about is fair play. When do we leave?"

"Get together with Archie and Blue and draw the gear you want," the major directed. "We don't have to move too fast on this. Departure any time in the next half hour should be sufficient."

A chorus of groans followed him to the door.

ARVN Lt. Andrea Thuy walked through the door of the barracks at that moment, and Robert Falconi invited her to join her fellow Black Eagles on the tiger hunt, but she politely declined.

"She can't be bothered with this small stuff," Archie commented with a leer, giving a sideways glance toward Robert Falconi. "She's a big-game hunter."

Andrea beamed, but Major Falconi eyed him darkly.

They loaded their gear into the truck and waved good-bye to Andrea. The leave-taking took on an ominous aspect for her. She could not fathom the feeling. She was well aware that Robert Falconi hunted men for a living. A tiger should not present any more of a danger to him. Besides he was such a tiger himself.

But, the feeling persisted that she would not see him again.

Andrea shivered in the tropical heat as she walked to her car.

The deuce-and-a-half truck is the mainstay of the United States Army for personnel and equipment transport. It is so named because of its two and a half ton rated carrying capacity. There are certainly larger trucks and some with more capacity but none so ubiquitous. It is sometimes called a six by six or a ten by ten depending on how many tires are mounted on it. The deuce-and-a-half actually has more traction than a jeep and can climb steeper hills because it has more tires, and each tire is driven at all times.

The truck carrying the truncated Black Eagles team lumbered confidently over the deteriorating road which got worse the further it got from Saigon. The vehicle had no armor as such but was very sturdily built and closely resembled an outsized Tonka truck.

An hour after they left the gates of Tan Son Nhut Air Force Base the Black Eagles arrived at Strategic Hamlet number seventy-eight, called Trangville, in Vietnamese.

Trang Van and his wife Cam were present to greet Major Falconi and his party. The village appeared to be a loose collection of thatch walled huts of solid construction with dirt floors. The layout of the village, however, had been carefully planned to take advantage of the local flora and relief features for the purposes of observation, defense, and, if necessary, rapid evacuation.

The faces of the villagers, that were visible to the four Americans, were shaded with sorrow and tinted with terror not usually observed before a V.C. attack. Terror

33

that was caused by the man-eater.

"Welcome to our village," said Trang Van. Cam bowed with her hands, palms together in a gesture resembling prayer, an archaic posture not often seen in modern Vietnamese women.

"We are grateful you could come to our aid in these unhappy times," she said.

With these words she left the group and busied herself inside with meal preparation. Her normal polite smile, usually unaffected by any adversity, was absent.

Trang Van explained to Major Falconi, "I'm glad that you have all come to help us, Major. Upon my return to our village I soon realized that my wife could not take up her life as before until the death of our daughter, Mei, is avenged, and the skin of her savage slayer decorates the village center. I apologize for the display of primitive behavior on her part. She is usually a more civilized person. In these dark moments she is lapsing under the influence of the non-Christian members of this village."

"Thank you for your explanation," Major Falconi responded, "but I see no reason to apologize. I think her point of view is very practical considering the circumstances and well understood by all of us here."

"I would be honored to have you stay in our house tonight and share a meal with us," said Trang Van.

"We would be honored to share a meal with you, but since the Viet Cong are uncontrolled at night we will make our camp out of sight of the village and recontact you in the morning," Major Falconi answered.

Well fed, and their senses slowed by mint-flavored rice liquor given to them by Van from the local moonshiner, the Black Eagles drove a couple of miles from the village and set up camp.

"Wait till you see the goodies we rounded up, major," said Eddie Barthe. "Blue, I still can't figure out why you wanted this point four-six-oh Weatherby Magnum. It's

34

more suited to elephant than tiger. The M-one Garand is a decent performer but a little heavy to carry. This M-fourteen is better because it is lighter and both can punch through the jungle growth better than the M-sixteen."

"Here's a Thompson forty-five caliber submachine gun. It has lots of stopping power, but is very hard to hold on target." Eddie held up a short-barreled shotgun. "This is a smart choice, a riot gun with a barrel rifled for twelve-gauge slugs. In addition we have standard anti-Viet Cong ordnance: Claymore mines; frag and willie peter grenades; and a couple of the original issue M-sixteens. That's good. Be careful to avoid the newer variety. They've been altered from the original design to meet the Department of the Army specifications meant for the M-fourteen. Therefore the new ammunition will be hotter than it needs to be because the recoil spring was altered for a higher rate of fire than the weapon was designed for. Both changes tend to jam the operating mechanism as well as cause premature breakdown. Also changed was the number of turns in the barrel resulting in larger groups on the target range."

"The M-sixteen is more suited for desert warfare than for the jungle. But if you can clean it every ten minutes it works fine."

"Thank you for the weapons summary, Sergeant Barthe," said the major. "Because this is an informal mission each man's specific role will depend on who and what we find while we are tracking down the tiger. Remember, we are in V.C. territory.

"Our primary target is a member of the family Felidae, genera *Panthera*, species *tigris*. He is the largest and smartest of the cats, weighing as much as five hundred pounds, standing up to five feet tall at the shoulder, up to fourteen feet long including the tail.

"I'm beginning to sound like a ringside announcer at a prize fight, but I wouldn't want to find myself inside the ring with this kitty. Considering all the folklore generated about this beast, our safest strategy is to assume the worst until we know better. Don't try to outswim or outclimb the tiger. He will beat you at both. Needless to say, you can forget hand-to-hand combat. Therefore we *will* try to outsmart him, but only as a team, following a preset plan. It's too late tonight to get into that with a question-and-answer period. We'll cover it tomorrow. Here's some information to sleep on.

"If you surprise the tiger, your best bet is to stand your ground. In addition, try talking to him. I heard an account of a tiger that found a man asleep and began dragging him away. Half awake, the guy yelled, 'Go away! Leave me alone!' The surprised tiger obliged him. Remember, these animals are heavily programmed by evolution. It is known that cats, especially cheetahs, cannot help but chase after a fleeing animal of prey. They are also prone to select one animal out of a herd and run down that one animal regardless of how the attack situation develops. That trait may come in handy."

Sergeant Blue Richards spoke up. "It sounds to me like if you act like a meal: small, frightened, helpless, and running away, you will be treated like a meal." Blue continued. "I am curious about one thing, Falc. Since this cat has become a man-eater, his habits have probably changed, become less predictable. So why don't we blow him away at first opportunity?"

"Good question, Blue," Falconi answered. "For one thing we don't know how close the Cong may be at the time. But if you find a righteous opportunity, don't pass it by. Use it!"

Eddie Barthe added, "Every animal, whether predator or prey, has a weak spot in its behavior. Major Falconi has pointed out a few. But there may be a trait waiting to be discovered by one of us at a critical moment. So, hang loose. Keep your eyes open!"

"Well put, Sergeant Barthe," the major said. "Our greatest advantage in this situation is our fighting spirit and willingness to change, to adapt."

Archie began to recite: "Yea, though I walk through the valley of death, I will fear no evil . . ."

And Blue picked up the chant: "For I am the biggest, meanest, toughest son of a bitch in the valley."

"Right on!" Eddie Barthe laughed. "That's the spirit."

"Hey Blue," said Archie, "what's your opinion of the notion that a man's chances of surviving depend on his willingness to die for what he believes in?"

"Bullshit," Blue replied. "It all depends on your ability to make the other guy die for what he believes in. That's called the *no heroes* rule of combat."

In the morning the hunting party broke camp and rode in the truck back to Trangville. Trang Van pointed toward where the tiger had last been seen. It was a fine morning. The oppressive tropical moisture and the atmosphere of dread in the village did little to dampen the enthusiasm of the group. It is true, they had not lost one of their own to the tiger yet. But they were men, confident in their abilities, with a definite problem to solve. That, plus being free to choose one's own path is often enough to turn a forboding task, full of danger, into an adventure.

Eddie Barthe was first to cut the trail of the tiger. The dampness of the disturbed earth within the pugmark told him that the tiger had been there an hour and a half before. Then the team began to pick up signs of human presence, crossing the tiger's trail fifteen minutes or so ahead of the cat.

Falconi said, "Archie, you go ahead and scout the unknowns. By the way, keep an eye out for the tiger while you're at it."

"I'll keep that in mind, Falc," Archie replied. "And I'll try to keep him at arm's length. I hear they're mighty nasty infighters."

With that he ambled forward, following the trail.

Major Falconi had briefed the group on the use of the ANPRC-6 hand-held radio, the "Prick-6." In combat, voice communication is too slow, too loud, and often confusing. Using the radio, a Morse code was substituted for voice. It was sent by keying the transmit button. The first series of clicks identified the sender. The one, two, or three clicks that followed described his situation.

Archie moved rapidly forward following the trail of the suspected Viet Cong. There were at least five sets of tracks. Some of the soles were from well-worn boots. A few were from Jesus sandals, and there was even one set of sneakers. Archie's suspicion that they were V.C. grew stronger.

Archie returned to his group an hour later. "They're definitely Viet Cong," he reported to the major. "I counted eight of them, fifteen minutes ahead of us beyond that saddle ridge. A couple of them have AK-forty-sevens. The rest have bolt-action rifles. And they're transporting some homemade anti-personnel devices."

The V.C. had adapted crude copies of American, Russian, and Chinese weapons to augment what the Russians gave them and what they could steal from the Americans.

"Eight of them to four of us," Sergeant Barthe remarked. "The odds are hardly even."

"Yeah! No fun at all," Blue said with a groan. "They need at least twice that number to make it a fair fight."

"What's the word on the tiger, Falc?" Archie asked.

"Sergeant Barthe reports that the tiger's heading will carry him on an arc that falls very close to where you located the V.C. I think we can accomplish our mission and have some fun with these people," said Major Falconi. "It's time for a commo check," he added.

Each man field-tested his Prick-6 radio. Then followed a cursory check of their weapons for dirt and other obstructions. It was assumed that they were cocked and locked.

"We will work the tiger in teams of two," directed Major Falconi. He was savvy to the stalking habits of the big cat. He knew that tigers responded unpredictably to a group of beaters. When a group of men are hired to beat the bush in front of a lion, this king of beasts will usually panic and allow himself to be driven straight into the hunter's blind. But tigers are more cunning, and often as not, would circle around the beaters and attack them.

"If the tiger hears your buddy before he hears you, he may run away or circle back on him. As long as we know what's happening we can make use of either response to lur or prod him where we want. We will work him toward the V.C. location. Once we get close enough I will break off from the team and arrange a present for that big kitty."

They moved rapidly through the tall grass, slapping their rifle butts and stamping firm ground where they could find it. Little noise discipline was necessary until they were closer to the V.C. encampment. Each man felt the tension building within him as he advanced, expecting to come face to face with the tiger at any moment.

"Blue! On your left. We spooked him. Barthe, close in a pincer behind him and draw him off Blue. Start using your radios unless you are close enough to hear your buddy's voice." Falconi finished instructing and moved to higher ground to observe the rippling grass at a better angle.

As the tiger began to close in on one of the Black Eagles, that man would freeze and his opposite number would take up the beat. Within two hundred yards of the saddle ridge Falconi spoke one last time into his radio.

"I'm going ahead to the encampment. You guys are on your own."

They worked the tiger like a pack of coyotes would drive an antelope, moving him constantly toward the saddle ridge.

Falconi followed Archie's directions and soon spotted the V.C. lookout. Archie had said that the remainder of the Cong would be grouped in a hollow on the far side of the hill from the guard. Falconi couldn't see his men or the tiger from his position but estimated them to be one hundred fifty yards out. Then he took a wicked-looking knife from his belt scabbard. The pint-sized samurai sword had been lent to him by the company sales representative that was promoting them.

"I won't have to worry about using it for playing mumbly peg," Falconi remembered commenting the first time he saw the knife. "The tip looks like it's already been busted off."

The blade was sharpened on only one side. It had a very heavy spine and came to a point with an abrupt taper. It was hollow ground and razor sharp.

The company rep explained, "It was designed with that shape and weight to facilitate slicing through meat without losing momentum."

Robert Falconi hefted the short heavy weapon. It had nine inches of blade and five inches of grip. He flanked the guard carefully and closed rapidly behind him. A few practice swipes against carcasses in the cold room of the company mess had convinced him of the effectiveness of the blade.

When he was within rock-throwing distance behind the guard, he paused and tested the air. The solder seemed totally unaware of his presence.

Major Falconi concentrated his *ki* in his center of gravity and directed the swing of the blade one foot beyond the man's neck. Falconi's breath exploded from clenched teeth at the end of the stroke.

The guard swiveled his hips, twisted his trunk and tried to turn his head toward the source of the sound. Falconi glanced at his knife to make sure there was blood on it and returned his attention to the V.C. just in time to see the man's hand attempt to reach up toward his neck. His head made the wet sound of a child's toy suction arrow giving way as it slid off his neck.

The major muttered, "That will teach you to shake your head at me, you Viet Cong slime."

Falconi grasped the still-standing body by the wrist. It followed him for two full coordinate steps before it fell. He dragged it behind him a distance of fifty yards through the slippery grass. He stopped to rest while he looked for signs of the tiger.

The major detected movement to his left, then right, and suddenly Sergeant Barthe appeared in front of him.

"The tiger is coming fast, Major," Eddie said, glancing warily behind him into the grass.

"Follow me!" the major commanded in a loud whisper after Dobbs and Richards converged on him.

"Let's shag ass out of here." He shook off the hand of the dead Viet Cong which somehow mysteriously came to grip his fatigues.

The group of Black Eagles moved, single file, toward the V.C. encampment. Halfway up the hill Major Falconi could be heard apologizing to his knife as he used it to hack a two foot length of hardwood branch into a pointed pole. Then he searched out the head of the dead V.C. and, positioning it with his foot, speared it upward, through the neck.

Holding it up in front of Sergeant Barthe, he grinned wickedly and said, "Put his hat back on. We don't want him to get sunburned. Follow my lead, men," Major Falconi commanded. "Our job, now, is to work them back toward the tiger."

They crept as skirmishers to within sight of the camp. None of the guerrillas seemed to have noticed that their guard was missing. Motioning his men to fall back along their trail, Falconi held up the head in such a way that the supporting pole was hidden behind the broad-leafed foliage and began a low moan which ended in a loud, plaintive howl. He gave the V.C. only a moment to glimpse the head. One of them questioningly shouted a name.

Seeing that this part of his plan was accomplished, Falconi ran back along the trail and waited.

The tiger padded cautiously forward, intensely curious about this prey that seemed to be everywhere but was, as yet, unseen. The constantly branching trail of the prey had the smell of his last meal. Then the cat came upon the body of the headless soldier, lying on the path, hand outstretched.

The smell of blood quenched the tiger's curiosity and brought into play his ancient, feeding-time behavior pattern. Major Falconi didn't have to wait very long. One of the guerrillas soon appeared and could be seen searching anxiously under the low-lying jungle vegetation.

Robert instructed Archie, "Fall the men back to the dead V.C. Then get into good ambush positions but don't fire until I do."

Seeking a better position, he followed their retreat for twenty paces and waited there until two of the enemy were visible. Holding up the head, one last time, he called out in high-pitched, whining Vietnamese, "He's eating me!"

Falconi moved out of sight, shook the head off the stick and rolled it onto the trail. Then he ran to join his men.

42

The body of the guard was gone, but a blood trail with scuff marks led to dense foliage nearby.

So far he is a very predictable tiger, Robert Falconi thought, and hoped that the beast would continue his cooperation for the final act. He paused as he passed the tiger's suspected position and saw Blue's arm beckoning urgently.

Reunited with his commanding officer, Blue pointed out Archie and Eddie in ambush positions and reported, "They are waiting for the first shot from you."

"Hang loose," Falconi replied. "Let's see if this works out the way I planned it."

The tiger heard the sounds of many feet on the trail approaching his position. He abandoned his meal momentarily to circle in on them and defend the kill.

The lead guerrilla burst through the bush and discovered his headless, partially devoured fellow soldier. The tiger, following his normal inclination, had selected the intestines, a rich source of vitamin C, for his first entrée. The guerrilla pointed his rifle nervously at the bush, fighting the rising gorge in his throat. He was soon joined by the others. The commander fanned them out into the jungle to flush the man-eater. He needn't have bothered.

Having flanked his pursuers, the tiger burst from the jungle and attacked the group of men, hoping to scatter them like a herd of deer.

Two swipes from his giant paws fractured a neck and broke the pelvis of another V.C., sending him ten feet through the air in a whip-cracking spin. Then the tiger performed the last of a series of fatal errors which had begun when he first fed on the body of the dead Viet Cong in Cambodia.

Instead of retreating into the safety of the jungle, he pounced on the back of the nearest fleeing guerrilla and closed his jaws on the man's neck, finally feeling the satisfying crunch of vertebrae. But, as many an ice-age tiger had discovered, to its severe disappointment, these strange apes didn't give up easily and they didn't play fair.

Given an instant's respite, most of the remaining V.C. pointed their ragtag collection of weapons, including the assault rifles, at the gigantic feline in his moment of triumph. The remaining Viet Cong guerrilla, terrified and fleeing, heard the prolonged, simultaneous firing of many weapons behind him.

The tiger took many hits from the two AK-47 automatic rifles. The impact drove him onto his side.

Bullets from Major Falconi's Thompson .45 sub-machine gun smacked into the bearer of one AK-47, and Blue Richard soon found the other with rounds from his M-14. The last guerrilla looked around at his fallen companions and searched frantically into the jungle for a target. Archie's single bullet from the .460 Weatherby exploded his brains from the remnants of his skull in a conical spray behind the man's head.

"Move out and assess the damage!" Major Falconi commanded.

"One of them got away," Eddie Barthe informed his commanding officer. "Do you want me to run him down, Major?"

"If you don't, he may never stop running," Blue Richards interjected.

"You got it, Blue," said the major. "And he might best serve our purposes by staying alive. Eight dead guerrillas wouldn't demoralize the rest of the V.C. as much as seven dead and one left alive to tell the tale later. I don't think he ever caught on that we were involved, and his terrified mind will find a way to rationalize any surplus gunfire he may have heard."

Falconi strode toward the supine beast. The tiger had no more energy to rise and fight. It gazed up at the tall

Black Eagle through a mist of blood, with a reproachful expression on its face, as if to say, "Why do you want to destroy me? I'm only doing the job I was designed for."

Major Falconi unlimbered the pump riot gun, its barrel rifled for twelve-gauge slugs, and said, "Well kitty, it's unfortunate that somewhere along the way you got ahold of the wrong menu."

Without remorse or guilt he pumped a shell into the chamber of the big piece and barrel-sighted between the tiger's eyes.

The dull boom of the twelve gauge was the last gunshot heard by the surviving Viet Cong, who, exhibiting a total lack of curiosity, continued his flight, never looking back.

"Too bad Galchaser couldn't make it on this mission," commented Archie Dobbs. "He was always looking for a little pussy."

Chapter Two

Maj. Truong Van sipped his tea and stared over the mug at the man seated at the desk on the other side of the office.

Truong smiled to himself. As a senior intelligence officer in the North Vietnamese army, he had plenty of responsibility. An order of battle specialist, it had been his main job to keep track of the new American units and their commanders who were beginning to show up in the south. Then he'd been abruptly pulled off his regular duties and assigned to work with the Russian who now shared his office.

Lt. Col. Gregori Krashchenko was from the Soviet KGB. He had begun his military career in the Russian army serving as a young paratrooper officer in several of their more elite units. At first it had seemed his career would be normal for an eager junior lieutenant, but he quickly caught the attention of his regimental commissar.

Not only did Krashchenko display a great amount of attentiveness in the political classes, he even wrote several treatises expounding the philosophies taught in them. The commissar sent papers to higher headquarters extolling the eager shavetail's qualities of loyalty with a recommendation that he be switched from the role of line officer to the political branch of the Russian army.

But Kraschenko did an even more "commendable" thing by turning in a fellow officer who had been making "unpatriotic" remarks regarding the institutions of Communism and particularly the current Russian government. This normally would have cinched the political officer's job, but Kraschenko was able to do even better than that—and for a very good reason.

The man he turned in was his own cousin.

Thus, Krashchenko came to the attention of the KGB. He was just their type of guy. In a political system that could not survive without snitching finks, the lieutenant was a natural.

After graduation from the KGB academy, Kraschenko was tested by being put into a counterinsurgency campaign in the Ukraine. He proved to be deadly efficient, even bringing in East German police to combine the massacre of local peasants with on-the-job training for the visiting krauts.

Kraschenko's career continued to soar. When news came out of North Vietnam of a special detachment of raiders led by an American officer, he was sent to gather intelligence on the group and begin the campaign to bring about their destruction.

The KGB agent used indigenous operatives in the south in combination with the North Vietnamese army's G-2, to first identify the group. This was when Maj. Truong Van was assigned to him as an assistant and interpreter.

Within a few months, utilizing Major Xong—the dry-cleaning truck driver—and his Saigon organization, they had blackmailed a South Vietnamese colonel named Ngai Quang into ferreting information on this group out of the Americans' Special Operations Group. Thus Kraschenko knew all about Maj. Robert Falconi and his Black Eagles.

What excited the Russian colonel the most was to learn that Falconi's mother was a Jewish refugee who had illegally fled the Soviet Union in the early 1930s. By Russian law she was still a citizen, and that meant her son Robert Mikhailovich also belonged to the Worker's and Peasant's Paradise—whether he wanted to or not.

Thus, if Falconi could be captured, it would be lawfully proper (under the Communist system) to take him back to Russia to be tried as a traitor and a war criminal. Then he could be shot or used as a propaganda ploy to embarrass the West.

Unfortunately, one effort after another had fallen prey to the skill and resourcefulness of Robert Falconi and his Black Eagles.

Chuck Fagin, the CIA case officer directing the Black Eagles for SOG, had assigned his unit to contact and recruit the Pings, a Chinese tribal group of mercenaries, to defend a strategic hamlet that would bolster the border of South Vietnam against the invading North Vietnamese army.

Kraschenko soon detected the characteristic combat profile of the Black Eagles at work. The KGB officer soon threw together a net of North Vietnamese soldiers, supported by a Czechoslovakian helicopter force, to trap the Americans.

Carefully and patiently he reeled in his net and would certainly have captured Major Falconi's unit. But Kraschenko's superior officer, Gen. Vlademir Kuznetz, the senior ranking KGB officer in Southeast Asia, jumped into the middle of the situation with both feet, seeking some of the glory for himself. But he succeeded only in confusing the application of Kraschenko's excellent field strategy.

The Black Eagles subsequently escaped the trap and successfully completed their mission.

Now, Colonel Kraschenko was waiting to be called into the office of General Kuznetz to be critiqued on his handling of that mission.

"Enter!" commanded the imperious voice of the general. Vlademir Kuznetz did not waste time telling Colonel Kraschenko to stand at ease.

"Colonel Kraschenko," the general began. "You may have learned some simple tricks on how to rise to power in the Communist party, but you will never advance beyond the status of a simple soldier because you have not learned, as the Americans say, to cover your ass. When our last mission to capture Major Falconi failed, I was immediately prepared to shift the blame onto you. You should have been willing and prepared, at that moment, to shift the responsibility further down the line. I was astonished that you did not have a contingency plan, similar to my own, for one of your subordinate North Vietnamese army officers."

Kuznetz gave Kraschenko no time to answer any of his charges and continued. "It is your primitive state of development, your political naivete, that bothers me. I know, perfectly well, how you came to be a member of the KGB. But wise up, man! How many of your relatives do you think you can turn in?

"In addition to thoroughly preparing yourself to carrying out your mission, you should also have been prepared to remedy the misguided idiocy of your commanding officer, even if that meant disobeying a direct order. The KGB needs wolves, not sheep. I expect you not only to cover your own ass but mine as well. I am beginning to have my doubts about your continuing usefulness to the KGB.

"However, in their infinite mercy, the party has, on my recommendation, decided to give you one last chance to end the career of this American nemesis. It is still our plan to capture Maj. Robert Falconi and to parade him in front of the citizenry of the U.S.S.R. We want him revealed for the traitorous, runaway-turncoat that he is!

"Start using your brain, Kraschenko. Get devious.

50

You have been attacking Falconi at his strong points while ignoring his weaknesses. For example . . ." Kuznetz began to raise his hands in emphasis several times, then paced the room with his chin in his hand, with the colonel hanging on his every gesture.

"For example," General Kuznetz finally continued. "Who does he sleep with? Unless he has a particular war wound or a penchant for boys that has escaped his fellow officers, he must be relieving his basic animal urges with someone. Your dossier on Robert Falconi is surprisingly blank on this very important characteristic.

"I am losing my patience, Colonel Kraschenko. If you fail to bring me Major Falconi this time we will have to consider an honorable disposition to your KGB career. You may find it motivating to read the Bible . . ."

Kraschenko managed to feign shock.

"And investigate," Kuznetz continued, "how King David resolved the problem of Bathsheba's husband. I'll give you a hint. There are numerous North Vietnamese army units, at this moment enjoined in battle with the forces of the Wall Street imperialists warmongers, who are crying for an officer of your training and ability. Of course their casualty rate is almost prohibitively high for us to normally consider such a transfer.

"It has also come to my attention that you are responsible for deteriorating relations with our North Vietnam comrades. Remember that they are our allies. We are here at their request and, considering their hatred of the Chinese, I doubt that your bad manners alone could alter that fact.

"However, I am giving you a direct order to secure a rapproachment with your counterpart Maj. Truong Van so that you can work together toward one goal: the capture of Major Falconi. I expect a progress report within the week. You are dismissed!"

51

Chapter Three

Colonel Kraschenko returned to his office and sorted through his files to locate his notes on the South Vietnamese army (ARVN) lieutenant, Andrea Thuy, the administrative coordinator of the Black Eagles. He found the file, originally titled "Unknown Woman," and began to review his notes. General Kuznetz had not given him an opportunity to relate what he suspected about Andrea Thuy and Robert Falconi. All the better, he thought. When he displayed the fully developed idea of Kuznetz it would appear to be completely inspired by his superior officer.

The unknown woman had been linked to the assassination of no less than three high-ranking personages in North Vietnam before mysteriously disappearing. There was no doubt it was the same woman. The description in all cases matched. Her method of operation was to appear in places where she could make contact with important people. Then, using sex, she would neutralize the individual with gun, knife, or drugs. The subject was an Asian woman in her twenties, beautiful, and rather tall. In fact, she was taller than most Oriental men.

When Maj. Truong Van compared the information to a dossier of a South Vietnamese army woman, he had exclaimed, "Why, comrade! It appears as if the unknown

53

woman is none other than the administrative coordinator of the Black Eagles—Andrea Thuy."

The data was soon verified through a new source of intelligence, a disgruntled ARVN lieutenant named Loc who was a guard officer at MACV headquarters.

Having reviewed this information, Colonel Kraschenko immediately placed Andrea Thuy at the top of his list as a possible sexual liaison with Robert Falconi.

"Ach!" he exclaimed to Maj. Truong Van, seated across the office. "Her abduction will serve double duty. We can remove a deadly adversary to the North Vietnamese army and lure a traitor of the Soviet Union into a trap. I think I will call this mission *Operation Snatch.*"

"Indeed," said Maj. Truong Van, once again impressed with the creative powers of Kraschenko, "I have a torture-master who will be most anxious to put her to the knife."

"No, you don't!" contradicted Colonel Kraschenko. "I will have none of your sadistic, primitive Oriental methods. The woman will be interrogated properly by a progressive, scientifically trained KGB official."

"I warn you Kraschenko," said Truong Van in an angry fit of frustration, "this is not the first time you have meddled unsuccessfully in the military affairs of North Vietnam. But it will most assuredly be the last. This woman is ours."

The disturbed officer momentarily lost his Oriental inscrutability and endless patience. Forgetting proper military etiquette, he stamped out of Colonel Kraschenko's office without taking leave of his superior officer.

"Your time will come soon, you insubordinate wog," Kraschenko continued to himself. "Given one week with this woman, my interrogator will have her so confused she will beg to tell him everything she knows merely to regain her own identity."

As Maj. Truong Van strode out of the office he whispered to himself, "Primitive Oriental methods indeed! Our torture-master comes from a long, honorable tradition going back two thousand years. He trained under the decadent, pre-communist Chinese. To him, the *Death of a Thousand Cuts* was an apprenticeship exercise. The traitorous woman will beg to die long before he has extracted every last, useful bit of information from her."

Maj. Yuri Sakharov was of White Russian extraction, with blond hair and blue eyes. He was no relation to the Russian dissident but suspected, at times, that his career in the KGB had suffered from the name association, an example of his superior's anti-cultural reactionism.

As a citizen and military officer with a scientific background, he had gone to the best schools and was accustomed to the best treatment. He was a specialist in his job as an interrogator in the KGB, trained in the best Pavlovian traditions of conditioning psychology.

Unlike his superior officer, Gregori Kraschenko, Yuri had never found it necessary to turn anyone in to guarantee his position. Such was the State's investment in him that he was relatively free of the day to day worries of political infighting.

Major Sakharoz was placed in a supervisory role over Major Xong of North Vietnamese counterintelligence, who was nominally his military peer. Together, they were rseponsible for the successful abduction, ex-filtration, and interrogation of Andrea Thuy. General Kuznetz knew that Sakharov was an expert in dealing with politically sensitive prisoners. The KGB officer had demonstrated that he could grab them, soften them up, and make them talk.

When Yuri was introduced to Major Xong, whose code name was Comrade Bua, he outlined his role in the mission.

"Because of my expertise in these matters, I will be in overal charge of the mission. However, due to the psychological role I will play in the interrogation of the prisoner, it would be optimal if her first contact with me occurs under controlled conditions. I am not to come into contact with her until she is safely transported to the debriefing facility in North Vietnam. You will be allowed to soften her up but not to harm her permanently.

"Initially we will employ a stick and carrot or good guy-bad guy strategy, to make certain that she has no confusion in her own mind who she should hate and fear. I have studied her history and have determined that she will be particularly vulnerable to a father figure because her own father has been absent most of her life."

Major Xong was not impressed with this arrogant KGB advisor.

"I must caution you, Major Sakharov, many of our women have been exposed to the harsh realities of life. They are not sheltered but rather encouraged to assume responsible positions in their daily lives. She may not be as vulnerable as you assume."

"This is the last time I will repeat myself, Major Xong," replied Major Sakharov emphatically. "I said that this would be our *initial strategy*. If she still cares to make judgements about your competency after you have ex-filtrated her, I would rather she viewed you as buffoons."

Xong thought to himself, *And, if you fail with your initial strategy and your subsequent strategies, our torture-master will be happy to subject that portion of her mind which survives your efforts to destructive analysis.*

Chapter Four

Andrea waved to the guard as she drove through the gates of Tan Son Nhut Air Base near Saigon and drove toward her apartment in the Colonial's Quarter. The memory of her previous night with Robert Falconi would be all she would have to keep her company for the next few days. She could not bring herself to regret breaking her word to Chuck Fagin that she would not become involved with the leader of her unit, the Black Eagles, again. But if their liaison were to get back to the CIA case officer, she might have to forgo participating in field missions with her unit for a long time to come.

Her car had traveled a kilometer of distance when the all too familiar sound of exploding mortar shells assaulted her ears. Then Andrea spotted the burning wreckage of an automobile blocking the road ahead of her.

A woman was running away from the fire toward her with what appeared to be an infant wrapped in a blanket. Blood was dripping from her fingers, staining the sleeve of her white cotton coat.

The terror that Andrea had experienced in her earlier years came back to her swiftly. But she realized that she was no longer the little girl who was forced to suffer the unspeakable, mutely and helplessly.

She slowed her car as it approached the running

woman. In the rush of events Andrea attributed the woman's indecisive behavior to confusion due to the shock of her wound. Lieutenant Thuy sorted through the contents of her purse and swiftly located the Colt ACP and the frag grenade beside it. The .45 was also the favorite pistol of many of her fellow Black Eagles. Although her small hands could barely grip the hefty piece, she found it a much more stable weapon on the firing range than the smaller, lighter detective model of the .38 Special that jumped uncontrollably and twisted in her hand with every shot. It was also a well-known fact that a .38 Special often could not even penetrate an automobile windshield.

Seeing that the woman was making good progress, Andrea turned the steering wheel and performed a one-eighty, then sounded her horn to get the woman's attention and threw open the passenger door.

At this point the woman seemed to stumble, twist, and fall on her side, cradling her baby protectively in her arms. She appeared to make an effort to rise, then fell back. Andrea gunned the car engine to move closer to the woman, but at that moment automatic gunfire ripped into the rear of the car, and she heard the sound of a tire exploding.

"That tears it," Andrea said to herself. She stood outside her car and gripped the pistol tightly in both hands, assuming a frontal horse stance to the attacking rifleman. Without using her sights, she shot the closest target twice in rapid succession. The first round took him in the groin, exploding flesh and blood down and backward behind him. Before he could pitch forward, the second round, elevated by the rise of the barrel, smacked him square in the sternum. He was driven onto his back, arms outstretched, with his rifle spinning sideways from his hand.

Taking careful aim this time, Andrea squeezed off a

round at another Viet Cong rifleman who was so careless as to let himself remain in her sight picture for longer than a half second. The bullet hit him in the shoulder and spun him around three times before he dropped to the ground, motionless. The remaining riflemen assumed very low profiles.

The woman moaned and appeared to make an effort to rise. Although the car was no longer functional Andrea wanted to use it for cover and as an armrest for her pistol, but the odor of gasoline was strong in the warm humid air. Knowing that the car could become a funeral pyre at any second, she ran toward the woman and kneeled protectively in front of her, fully exposed to gunfire.

The blood on the woman's sleeve was drying rapidly. *Good!* Andrea thought. *There is no new blood. Perhaps the wound is not very serious.*

Suddenly the V.C. charged again, but their shots were not hitting anywhere near her. Losing two companions doesn't usually shake them that much, she mused, but shrugged the thought away and thanked her stars for her luck. Without a car her retreat appeared hopeless. She remembered the words of the big Sioux Black Eagle, Ray Swift Elk: "Hoka Hey, it's a good day to die." She supported the big pistol on one knee and prepared to fire on the Viet Cong again.

Andrea dimly perceived a dull pain in her head. The pain grew and then faded. Her perceptions became a mixture of the present confused with the recent past. Then all was gone.

"Be careful, she may regain consciousness quickly," directed Major Xong. "Fetch that anesthetic mask and place it over this lethal young lady's face. It's time to call in the ambulance. Hurry up!" Major Xong exhorted his team. "Do I have to coordinate everything? Make sure she is securely tied."

Andrea regained consciousness to discover herself

inside a van of some sort, bound, spread-eagled to a wooden stretcher with soft leather and foam rubber medical restraints. She felt a dull, throbbing ache on the back of her head and a sharp pain in one spot which eased when she shifted her scalp away from it.

So that's what happened, she thought.

"Ah, Miss Thuy, you are with us once again," said the nondescript little man in workman's clothes. Andrea thought he looked familiar but couldn't place him immediately.

"Don't you remember?" he reminded her. "The deliveryman from the air base laundry supply?"

Andrea once again felt the portent of doom. Obviously he wasn't worried that she would ever again have the opportunity to reveal his identity.

"We have been waiting for you a long time," continued Major Xong. "But there is no hurry now."

"What do you want of me?" Andrea asked. "I am only a secretary at the base. I can't even get you inside."

"We know who you are and what you are, Andrea," said the little man. "In fact we require no further information from you at all. Your mere presence will be enough. And we have carefully checked your body and clothing for any sort of suicide device."

What I have for you is far better than cyanide, she thought. Then her gaze took in the two, well-muscled, ambulance attendants.

Probably Viet Cong, she concluded. Recalling her experiences at the hands of the V.C., she wished she had had the time to slip a razor blade into the appropriate orifice before they knocked her out. She was puzzled how they managed to sneak up behind her.

Andrea began to reassemble in her mind the scenario given to her at the last Survival, Escape, and Evasion monthly update briefing, two weeks before.

"The secret to survival as a captive," the instructor

emphasized, "is to make an intelligent guess as to what you can expect from your captors; that is to say, what they want from you, what role they are expecting you to play. Then take the initiative and direct the action in whatever small way you can. You must seek to distract their attention from you and to reduce your hostage value as much as possible. Try to make them identify with you as a person, a human being. Don't let them reduce you to an object. An object is easy to abuse, a person is much more difficult. They will try to humiliate you and make you feel helpless by eliciting within you the feelings of pain and terror in order to break down your will to resist.

"You must seek to avoid pain as much as possible by giving them what they think they want."

What they think they want. The words echoed in her memory. Andrea's mind continued to reassemble the scenario.

But they say they don't want anything from me, she thought. *That's impossible. If they didn't want me, I wouldn't be here.*

Abruptly the two attendants turned the stretcher over, placing her on her stomach, so that she could see out the back of the van. The vehicle was moving at a moderate speed through the northeastern outskirts of Saigon. The driver was in no particular hurry. The faces of the people were especially disturbing, so unconcerned.

Of course, her mind knew, they had no way of knowing of her predicament. But the emotion evoked within her was exactly what Major Xong had hoped for. A lost quality, a hopelessness that grew with each passing mile.

"You see," said Major Xong. "Freedom is so close but there is no one who will help you. There are people all around, but for you—not a friend in the world."

And for a brief moment she did feel terror and helplessness.

"Take a good look," he repeated. The stretcher was again abruptly lifted, and she was turned and dropped painfully on her back.

"Did that cause you discomfort my dear?" he said. "I will examine you. This appears to be a head wound."

He manipulated her scalp roughly with his fingertips, prying the edges of the wound further apart. She tried to repress her gasp of pain. Then he grabbed her roughly by her shiny, jet-black hair and yanked her head back.

"I said we have plenty of time, Miss Thuy. My companions, on the other hand, have been waiting long enough for their entertainment."

One of the attendants reached for the waistband of her dress and tore it, along with the fragile undergarment beneath, ripping it from her body.

Make them think they are getting what they want, she remembered and cried out, "You bastards!" as the first one mounted her.

Chapter Five

Feeling the satisfaction of a job well done Major Falconi watched the jungle pass his point of view from the shotgun position in the cab of the deuce-and-a-half. His head was still fuzzy from the mint-flavored moonshine served during the revelry of the victory celebration last night. But Falconi was satisfied that the villagers could now content themselves, once again, with leading normal lives, and worry about nothing more than the usual lethal harassment from the V.C.

The tiger's skin had been scraped and hung out to dry after being stretched onto a hoop framework of bamboo rod in the center of the village.

Before the hunter's return, the storytellers of the village had already begun fabricating the myth of the tiger hunt that would become part of their folklore.

Sergeant Barthe was very popular with the village children after he participated in the shadow theater in which shadows were cast by firelight against a sheet of fine fabric using stylized, cutout figures with articulating limbs that were controlled by the shadow-master. Eddie had diplomatically asked the shadow-master if he could join in the next performance. His knowledge of the Vietnamese language was practical and sketchy at best. He added words to his vocabulary that night simply by listening to the constant retelling of the tale. Hence his

63

participation graduated from rendering the sound effects of the tiger and the cries of the wounded Viet Cong to narration of the verbs of action. Finally he was granted the opportunity to work the articulated arms and legs of the figurines which cast the unfolding drama of the hunt for the tiger.

Oohs and ahs were elicited from the children of the audience for his performance that night.

Upon their arrival at their barracks, Major Falconi lowered the tailgate of the truck and assisted the three Black Eagles in unloading their gear onto the hot tarmac beyond the Special Operations Base entrance at Tan Son Nhut Air Base.

He hadn't expected Chuck Fagin to be waiting for him at the door of the Headquarters building. It was Fagin's total lack of reaction and expression that put Falconi on guard.

"You men store your gear," he said quietly to the others. "I will be with you shortly."

Chuck Fagin turned curtly and disappeared inside the office. Falconi followed. Inside, Fagin faced him squarely and announced, "Andrea is missing. She appears to have been abducted."

Still basking in the previous day's triumph, Robert Falconi was caught off guard and emotionally totally unprepared for the news.

"Where—when—" he stammered. Then his organizationally trained mind shifted into high gear.

"What are the details?" he asked.

"The guards at the base said she left the base about two hours after you did," Fagin replied. "There was a brief firefight, probably a diversion, approximately one kilometer from the base. When we arrived, two of Andrea's tires had been shot out, and there was another car, still burning, fifty yards away. There was some blood

64

on the ground, but no where near her car. No bodies were found."

"Did it appear to involve her current work?" Major Falconi asked. Andrea was often working on special operations that he knew nothing about.

"I don't think so," Fagin replied. "I highly suspect that the ultimate target of the raid was the Black Eagles themselves, you in particular. And I don't need to tell you where that conclusion comes from."

Robert Falconi remembered well Chuck Fagin's previous admonitions not to become sexually involved with the female member of his team.

Fagin had thought that Robert Falconi and Andrea Thuy had completely broken off their past liaison. The CIA case officer had once heard a navy chief put the problem of romances in a professional relationship into a nutshell when he remarked, "You should get your meat and potatoes in different places."

Robert Falconi could not meet the steady gaze of his supervisor.

Fagin continued, "I've left word with the Military Police to pick up the remaining Black Eagles in case Andrea was not the only object of the kidnappers. I want your unit in isolation until we clear this thing up one way or the other."

"What kind of effort is SOG planning to track down her captors and rescue Andrea?" asked Falconi.

Then it became apparent to Robert that Chuck Fagin was becoming more angry with every passing second. With the major's last question he exploded.

"Damn it! Falconi. Where do you get the idea that Special Operations Group exists solely to pull your nuts out of the ringer because your girl was stolen while you were out chasing pussy elsewhere? We don't do things that way in this outfit. You seem to have forgotten that

65

we have a mission to perform. You were specifically warned what could happen if you didn't completely break off your liaison with Lieutenant Thuy. Such relationships serve as a red flag to enemy counterintelligence. They are a weak link in any chain.

"If this were Yugoslavia back in World War Two, I'd have you shot for this." Fagin relented a little. "Or at least court-martialed. Lieutenant Thuy is an officer in the ARVN and a dedicated SOG operative. But she seems to be the only one of you two who had any idea what you were getting into."

Then Chuck Fagin simmered down and addressed the question at hand.

"If plans are being formulated to deal with this incident, they will be made following standard operating procedure by professionals who are trained and proven in their ability to responsibly follow such procedures. You, evidently, are not. Your unit will be informed of their conclusions at the proper time. When I get your entire unit together I will have a short briefing for all of you. You are dismissed!"

Major Falconi managed to retain his composure long enough to execute a sharp salute and about-face. His thoughts were dark as he strode back to the isolation barracks to break the bad news to his men.

A jeep with MP markings pulled in front of the tall, husky man who had been double-timing along the side of the road. One of the two military police called out, "Are you M. Sgt. Duncan Gordon out of the Special Operations Group?"

"Yo! That's me," replied Sergeant Gordon. He stepped forward and stopped across from the driver, one meaty paw resting on the jeep hood, the other against his hip.

He was barely breathing hard after running two miles.

"Hop inside Sarge," directed the soldier riding shotgun. "We'd like you to come with us while we pick up one of your men by the name of McCorckel at the brig."

"Sergeant McCorckel? That sot!" exclaimed Sergeant Gordon. "I was positive he could stay out of trouble for at least a half an hour." ●

"Oh, he's in no trouble," explained the driver. "And neither are you. Your unit has been recalled and is scheduled for isolation until further notice. Aren't you SOG boys usually warned of these things in advance?"

"I certainly thought so," Gordon answered. His brows knitted in puzzled anger as the jeep bounced down the dirt road.

The introductions to Sergeant Barthe, that day at the briefing, were hasty and distracted. He watched the faces of his fellow Black Eagles carefully as they received the news of Andrea's abduction.

"Andrea kidnapped?" M. Sgt. Chun Kim couldn't believe his ears. His usual Oriental inscrutability slipped momentarily as his face revealed concern.

"What's the plan for getting her back, Falc?" asked Sfc. Malcomb McCorckel, the unit medic.

Chuck Fagin stood propped against the wall, his arms crossed on his chest. His face was a study of somber toughness. He pursed his lips and walked, eyes cast down, to the podium in the center of the briefing room.

Chuck gripped the sides of the podium. When he looked up again his eyes were full of fury, and his voice rang with authority in the small room.

"Until you hear further, this detachment of Special Operations Group is in a stand-down condition. You are all in isolation. I don't want to see any of your faces outside the company area."

Fagin paced rapidly from the room, leaving stunned silence behind him.

Sfc., Ray Swift Elk stopped on his way out of the room in front of Major Falconi and asked in halting confusion, "Well, what can you tell us, Major Falconi?"

"Not much," Robert answered in a soothing conversational tone. "I don't know any more than you do at this point, Ray. I'll see you guys soon back at the barracks."

Twenty-four hours later the shock felt by the Black Eagles had turned into restlessness and indignation.

"The troops feel they're being punished for events that were beyond their control," related Top Gordon. "And they are being prevented from doing anything to remedy the situation."

"I realize that," responded Robert Falconi. "If anyone is responsible, I am. I think it's time for another visit to headquarters."

Chuck Fagin had not secured additional personnel to replace Andrea as his administrative assistant. Escorted by an MP, Major Falconi knocked on the office door and requested permission to enter.

"Come in, Major," answered Chuck Fagin. "I think it is time you became acquainted with the way the other half lives in Special Operations Group. The kind of work that Andrea was trained in. I often hear complaints that you direct ops people are the glamor pusses of SOG. The way I hear it, you get all the limelight, all the glory. When the people who select your missions do their research in the dark, stinking corners of Saigon or are sent into the jungle on recon missions, they are not allowed to retain their own identities much less carry weapons for fear it might give away our intentions if they are captured. They are constantly out there dying anonymously so the Black

Eagles can drop in at the last minute in their cute little uniforms and jaunty berets to add the final touch.

"Well, you will be glad to hear that we have no intentions of wasting your talents. It's about time you got a taste of some down and dirty intelligence work. I think we've had a break in Andrea's disappearance."

Falconi's posture straightened and his ears perked up.

"One of our field contacts turned up a lead. She is a call girl who was recruited, ironically, by Andrea, who was working undercover as a prostitute to get the goods on Tsing whose gang was subsequently busted up by the Black Eagles in Saigon.

"The call girl, whose name is Giselle, recently had occasion to service one of our security guards. She realized he had no legitimate source of income, from either family or employment, to afford her services. In addition, his drug habits and the exotic sexual practices he was introduced to by her loosened his tongue. What he related to her about his role in Andrea's abduction was as good as a signed confession.

"She is requesting a meeting with an SOG operative so she can personally give us the traitor's identity. I'm assigning this mission to you, Robert. But the most difficult part of it, for you, will be restraint. No matter who this man is or how you feel about him, he must not be harmed or in any way warned that we are on to him until we are ready. Andrea's safety depends on this. It could be a dirty, frustrating task. And if you don't think you will have the patience for it, you'd better develop it.

"Since you appear to have been determined to get yourself into this mess I'm going to give you the chance to dig your way out of it.

"That's it, Major," said Chuck Fagin in conclusion. "Get this information and get it back to me as quickly as possible. The sooner I get it the faster the Black Eagles can be dismissed from sixteen hour a day equipment drill and get back into the field."

Robert Falconi traveled by taxi to the address given to him by Chuck Fagin in the Colonial Quarter of Saigon. He was stopped and questioned before he was allowed to enter by a large Chinese guard wearing a suit with a slight but ominous bulge under the armpit. From his formidable appearance Robert assumed that he rarely had to resort to his pistol.

When Robert informed the guard of his appointment with Giselle, the man smiled and said, "Ah, yes, the flower of the morning. I will call ahead for you."

He opened a wooden box mounted on the wall, picked up the telephone inside, dialed two numbers and spoke softly.

As he passed Falconi through the electronically locked gate he said, "May you enjoy your days in peace and harmony, sir."

Major Falconi had only attained the threshold of the doorway and hadn't had time to pull the intricately weaved sash linked to an elaborate set of wind chimes when the front door opened.

"Major Falconi?" The musical voice floated upward to him from the mouth of an exotic but tastefully attired young girl.

"Yes, ma'am," Robert answered the well-dressed girl with a mischievous air about her demeanor. He eyed the area around them and said, "Even though this is a well-guarded, secure apartment complex, your mother should not leave you here alone for any length of time. Besides, aren't most girls your age in school this time of the day?"

She hasn't yet lost her baby fat, he thought.

"My mother?" She looked at him quizzically. "I have not seen my mother for a long time. As for school, everything I need to know to engage in my profession may be elicited by pushing the right button," she said, putting her thumb over her navel. "It is me, Giselle, that you have been sent to contact, Major Falconi. Do not be disappointed in yourself. Many people have made the same mistake. If I did not look so young and tender, I would not receive a tenth of the business I enjoy. Perhaps Andrea Thuy would not have taken me under her wing."

She led him inside and motioned him to sit down on the danish-modern sofa.

"Will you share tea with me?" she asked, leaning forward in a bow with her palms together. Robert assented. As she prepared tea, Giselle's musical voice floated out to him from the kitchen.

"Is it not Andrea who is the purpose of our discussion?" She brought the tea to the table, sat it down and asked, "For what purpose has this meeting between us been arranged, Major Falconi?"

"I've been sent to dicker with you, ma'am," Robert answered with a grin.

"How fascinating," the young girl said and giggled. "Do you have a first name, Major?"

"It is Robert," he answered.

"Well, Robert," she began. "If I had no one else to look out for but myself, I would be ashamed to set a price on the information I will be gathering for you."

"You see," she continued, "I have an infant son. He is half American, and illegitimate, as you would say."

"Lady." Falconi sighed. "I've hardly said a word since I came in here."

"Well." She smiled. The expression suited her name: Flower of Morning. "Others would use such terms. I care for my son very well here, but his opportunities in the U.S. would be far greater than any I can give him. This outweighs my love. However, I have met with considerable . . . what do you say? Red tape?"

"And you want me to help cut that tape to get your son to America." Falconi nodded. "I can't promise anything, except that I'll try."

"I can ask no more of you," she said, nodding in reply. "I require these conditions from you because I no longer live only for myself. Of course, both of us are joined in this bargain for the sake of the ones we love. I can see that Andrea means a great deal to you, Robert."

"That's why I'm here," he admitted. "And that's why I sat through a grand ass-chewing from a control officer with my mouth buttoned shut. He's upset about Andrea too and not for purely professional reasons as he claims. If he wants to let off some steam on me, that's okay."

"Andrea Thuy is a most special person. My son would have died, and I would have been left on the street without a home if it had not been for Andrea. After her mission in Tsing Chai's establishment was completed, she took care of me."

She put her teacup aside. Giselle had reached a decision.

"Because Andrea came to my aid," she said, "I will come to hers and help you with your assignment."

"Thank you, Giselle," the major replied.

She leaned back against the sofa and looked at him in a suggestive manner. Under different circumstances, Falconi would have found Giselle irresistible. He had thought that Andrea's beauty was matchless, but Giselle was certainly her equal. Indeed, this sixteen-year-old sex goddess was also forbidden fruit which added to her appeal. Would Falconi have partaken in the wondrous pleasures the girl had to offer? Back in the States she was jail bait, but in Vietnam she was a commodity. The only prohibition of partaking of what she offered was price, not morality.

However, Falconi's mind was preoccupied with

Andrea's safety. He felt a strong attraction to Giselle's rare combination of innocence and desire, yet he could not lie down with another woman while Andrea's life was in mortal danger.

"I'd better be leaving now," Falconi announced.

"A pity." Giselle smiled once more. "Please do return when you have more time."

Chapter Six

Major Falconi was once again escorted by the MP to Chuck Fagin's office. Chuck waited quietly until the MP left.

"Sir," Robert Falconi began. "The security guard who gave Andrea to the Viet Cong is none other than the commanding officer of our ARVN base security, Lt. Trung Uy Trang Loc."

"That sounds logical," answered Chuck with a sigh. "Nothing I could say would excuse his behavior, but an analysis of that behavior may give us information that would be of use in rescuing Andrea.

"The French have occupied this area as a colony for nearly ninety years. In the process, they undermined the supremacy of the Confucian Mandarin bureaucracy, as well as the authority of the village chieftain and the cohesiveness of the family unit. Currently, Communist-directed terrorism and subversion has destabilized individual values as well. We are seeing an increased number of people who are self-centered and self-seeking. They no longer see themselves in perspective with their supportive social structures.

"The Communist are always ready to take advantage of resentments and frustrations and the outright emergencies in our lives. I'm sure this is what happened to Loc. Too bad, but he's made his own bed.

"I wish I could give him to you this instant, Robert," Chuck continued. "But he has a couple of important jobs to do for us first. However, now that we are in a position to learn the identity of his control, I should be able to throw you a juicy bone in consolation to make up for not being able to put the touch on Loc.

"Listen up and commit this to memory, Major Falconi, because what you are about to hear will never appear on paper unless preceded by the heading, 'Burn Before Reading.'

"The capture of any one of us on this base would be a potential intelligence coup for the foreign powers we're working against. We play games, Falc, that plot out circumstances under which a given member of our personnel could be so thoroughly discredited that he or she would lose all intelligence value to the enemy, or, as in Andrea's case, we hope to confuse the enemy momentarily, long enough to keep the prisoner alive until we can rescue them.

"Every month it's a new game, new circumstances, so the enemy won't be able to break our cover story and see through us too quickly before the rescue is accomplished. We call it our 'scenario.' This month the scenario called for you to be a double agent for Red Chinese counterintelligence."

"But how long will it take you to set up the confirmation in the field?" asked Major Falconi in a daze. His head was beginning to spin.

"We set it up every month," answered Chuck, "when we change the scenario. Your story was fed into a few bars in Saigon and various other outposts in South Vietnam and Cambodia.

"You'll be working with Mr. Chang on this assignment. He is a Chinese rice merchant who went bad and became involved in the black market. We saw a good prospect for future covert ops when he first came to our

76

attention. Mr. Chang thinks we did him a favor and wants to pay us back. Take care not to do anything to disillusion him. He has had some contact with the Red Chinese and will make a plausible double agent.

"But it's not enough to lay a couple of false trails for the Cong to discover at their leisure. Andrea hasn't got enough time for that. So we will rub their noses in it. We will thoroughly and brutally confuse them. Whoever is holding Andrea must develop a case of severe ambivalence and indecision. We need to reduce her usefulness to them, but not to the point where they kill her out of hand.

"If everything goes as planned on your next assignment, they will put everything on hold. That will be the time to grab Andrea and nail them all."

"Sounds interesting," commented Major Falconi. "What do you have in mind Chuck?"

"It should be a tension reliever for you and your team, if not downright fun. Take as many members of the Black Eagles as necessary and, of course, Mr. Chang for authenticity.

"We will set up the situation so you can corner Loc when he is with his control. If you can't convince him that you are a Chinese double agent, I want you to at least scare the hell out of him.

"In combination with our preparatory field work on your false identity, these actions should cause enough red lights to flash on the control boards where Andrea is being held that they won't dare make any further moves until they can confirm the facts with Comintern, Red Chinese counterintelligence. And the Red Chinese are never very enthusiastic about cooperating with the Russians or the North Vietnamese anyway. They should play right into our hands."

* * *

I haven't lost count yet, Andrea thought. It was her fourth day of travel, four days and as many vehicle changes. The vehicles may have been different, but the player and the action were the same. Once, Andrea caught sight of the woman she had tried to rescue. The woman's arms were bound tightly behind her at the elbows and wrists.

Andrea was convinced that they wanted more from her than her mere presence. This must be the softening-up phase, she concluded. They were giving her barely enough water to meet her needs and no food. Soon hunger would become a factor in her will to resist.

She decided that there was little to do under the present circumstances but remember. So Andrea steered her thoughts toward her youth to give her strength and to Robert Falconi to give her comfort.

Andrea was born in a village west of Hanoi in the late 1940s. Her father, Dr. Gaston Roget, was a lay missionary physician of the Catholic church. Deeply devoted to his native patients, the man served a large area of northern French Indochina in a dedicated, unselfish manner. The man did not stint a bit in the giving of himself and his professional talents.

He met Andrea's mother just after the young woman had completed her nurse's training in Hanoi. Despite the difference in their ages—the doctor by then was forty-eight years old—the two fell in love and were married. This blending of East and West produced a most beautiful child, young Andrea Roget.

Andrea's life was one of happiness. The village where she lived was devoted to her father, and this respect was passed on to the man's wife and child. When the first hint of a Communist uprising brushed across the land, the good people of this hamlet rejected it out of hand. The propaganda the Reds vomited out did not fit when applied to the case of the gentle French doctor who devoted his time to looking after them.

This repudiation of their ideals could not be ignored by the fanatic Communist movement, so the local Red guerrilla unit made a call on the people who would not follow the line of political philosophy they taught. To make the matter even more insidious, these agents of Soviet imperialism had hidden the true aims of their organization within the wrappings of a so-called nationalization movement. Many freedom-loving Indochinese fervently wanted the French out of their country so they could enjoy independence. They were among the first to fall for the trickery of the Communist revolution.

When the Red Viet Minh came to the village, they had no intentions of devoting the visit to pacification or even of winning the hearts and minds of the populace. They had come to make examples of areas of the population that rejected them—they had come to kill and destroy.

Little Andrea Roget was only three years old at the time, but she would remember the raping and slaughter the Red soldiers inflicted on the innocent people. Disturbing dreams and nightmares would bring back the horrible incident even into her adulthood, and the girl would recall that day with horror and revulsion.

The first people to die were *Docteur* and *Madame* Roget. Shot down before their infant daughter's eyes, the little girl could barely comprehend what had happened to her parents. Then the slaughter was turned on the village men. Shot down in groups, the piles of dead grew around the huts.

Then it was the women's turn for their specific lesson in Communist mercy and justice.

Hours of rape and torment went on before the females were herded together in one large group. The Soviet burp guns chattered like squawking birds of death as swarms of steel-jacketed 7.65 millimeter slugs slammed into living flesh.

Then the village was burned while the wounded who had survived the first fusillades were flung screaming into the flames. When they tried to climb out of the inferno, they met the bayonets of the "liberators."

Finally, after this last outrage, the Communist soldiers marched off singing the songs of their revolution.

It was several hours after the carnage that the French paratroopers showed up. They had received word of the crime from a young man who lived in a nearby village. He had come to see Dr. Roget regarding treatment for an ulcerated leg. After the youth had heard the shooting while approaching the hamlet, he'd snuck up for a quick look. When the young Indochinese perceived the horror, he had limped painfully on his bad leg the fifty kilometers to the nearest military post. The French paratroopers, when they arrived, were shocked. These combat veterans had seen atrocities before. They had endured having their own people taken hostage to be executed by the Gestapo. But even the savagery of the massacre of this inconsequential little village was of such magnitude they could scarcely believe their eyes.

The commanding officer looked around at the devastation and shook his head. "The SS could take a lesson from these beasts!"

The French searched through the smoking ruins, pulling the charred corpses out for a decent burial. One grizzled trooper, his face covered with three days' growth of beard, stumbled across a little girl who had miraculously been overlooked during the murderous binge of the Viet Minh. He knelt down beside her, his tenderest feelings brought to the surface from the sight of the pathetic, beautiful child. He stroked her cheek gently, then took her in his brawny arms and stood up.

"Oh, poor child," he cooed to her. "We will take you

away from all this horror." The paratrooper carried the little girl through the ravaged village to the road where a convoy of secondhand U.S. Army trucks waited. These vehicles, barely useable, were kept running through the desperate inventiveness of mechanics who had only the barest essentials in the way of tools and parts. But, for the French who fought this thankless war, that was only par for the course.

Little Andrea sat in the lap of the commanding officer during the tedious trip into Hanoi. The column had to halt periodically to check the road ahead for mines. There was also an ambush by the Viet Minh in which the child was protected by being laid in a ditch while the short, but fierce battle was fought until the attackers tired of the fight and snuck away.

Upon arriving in Hanoi, the man followed the usual procedure for war orphans and turned the girl over to a Catholic orphanage. This institution, run by the Sisters of Charity, did their best to check out Andrea's background. But all the records in the home village had been destroyed, and the child could say only her first name. She hadn't quite learned her last name, so all that could be gathered from her baby talk was the name "Andrea." She had inherited most of her looks from her mother, hence she had a decidedly Oriental appearance. The nuns did not perceive the girl had French blood. Thus Andrea Roget was given a Vietnamese name and became listed officially as Andrea Thuy.

Her remaining childhood at the orphanage was happy. She pushed the horrible memories of the Viet Minh raid back into her subconscious, concentrating on her new life. Andrea grew tall and beautiful, getting an excellent education and also learning responsibility and leadership. Parentless children were constantly showing up at the orphanage, and Andrea, when she reached her teens, did her part in taking care of them. This important task was expanded from the normal care and feeding of the children to teaching school. Andrea was a brilliant student, and plans were being made to send her to France where she would undoubtedly be able to earn a university degree.

But Dien Bien Phu fell in 1954.

Once again, the war had touched her life with insidious cruelty. The orphanage in Hanoi had to be closed when that city became part of Communist North Vietnam. The gentle Sisters of Charity took their charges and moved south to organize a new orphanage in Attopeu, Laos.

Despite this disruption in her education, Andrea did not stop growing physically and spiritually. She was a happy young girl, approaching womanhood, being loved and loving in return as she performed her tasks with the unfortunate waifs at the orphanage.

Then the Pathet Lao came.

These zealots made the Viet Minh look like Sunday school teachers. Wild, fanatical, and uncivilized, these devotees of Marxism knew no limits in their war making. Capable of unspeakable cruelty and displaying incredible savagery and stupidity, they were so terrible that they won not one convert in any of the areas they conquered.

Andrea was fifteen years old when the orphanage was raided. This time there was no chance for her to be overlooked or considered too inconsequential for torment. She, like all the older girls and the nuns, were ravished countless times in the screaming orgy. When the raping finally ended, the Father Lao set the mission's buildings on fire. But this wasn't the end of their "fun."

The nuns, because they were Europeans, were murdered. Naked, raped, and shamed, the pitiable women were flung alive into the flames. This same outrage, as commited by the Viet Minh, awakened the memory of the terrible event for Andrea. She went into shock as the murder of the nuns continued.

Some screamed, but most prayed, as they endured their horrible deaths. Andrea, whose Oriental features still overshadowed her French ancestry, was thought to be just another native orphan.

She endured one more round of raping with the other girls, then the Pathet Lao, having scored another victory for communism, gathered up their gear and loot to march away to the next site in their campaign of Marxist expansionism.

Andrea gathered the surviving children around her. With the nuns now gone, she was the leader of their pathetic group. Instinct told her to move south. To the north were the Red marauders and their homeland. Whatever lay in the opposite direction had to be better. She could barely remember the gruff kindness of the French paratroopers, but she did recall they went south. Andrea didn't know if these same man would be there or not, but it was worth the effort.

The journey she took the other children on was long and arduous. Short of food, the little column moved south through the jungle, eating wild fruit and roots. For two weeks Andrea tended her flock, sometimes carrying a little one until her arms ached with the effort. She comforted them and soothed their fears as best she could. She kept up their hope by telling them of the kind people who awaited them at the end of the long trail.

Two weeks after leaving the orphanage, Andrea sighted a patrol of soldiers. Her first reaction was of fear and alarm, but the situation of the children was so desperate that she had to take a chance and contact the troops. After making sure the children had concealed themselves in the dense foliage, Andrea approached the soldiers. If they were going to rape her, she figured, they would have their fun but never know the orphans were concealed nearby. Timidly, the young girl moved out onto the trail in front of them. With her lips trembling, she bowed and spoke softly.

"Chao ong."

The lead soldier, startled by her unexpected appearance, had almost shot her. He relaxed a bit as he directed his friends to watch the surrounding jungle in case this was part of an insidious Viet Cong trick. He smiled back at the girl. *"Chao co.* What can I do for you?"

Andrea swallowed nervously but felt better when she noted there was no red star insignia on his uniform. Then she launched into her tale about the nuns, the orphanage—everything. When the other soldiers approached and quite obviously meant her no harm, she breathed a quiet prayer of thanks under her breath.

She and the children were safe at last.

These troops, who were from the South Vietnamese army, took the little refugees back to their detachment commander. This young lieutenant followed standard practice for such situations and made arrangements to transport Andrea and her charges farther back to higher headquarters for interrogation and eventual relocation in a safe area.

Andrea was given a thorough interview with a South Vietnamese intelligence officer. He was pleased to learn that the girl was not only well acquainted with areas now under occupation by Communist troops but was also fluent in the Vietnamese, Laotian, and French languages. He passed this information on to other members of his headquarters staff for discussion as to Andrea's potential as an agent. After a lengthy conversation among themselves, it was agreed to keep her in the garrison after sending the other orphans to Saigon.

Andrea waited there while a thorough background investigation was conducted on her past life. They delved so deeply into the information available on her that each item of intelligence seemed to lead to another until they discovered the truth that even she didn't know. She was an Eurasian, and her father was a Frenchman—*Monsieur le Docteur* Gaston Roget.

This led to the girl's being taken to an even higher ranking officer for her final phase of questioning. He was a kindly appearing colonel who saw to it that the girl was given her favorite drink—an iced Coca-Cola—before he began speaking with her.

"You have seen much of communism, Andrea," he said. "Tell me, *me chere,* what is your opinion of the Viet Minh, Viet Cong, and Pathet Lao?"

Andrea took a sip of her drink, then pointed at the man's pistol in the holster on his hip. "Let me have your gun, *monsieur,* and I will kill every one of them!"

"I'm afraid that would be impossible," the colonel said. "Even a big soldier could not kill all of them by himself. But there is another way you can fight them."

Andrea, eager, leaned forward.

"How, *monsieur?*"

"You have some very unusual talents and bits of knowledge, Andrea," the colonel said. "Those things, when combined with others that we could teach you, would make you a most effective fighter against the Communists."

"What could you teach me, *monsieur?*" Andrea asked.

"Well, for example, you know three languages. Would you like to learn more? Tai, Japanese, possibly English?"

"If that would help me kill Pathet Lao and Viet Cong," Andrea said, "then I want to learn. But I don't understand how that would do anything to destroy those Red devils."

"They would be skills you could learn—along with others—that would enable you to go into their midst and do mischief and harm to them," the colonel said. "But learning these things would be difficult and unpleasant at times."

"What could be more difficult and more unpleasant

85

than what I've already been through?" Andrea asked.

"A good point," the colonel said. He recognized the maturity in the young girl and decided to speak to her as an adult. "When would you like to begin this new phase of your education, *mademoiselle?*"

"Now! Today!" Andrea exclaimed, riding to her feet.

"I am sorry, *mademoiselle*," the colonel said with a smile. "You will have to wait until tomorrow morning."

The next day's training was the first of two solid years of intensified schooling. Because of being able to mask her true identity, South Vietnamese intelligence decided to have her retain the name Thuy—as the Sisters of Charity had named her.

Andrea acquired more languages along with unusual skills necessary in the dangerous profession she had chosen for herself. Besides disguises and a practice at mimicking various accents and dialects, the fast-maturing girl picked up various methods on how to kill people. These included poisons and drugs, easily concealable weapons and the less subtle methods of blowing an adversary to bits with a plastic explosive. After each long day of training, Andrea concluded her schedule by pouring over books of mug shots showing the faces and identities of Communist leaders and officials up in the north.

Finally, with her deadly education completed, seventeen-year-old Andrea Thuy *nee* Roget, went out into the cold.

During two years of operations, she assassinated four top Red bigwigs. Her devotion to their destruction was to the extent that she was even willing to use her body if it would lower their guard and aid her in gaining their confidence. Once that was done, Andrea displayed absolutely no reluctance in administering the *coup de grace* to put an end to their efforts at spreading world socialism.

When the American involvement in Vietnam stepped up, a Central Intelligence Agency case officer named Clayton Andrews learned of this unusual young woman and her deadly talents. Andrews had been tasked with creating an elite killer/raider outfit. After learning of Andrea, he knew he wanted her to be a part of this crack team. Using his influence and talents of persuasion, he saw to it that the beautiful female operative was sent to Langley Air Force Base in Virginia to the special CIA school located there.

When the Americans finished honing her fangs at Langley, she returned to South Vietnam and was put into another job category. Commissioned a lieutenant in the ARVN, she was appointed a temporary major and assigned to Special Operation Group's Black Eagles which was under the command of Robert Falconi.

Andrea accompanied the Black Eagles on their first mission. This operation, named Hanoi Hellground, was a direct action type against a Red whorehouse and pleasure palace deep within North Vietnam. Andrea participated in the deadly combat that resulted, carrying her own weight and then some, in the fire fights that erupted in the green hell of the jungle. There was not a Black Eagle who would deny she had been superlative in the performance of her duties.

But she soon fell out of grace.

Not because of cowardice, sloppy work, or inefficiency, but because of that one thing that seems to be able to disarm any woman: love. She went head over heels into it with Robert Falconi.

Clayton Andrews was promoted upstairs, and his place was taken by another CIA case officer. This one, named Chuck Fagin, found he had inherited a damned good outfit except that its commander and one of the operatives were involved in a red-hot romance. An emotional entanglement like that spells disaster with a capital D in the espionage and intelligence business.

Fagin had no choice but to pull Andrea out of active ops. He had her put in his office as the administrative director. Andrea knew that the decision was the right one. She would have done the same thing. She or Falconi might have lost their heads and pulled something emotional or thoughtless if either one had suddenly been placed into a dangerous situation. That sort of illogical condition could have led not only to their own deaths but to the demise of other Black Eagles as well.

The short, nondescript man in workman's clothes drove the laundry truck to the house of Mr. Ngoc, the wealthy Vietnamese businessman. He parked at the servants' entrance.

"Laundry for Mr. Ngoc." He smiled to the ancient crone who opened the door.

"Leave it there," screeched the woman.

"Mr. Ngoc left specific instructions with my superior. He is to be informed immediately of the arrival of his laundry. I will wait until I know you have given him this message."

Soon, a roly-poly, middle-aged, well-dressed Vietnamese gentleman came to the door.

"Thank you for being so prompt with your delivery," said Mr. Ngoc. "Please follow me. I have a gratuity for you."

The laundryman followed Ngoc to his office.

"Comrade Bua, welcome to my humble home," said Ngoc.

Major Xong did not acknowledge the salutation but proceeded immediately to the matter at hand.

"I've come personally to deliver essential information. I am about to be called away on an important mission. I will no longer be here to give you strategic guidance in controlling the Black Eagles' security guard. I am confident of your ability to habituate him to the pleasures of Saigon high society. But the Black Eagles are sure to come up with unique and difficult responses to our efforts to destroy them. Therefore, I will set up a meeting between you and the Soviet control who has been appointed to take my place while I am gone."

Russian control? mused Ngoc, thinking to himself. But the expression of puzzlement disappeared quickly from his face.

"In fact," continued Bua, "I have decided to eliminate the necessity for two separate meetings. You may as well bring along the security guard, Lieutenant Loc. You can both meet the control at the same time. His name is Maj. Vassily Ivanovich. This will be Major Ivanovich's first assignment in Vietnam, but he has run agents in Hong Kong and South Korea. I expect you will lend him your every assistance and insure that his stay here generates nothing but good reports to our superiors."

"Of course, Comrade Bua. I will insure that everything proceeds without difficulty," replied Mr. Ngoc. Then he accompanied the laundryman to the back door and waited vigilantly until the delivery truck was out of sight.

"Good morning, gentlemen," greeted Major Falconi to the assembled group seated before him. "There will be no formal briefback for our next assignment since it is more in the nature of an errand than a mission.

"According to Giselle, the call girl who was recruited by Andrea, we will be doing this job just in time. The NVA's informant is about to have his control transferred to a member of the Soviet Socialist's Intelligence Apparatus. Our man will be meeting with a sympathizer of the V.C. and a Russian tonight in Saigon."

"How'd Giselle get the information out of him, Major?" drawled Sgt. Blue Richards.

"Perhaps Sergeant McCorckel can answer that question better than I can," answered the major. "He is better acquainted with the medical aspects of interrogation."

"Well, uh . . ." stammered Sergeant McCorckel, "I believe she used a combination of drugs and sexual technique to manipulate his will to resist."

Sgt. Archie Dobbs glanced in the direction of M. Sgt. Chun Kim and whispered loudly, "He was so high on cocaine that when she pulled that knotted rope out of his ass, he spilled a lot more than his prostrate."

The occupants of the room were broken up with laughter. It wasn't often that they could view the art of field interrogation humorously.

Major Falconi addressed the team once again.

"Tonight should be easy or agonizing, depending on how you look at it. First I'll give you the good news. Only one of the members of the other team absolutely has to survive the night. Now, the bad news: He is the same man who betrayed Andrea to the Viet Cong. He is our commander of ARVN security detachment, Lieutenant Loc."

Surprised mumbling gave way to baleful expressions from a few members of the team. They shortly resumed their expectant silence.

"Our assignment, in the words of Chuck Fagin, is to utterly convince Lieutenant Loc that Andrea and I were turned by the Communist Chinese and now work the black market for them, here, in Saigon. In the process of doing this we are allowed to scare the holy hell out of him. But the subject is not to be aware that any of us in this room are participating in this exercise with the exception of me and Mr. Chang."

Mr. Chang stepped forward and put one hand on the podium. He briefly established eye contact with every man in the room.

Major Falconi continued.

"Mr. Chang graciously offered his services and assistance to the Special Operations Group during this assignment. He comes from a long line of rice merchants, and his abilities stem from, but are not limited to the sharp and often illegal marketing practices of that group."

Chang's stocky body filled, almost to overflowing, his extra-large, gray wool, pin-striped suit. But there was not an ounce of fat on him. It was a body that would look more at home on a longshoreman or a labor organizer. In reality, he was a member of the Tong, the Chinese equivalent of the Mafia. His gaze was frank. He did not squint or show hesitation in any way. His eyes appeared as large and round as the epicanthric fold of his eyelids would permit. To say that his presence commanded authority would be an understatement. He was careful not to stare at any one man for too long. To be subjected to his continuous scrutiny left one with two choices: to kill Chang or to leave the room.

"Mr. Chang and his organization have given considerable logistical and intelligence support to us on this assignment," said Major Falconi. "His main role, however, will be to lend authenticity by his very presence, to the notion that I am a Red Chinese double agent.

"I wish that I could give you a step by step op plan for this mission. But outside of the meeting house it will be a classical hunting exercise. You all know each other by sight. Anyone you don't recognize is dead meat.

"Once we get inside, Mr. Chang and I will play it by ear. Our cover story is that we are enforcers for the local syndicate or Tong, which is sponsored and directed by the Comintern. We have been sent by them to the meeting place to deal with an unidentified rival gang who is suspected of trying to move in on our operation. This will give us an excuse to deal very harshly with those we find inside.

"In the way of hand-to-hand weapons, you can use anything you are comfortable with: blackjacks, brass knuckles, trench knives, etc. For handguns we have obtained extra long replacement barrels for our forty-fives, machined and tapped to take silencers. We've also borrowed several silenced Sten guns.

"For communications," Falconi continued, "we will stay with the venerable Prick six. You can pick up the crystals for the frequency we will be using from me. Because of the short range, a base station radio will not be needed."

When Mr. Chang spoke, it was perfect, unaccented English.

"A number of my men will be positioned around this location at a distance of two blocks. If we are attracting undue attention, I will be signaled on this small and highly useful communications device you call a beeper."

Chang held up a one by two inch metal object resembling an undersized cigarette case.

"And since I must leave you now, I wish you each the best of luck."

Chang's face broke into a humorless smile and, as one predator to another, he shook the hand of each Black Eagle once. Then he departed.

The Black Eagles and Mr. Chang waited for word to start their mission in a blacked-out school bus three blocks from the target.

Top Gordon relayed the word.

"One of Chang's men has signaled that the principal players are on station. It's time we move."

Major Falconi's team rode to within two blocks of the

south side of the house. Master Sergeant Gordon's team occupied a complementary position on the opposite side of the house.

Sgt. Malcolm "Malpractice" McCorckel, the medic, and Master Sergeant Kim stayed with the bus, keeping it ready for quick maneuvering. Kim was still recovering from a wound to his deltoid muscle, incurred while fighting with the Pings. They both prepared for word of any Black Eagle casualties.

Falconi and Gordon soon discovered positions which, like lanes of fire, allowed them to keep the roving enemy guards in sight through most of their circuit.

As scout and point man, the role of Sgt. Archie Dobbs in this mission was to locate and rapidly penetrate the defenses of the Soviet control and report their positions back to the leader of the command element. His ANPRC-6 transceiver was equipped with a standard, transistor radio type earphone so that an accidental transmission by any member of the team would not audibly break the squelch and give away his position.

"I'd like to give you all the time you need, Arch," Falconi had told him, "but if you don't penetrate rapidly, all the parties of interest will have packed up their bags and gone home."

Sergeant Dobbs comforted himself with the thought that, once he got inside their defensive guard, he wouldn't have to worry about getting out undetected. Since it was essentially a snuff mission, there would be no one left to detect him.

He spotted the first guard one block from the target. Dobbs whispered into his radio, "One of the unfriendlies has passed my position, moving south. I'm going in behind him and going off voice transmission. Keep your eyes on the skyline and click me a warning if you see anyone on the roof."

The lighting between the houses that bordered the

meeting site was designed for landscaping rather than illumination. Archie Dobbs scanned the area in front of him for natural cover, evaluating and rejecting positions. He rapidly formulated a checker-hopping route to the target. He moved like a graceful silent dancer from position to position, ending beneath a roof overhang next to a window that was partially obscured by a banana tree. In his mind's eye, Archie could see Major Falconi inspecting the roof. Dobbs waited for the static-burst code through his earphones that would confirm the presence of a guard above him.

At the same time Sgt. Ray Swift Elk was carefully surveying his assigned area on the opposite side of the house.

They all continued to search, in vain, for the guard on the roof.

Then Top Gordon said, over the radio, "I see him coming out of the roof entrance, Major Falconi. He's moving toward you. You should be able to see him any time."

"I spotted him," confirmed Falconi. "He was probably taking a leak. Good! He's moving to the opposite side of the roof from Archie.

"Arch!" Falconi whispered into his radio, "he's on the other side of the roof. Check out the inside for more guards. And keep an ear open for my warning if the roof guard moves."

Two bursts of static acknowledged Major Falconi's message. Raising the fronds of the banana tree for cover, Dobbs stood slowly and peered through the partially opened window through which he could hear voices.

Ngoc, the businessman, was speaking to Lieutenant Loc.

"The man you knew as Bua was called away. Since my role merely entailed guiding you into the upper society of Saigon, another person has been sent to take Bua's place in order to instruct you, should we need any further information or actions on your part. He will be known to you as 'Gregor.'

"The man standing behind me and others outside are members of my personal bodyguard. They are patriotic members of the Viet Cong."

In fact, they were North Vietnamese army regulars. The Viet Cong had been decimated by recent American operations.

Lieutenant Loc viewed the round-eyed, pudgy, Slavic face before him with suspicion.

KGB Maj. Vassily Ivanovich's hair was combed straight back over the top of his head after the manner of Stalin. At times his classically Russian peasant face had been both an asset and a liability for him. While it was true that he would never charm information out of female prisoners like Capt. Yuri Sakharov, his countenance never raised suspicions of decadent western tendencies from his superiors.

In this way his appearance was a self-fulfilling prophecy, and he had been more than willing to take advantage of it.

"Comrade Bua told me that you are an excellent observer," began Gregor. "I intend to continue the lucrative and productive association you had with him."

Major Ivanovich removed a large envelope, stuffed fat with currency, from the breast pocket of his coat and handed it to Lt. Trung Uy. The lieutenant's eyes glazed over momentarily at the size of the envelope.

Archie Dobbs's quick glance took in the group inside the window. He marked, like a retriever, the man standing next to the wall with his arms folded across his chest. When the signal came, this man would be among the first to go down.

Noting the position of the circuit guards one last time, Falconi told Chang to be ready to move out. Then he

95

contacted Sergeant Swift Elk on the radio.

"Ray, the guard on the roof is yours. The second you take him, Blue can have the circuit guard on his side, and Calvin can have the opposite number. Then Top and Eddie will advance rapidly on the house and assist Archie in securing it. Wait for my signal.

"You got that, Archie?" Falconi asked. "When I signal, you assume the roof guard is out, and you take care of business inside."

Two static bursts signaled Archie's acknowledgement.

The conversation inside the window again occupied Archie's attention. Major Ivanovich continued.

"We shall require more information on the woman Andrea Roget to aid in her interrogation."

The ersatz Viet Cong guard on the roof glanced over his shoulder, behind him, then straight north directly in front of him over the edge of the roof. The circuit guards were even with his line of observation. He waved his hand to signal the northern guard when Major Falconi's thumb keyed the transmit button.

Sergeant Swift Elk held the silenced, .45 caliber, automatic colt pistol directly in front of him, arms extended in a two-hand grip. The roof guard's chest occupied his sight picture. The burst of static from his ear phone triggered the weapon. The .45 coughed, and flame leaped from the barrel. The guard's AK-47, held at port arms, leaped from his fingers and spun away out of sight.

Damn! Swift Elk thought. *The bullet ricochetted off his rifle.*

Before the startled guard could lower his hands, the .45 coughed again. The impact of the bullet, fired at an angle from below, lifted the guard off his feet.

Sgt. Blue Richards had positioned himself on the far side of the circuit guard, away from the house. Blue heard the signal from Major Falconi and waited for the muffled sound of Swift Elk's weapon. He timed his approach from the rear carefully. The guard was drawn to the sound of the silenced pistol. Blue danced smoothly forward and grasped him from behind in the classical midnight commando's embrace of death. One hand firmly grasped the man's chin and mouth, tilting the head and pulling him backward off his feet. The other hand, wielding a Randall model 2 fighting knife, came around the victim's shoulder and sliced across his exposed throat, laying bare and neatly severing both jugular veins and carotid arteries. The knife hand had completed its arc and moved out of the way before the cascading spurts of arterial blood splashed onto the ground.

The mortally wounded man surrendered a deep sigh before lapsing into terminal unconsciousness.

On the other side of the house Sgt. Calvin Culpepper, one of the Black Eagles' demolition specialists, was reminiscing the gentle chiding of Blue Richards earlier that evening as Calvin began to apply his black-face makeup.

"What do you need that stuff for?" drawled Blue in friendly humor.

"It hides de shine, man," Calvin jived back, then lapsed into an Al Jolson routine. "With this stuff, you ain't seen nothin'."

Calvin didn't have the choice of position available to Blue Richards. This time around, Calvin's guard had taken a wider path, placing the Black Eagle between him and the house.

Culpepper drew his trench knife and anxiously awaited Major Falconi's signal.

The trench knife was a favorite of Calvin's father from World War One. Its double-edged chrome blade was ten inches long. The brass knuckle handgrip guard was studded with pyramidal spikes on each knuckle with an additional spike at the base of the handle.

When Calvin heard the burst of static in his ear he decided to wait for an opening.

Shortly thereafter, he and the guard heard the cough of the silenced .45 simultaneously and, from the corner of his eye, the guard caught the flash of flame leaping from the barrel. The man began to run toward the suspicious activity. His forward momentum carried him directly toward Culpepper's position. Calvin's hand exploded upward. His overhand right punch drove the brass spikes of the trench knife into the bone of the guard's forehead, dropping the man abruptly to his knees, his rifle still at port arms. Calvin finished him with a blow to the top of his head. The stud at the base of the knife handle fractured his skull. Before the dead man's face hit the street, Calvin was running forward to help Ray Swift Elk.

When Major Falconi's signal sounded in his earphone, Archie Dobbs took a step back from the window, raised his silenced pistol in both hands and slowly, calmly squeezed the trigger, sending the round into the chest of the man standing behind Mr. Ngoc. The window shattered, and the bodyguard's back bounced off the wall. Still standing, his body rebounded forward. His hips collided with a chair, and he sprawled onto the table in the middle of the three conspirators. They were taken completely by surprise.

Major Falconi spoke firmly to the occupants of the room, first in Vietnamese, then in English.

"Don't anybody move!"

Major Falconi and Mr. Chang swiftly entered the room.

Chang immediately seized the roly-poly Ngoc and lifted him out of his chair.

"You were warned," Chang hissed in Vietnamese, loud enough for Lieutenant Loc to hear. "I warned you not to operate your black market activities from this location without first arranging payment to the Tong."

Ngoc protested as he was seized by the head. "But we are not involved in the Black Market!"

Then Chang pried with his thumbs on the inner corners of each eye socket. He popped out Ngoc's eyeballs, leaving them dangling from their nerve stalks. Ngoc screamed in agony.

Although Lt. Trung Uy Loc was no stranger to backroom interrogations, his face blanched a pasty white. He recognized the work of the Tong for its characteristic sudden viciousness.

"What . . . what are you doing with this Tong?" Loc asked.

"I was captured by the Chinese during my tour of duty in Korea," he explained. "I was turned from my folly and enlightened to the wisdom of the masses by an officer in Chinese intelligence, the Black House. I was convinced that I should spend the rest of my life working with my brothers in the fields in a program of agrarian reform but my Chinese teacher redirected my thinking and showed me that I could better aid our cause by working as a mole in my own country's forces."

"But the Russians," Falconi said with scorn, looking at Vassily Ivanovich, "are relatively new to this business. They were still dashing each other's brains out with clubs when the Chinese had developed advanced civilizations capable of astounding public works."

Taking Loc by the shoulders, Falconi looked him straight in the eye.

"We are well aware of your youthful mistake. You gave your sister worker, Andrea, over to the Russian Bear, not knowing that she was already employed by the Chinese Sages. But the party does not take your sin personally. After all, your country, in this stage of its development, is in political turmoil.

"I think I can convince Mr. Chang to overlook your

99

involvement in this scheme if we can see some indication of reform on your part. You must study the history of your country carefully and look deeply into your heart."

"Don't believe a word of this, Lt. Trung Uy," demanded Major Ivanovich. "This is not a game of poker. They cannot bluff me," he protested, eyeing the Tong chieftain warily.

Robert Falconi turned toward him and answered, "We're not bluffing, you KGB imbecile. We're buying the pot and you're buying the farm."

Falconi lashed out with a twisting punch from his hip, directing the first knuckles of his index and middle finger into the unsuspecting Russian's soft gut. The punch penetrated the untensed, yielding muscles. Falconi felt his fist ram home against the front of the man's spinal cord. Although Ivanovich wasn't aware of it, he was already mortally wounded from internal injuries. Then Falconi hit him on the bridge of the nose, breaking the cartilage, and used the heel of his hand in a swift, upward stroke to drive the sharp fragments into the KGB agent's brain.

The Russian toppled straight forward and hit the floor with a meaty thud. His legs continued to twitch spasmodically.

Chang now addressed the thoroughly terrorized young lieutenant.

"A study of your history will reveal to you that the Vietnamese have had to deal with the Chinese repeatedly. And when the Russian Bear abandons you," he continued, indicating the fallen KGB agent, "you will have to deal with us once more."

Suddenly a shot sounded nearby.

"More company," Chang remarked quietly.

"Let's boogie," directed the major. "We no longer have any reason to stay here."

He grabbed Lieutenant Loc and shook him once more.

100

"Remember what I said," Falconi warned him. "We'll be back. You'll never know when, but we'll be watching."

Falconi and Chang exited the room and followed the rapidly retreating Sergeant Dobbs. Top Gordon joined them from his anchor position to the north of the house, accompanied by Blue Richards.

"We have problems to the north," Top reported to Major Falconi. "I suggest we tell the bus to hold position until we can join them."

"Good idea," Falconi said, reaching for the radio.

"*Hau bu hau!*" a voice rasped. One of Chang's men appeared from the shadows. The Tong henchman spoke to his leader in rapid Cantonese. Chang nodded and turned to Falconi.

"The Russian agent inside the building left a field operative as a roving guard. He managed to get off a shot which wounded one of my men."

"What about the Russian?"

"My other men took care of him," Chang reported, drawing a finger across his throat.

"We'd better part company now, Mr. Chang," Falcon said. "Thanks for helping. Couldn't have done it otherwise. We'll catch you at the debriefing. And thanks again for your help."

"It's a favor well returned," replied Chang.

Lieutenant Loc ran five blocks pell-mell before regaining enough presence of mind to hail a cab which he rode the rest of the way to his apartment. Then Loc picked up the phone and called the number given to him for emergencies before Xong's departure.

Loc's fear-ridden voice poured into the phone.

"They are all dead," he reported. "Mr. Ngoc, Gregor, and all the guards. Major Falconi is in league with the Chinese Communists and—"

The man listening at the other end of the phone cut Loc off.

"Are you injured? Are you in danger at this time?"

"No," answered Loc. He pulled over a chair and sat down, feeling weak.

"Do not call this number again," instructed the speaker. "We are abandoning this outpost. This phone number will no longer be operative. Do not change your daily routine. We will be contacting you soon."

Lt. Trung Uy Trang Loc rested the phone on its base and tightened his grip to prevent his hand from trembling.

Chapter Seven

Twenty-four hours later Chuck Fagin called another meeting. When Major Falconi arrived, an MP escorted them into one of the back rooms of the telecommunications branch of the SOG base. Fagin introduced the two men.

"This is Capt. Ross Barnett. He will explain the mechanics of the technique that was used to trace the location of Andrea's final destination."

Robert Falconi shook the hand of the tall, lanky Texan.

"Follow me, Major," he said. "I'll describe how this technique works." The sandy-haired captain pulled a Bering cigar from his shirt pocket and bit off the end. His only concession to gentility was to carefully pull the remnant from between his teeth and deposit it in a trash can instead of spitting it out. His hair was cut in a flat-top. Bone and muscle competed for locations to occupy on his lean and well-developed body. Barnett removed a wooden fireplace match and ignited it with a flick of one thumbnail. With a wave of the hand he indicated the room around them and said, "This is where we work. Sorry we don't have any computers or flashing lights. It's all done organically," he explained, pointing to his head. "The radio gear is kept in a separate facility. It's so sensitive that we would have to maintain clean room discipline to be anywhere near it."

The office looked like the workplace of accountants rather than the storybook picture of intelligence analysts.

"I understand you had some fun with a couple of Rooskies last night," said Ross Barnett, eyeing Falconi with a ruthless grin.

"Chuck indicated to me earlier that we had to play hardball because they refused to deal for Andrea," Falconi answered. "The North Vietnamese army has the misconception that they are the meanest sons 'a bitches in the valley and tried to prove it by not trading for the life of one of their agents. There's nothing the Russians can do about it if the North Vietnamese won't play ball."

Captain Barnett indicated his understanding with a Gallic shrug. "Well, then, what I am about to describe to you closely resembles a method we used in World War Two in the Pacific Theater immediately before the Battle of Midway. Our intelligence people wanted to uncover whether the Japanese intended to attack Midway or the Aleutians. We broadcasted, in the clear, a piece of information that we knew would be easy to recognize once it appeared on their radio traffic. We let it be known that the water condenser on Midway was not functioning. Whether it was true or not was immaterial.

"Shortly thereafter, we monitored a transmission that the water condenser on target red was out. So we knew that target red was the code word for Midway.

"In a similar fashion our analysts have been pouring over transcriptions of enemy transmissions. In this way we slowly accumulated the code words for every major North Vietnamese army installation in North Vietnam. All it took was some intelligent guessing to ferret out the code name for Andrea."

Barnett picked up a folder marked classified and said, "Take a look at these transcripts. Let me give you some background on it. The transmission originated somewhere in Saigon. It was transmitted at night, and on a frequency that was picked up by sender to travel over three hundred miles. Let me explain further . . ."

Chuck Fagin eyed him impatiently.

"A given range of radio frequencies will tend to hug the ground or travel through the air. They are called ground waves or sky waves. Sky waves can interact with the atmosphere at various altitudes in characteristic ways. By checking with several other people receiving at different locations, the sender can quickly and efficiently pick the right frequency for the distance. And since those frequencies and distances will be the same for anyone in the region, that's how we know that this transmission was intended for a receiver over three hundred miles away.

"That's not enough to triangulate the location, but together with other information, it will do the job."

Captain Barnett had done his best to break down a difficult technical subject for Major Falconi, whose only experience with radio consisted in picking out the right crystals for the desired frequency and putting his finger on the transmit button.

Fagin interrupted. "Ross, let's not get so involved in intelligence techniques that we forget why we brought the major here."

"Pardon me," Barnett corrected himself. "Where were we?" He laid the folder down in front of Major Falconi. "Here's the material that's of interest to us. You can see several references in this transmission to an 'unknown woman' in connection with a casualty report of two Russian field operatives.

"On the strength of this we reexamined transmissions from the time period immediately after several of Andrea's wet work missions into North Vietnam. You see? Here and here." Barnett indicated. "So we are fairly certain that this is the code name for Andrea. This latest transmission indicates an unknown woman being transported to a former Buddhist temple that has been converted into a prisoner of war camp near the village of Xuan Hoa. It is situated five miles up a former tributary of this river next to a reservoir. An earthenware dam was constructed on this site in 1955, and a hydroelectric power generator was set up by Soviet advisors."

"You have my thanks for your excellent briefing, Captain Barnett," said Chuck Fagin, ending the presentation abruptly.

Chapter Eight

We must be across the DMZ by now, Andrea thought. The roads were not as well paved. She made it a game to remember every detail of her journey.

"Boredom and despair will eat away at your will to resist," echoed the words of the Survival, Escape, and Evasion instructor from her memory.

The journey had been relatively unimpeded before the change in the roads. Andrea's suspicion that the truck had crossed into North Vietnam was confirmed with the first air strike. The exit from the road during the attack from the air was so reckless that several young trees were wrenched from the ground exposing their roots. Assistance was required from the local militia to extract their truck from the ditch.

Major Xong seemed unaffected by the subsequent rocket explosions nearby. But the color returned to his face slowly, and Andrea could still detect a gray cast to his complexion when he faced her and spoke to her.

"I can see from your eyes, my fiery Miss Thuy, that you do not fear death. In fact I think you would welcome it. Poor girl," he cooed softly as he brushed an errant strand of hair from over her eyes. "Good fortune has fled from you."

Indeed, she began to welcome the attacks from the air. The frequency with which they raped and beat her decreased immediately after each bombing. Major Xong paraded the bound South Vietnamese woman in front of her more often as the days passed.

"Why did you take her captive?" Andrea asked. "She has done you no harm." Andrea still had not guessed that this woman was a shill in the kidnap game.

Major Xong turned his head so Andrea could not see the triumph in his eyes. Andrea still did not have the slightest suspicion that the fettered South Vietnamese woman who accompanied them was, in reality, an operative of the Viet Cong. She was the same woman who had lured Andrea into the trap and rendered her unconscious with a blow to the head while Andrea's attention was focused on the attacking infantrymen.

Bringing the female V.C. along was merely another contingency plan that Major Xong had little expectation would succeed. But he had planned that any of Andrea's behavior which showed a hint of decency would be noted immediately as a weakness and, if possible, used against her.

Subsequently, Major Xong arranged for the woman to be the object of a mock sexual attack in Andrea's presence.

"You will never get your baby back," the former ambulance attendant taunted her. "Until you learn your true place in the revolution."

The Russian cossack, Sakharov, with his scientific superiority and his racist arrogance, reflected Major Xong, *thinks we are here merely to run his errands for him as if we don't know how to properly carry out an interrogation of a female agent by ourselves. At least we have carried out our orders to the letter. If it were possible to soften her up, we should have done so by now. But she has stood up well under our initial efforts. For the Russian's sake,* Xong thought. *I hope that this technique called chemical interrogation is everything it was promised to me. He will need it on her. She is tough.*

Xong had no particular like or dislike for the subjects of his missions. They were nothing but military assignments to him. A given prisoner's ability to stand up under interrogation depended on the subject's training and preparation. Hard times created hard people. But Xong was ready to do anything in his power to deliver Andrea and the information she possessed to his superior officers.

Upon Andrea's arrival at the Buddhist temple, she was shackled, hand and foot, and thrown naked into a stone-walled cell.

Xong berated her. "This will be your new home. Indeed, your last home, you half-breed witch. Here, you can make all the plans you wish to betray the revolution. If, that is, you still have the strength," he finished, with a laugh.

The woman, Mrs. Ky, was allowed to see Andrea twice a day through the bars of the window. Mrs. Ky and Andrea shared the same meager rice gruel and broth rations. It was Andrea's seventh day without a proper amount of food.

It was day number two at the temple. How long could she hold out? Andrea woke up to find herself in another cell with no windows and a single, naked light bulb overhead and out of reach.

Andrea couldn't believe that Yuri had given up after only two days. He must have something else up his sleeve. Now she had no reference to day or night.

"You must not lose track of time," the instructor had said. "It is another factor that will weaken your will to resist. How can you keep track of time when you have no control over anything in your environment but your body?"

"Count your bowel movements," answered one student.

"That's a good beginning," countered Andrea. "But the frequency of your defecations can be controlled by not only drugs but by simple things, like enemas."

"Yes, Andrea." The instructor accepted her offering. "A woman's body is a twenty-eight day clock, but we also have drugs that can start or stop your monthly periods." Then one of the students with experience at tracking spoke up.

"We determine the age of a track by making our own tracks, then sit by them patiently for eight or more hours, and also check them daily to learn how the passage of time has left them eroded and weathered."

"That's exactly what we are looking for," pointed out the instructor. "We haven't the time to pursue this subject further today, so I want everyone to take some time and think about this. Find some bodily function that is not easily detectable or alterable by drugs or other methods."

Lying in her cell and looking at the naked light bulb, Andrea forced herself to bite down on the inside of her mouth, against her cheek. After that day at the briefing session, Andrea had kept a log, noting how the various characteristics of her bite wound changed with time. As the tracker had trained himself to notice the weathering of tracks, Andrea measured, every two hours, the size and feel of the wound against her tongue, the degree of painfulness to touch and the difference in its taste as it healed.

Andrea's preparations during that short briefing turned out to be very timely.

"Save physical torture for a last resort," Yuri had declared. "After all," he explained, "there are only so many physical appendages you can cut off. If everything prior to that fails, it will at least serve to soften her up."

"And, I repeat, I think you should begin with physical torture," reiterated Major Xong. "We have, at our service, a master in the art."

"Yes, I have met your freak," replied Major Sakharov, with disgust.

"He is not employed as a contestant in a beauty contest," retorted Major Xong. "I will say again that you are underestimating this woman. She is neither primitive nor weak. I hope you are not forgetting that the Vietnamese people have a history going back two thousand years."

"*Bosha moi,*" said Sakharov in exasperation.

"And we were playing these games with the Chinese when the Russians had not yet heard of Christianity, much less rejected it. Torture may be our only chance," concluded Major Xong.

The North Vietnamese army interrogation team came for Andrea when she was asleep. They injected her with a mixture of amphetamines and barbituates, known as a speedball. The net effect was confusion and helplessness. The amphetamine produced in Andrea a tendency to babble, while the barbs kept her from being uncomfortable.

"We have concluded that a sense of self is predicated on being able to accurately monitor one's environment, that is, receiving dependable feedback," intoned Andrea's instructor from her memory. "When you lose trust in your self you begin to lose your self. You need an anchor."

Andrea was thankful that she had carefully rehearsed

the scenario because the constant promptings of Yuri's team came very close to the truth. If not for the prepared story, at the tip of her tongue, Andrea would have given in and confessed everything, following their lead to her doom.

"You are lying," shrieked Xong. "It's all a lie."

"It's all right, Andrea," said the soothing voice in the French language of her childhood.

"Be logical, my dear. If we were going to hurt you, we would not have deadened your senses. We're your friends. You have nothing to fear from us."

Every fiber of Andrea's fatigue-laden, food-starved body longed to give in to his soothing voice.

"You must permit yourself to abandon your resistance now," Yuri argued. "You have fought the honorable fight, but no one can continue forever. How long do you think you have been holding out?"

The next time he came to her, the room was dark.

"Another day of senseless struggle." Yuri sighed. "After two weeks, surely your friends have given you up. You are a very brave girl, Andrea," he said, again in French. "If I had a daughter, I would wish her to have all of your qualities. We need people like you fighting for our cause. None of our present operatives could have lasted two weeks."

The scenario continued to unfold much as Andrea's instructor had predicted. Keeping her in a dreamlike state, they put her through periods of light and darkness. They fed her small amounts of food very frequently and put something in the food to stimulate her bowels.

They can't beat my clock, she thought. *Beat the clock, beat the clock.* The words repeated monotonously in her mind. The sensory input they permitted her through her drug-altered senses told Andrea that many days, perhaps a week, had passed. Yuri reinforced this confusion whenever he could.

Taste will tell, she thought. Yuri's team never caught onto the bite wound inside her cheek, her anchor on reality. Andrea's inner vision became a bird's track in the wet earth. Even though her sense of taste had been dulled by the drugs given to her, the taste in her mouth betrayed the truth. No more than two days had passed. Their attempts at hypnotic persuasion seemed to go on endlessly.

"Andrea, you must let me save you," Yuri pleaded. "We have to be sure of you. If our teamwork does not succeed, I have been ordered to try more drastic methods. You remember Mrs. Ky? She died for you, Andrea. You saw through her death, the torturer's art. Didn't she tell Minh Khoa everything she knew, anything he wanted to hear? How long do you think you will hold out under his knife? Your friends have abandoned you. Before you lies only her agony and death, flesh ripped asunder."

Andrea remembered Mrs. Ky in the hands of Minh Khoa. Andrea had long since guessed that Mrs. Ky was a plant. At first the Communist operative had cooperated in a marvelous job of playacting using plastic skin and tomato sauce. Even in her drugged state Andrea could tell the difference. Then, before Minh Khoa began the genuine torture, he cut the muscles and nerves to her tongue to insure her silence about her true role in the interrogation. Subsequently the only sounds that escaped from her mouth were endless screams that Andrea was forced to witness. After a day and a half Mrs. Ky's heart stopped beating in mid-scream. Minh Khoa looked genuinely disappointed and stomped angrily back to his quarters.

Suddenly, with no explanation, Andrea's interrogation team abandoned their efforts and left her alone.

"That is absurd," said Major Xong. "It is a trick, a monstrous lie. I am convinced that it is a ruse, concocted

113

in advance by Special Operations Group and memorized by her to buy time. We almost have her. We mustn't stop now or we will have wasted a week of effort. We will have to start all over again."

"My sincere apologies," replied Major Sakharov. "Remember, it was a week of my effort, as well. But this is a direct command from Gen. Vladimir Kuznetz, director of the KGB in this area.

"There exists a slight possibility, with only the sketchiest of confirmation, that the girl's absurd story is true. We have received independent confirmation from the field that the pirate-traitor, Maj. Robert Mikhailovich Falconi, is an agent of the Communist Chinese."

Minh Khoa was disconsolate even though Major Xong carefully explained to him that the delay in Andrea's interrogation would involve only a day or two.

Minh Khoa went to Andrea's cell and stared through the window at her. Having allowed his mind to become filled with bloodlust for her, he now seethed with frustration and anger.

"Bah!" he spat. "Cannot I merely begin the Death of A Thousand Cuts," he implored Major Xong. "She will hardly notice the first few strokes. Besides, what do we care that she might be an agent of the Black House? Many times I have wished for the opportunity to practice the arts they taught me on the Chinese themselves."

"Patience," answered Major Xong in a placating tone, laying a calming hand on the torturer's shoulder. "We all have our reasons for wanting to finish these traitors. We will let you have her soon."

Minh Khoa stood and stared at the sleeping form of Andrea for many minutes before he turned abruptly and returned to his quarters. He kneeled before the shiny red-lacquered wooden chest. After carefully lifting the top, he tenderly took out a small square box from which he

114

removed four packets and, taking one sheet from each packet, he laid them out in front of him.

Each square sheet of rice paper was embossed with a different arabesque pattern and hand painted with a pastoral scene as well. And, in one corner, each sheet bore a hexagram from the *I Ching*, the Chinese *Book of Changes*, an ancient literary work of Chinese culture and divination.

The art work was exquisite, he thought. Then Minh Khoa picked up one of the squares and began folding it to form an origami sculpture. Aside from his work, the Japanese art of origami was Minh Khoa's only vice. He indulged himself in it shamelessly. The embossed, hand-painted rice paper was the most expensive he could find.

Minh Khoa composed his mind. The first figure he finished folding was the delicate profile of a swan swimming on a lake. The next was a frog, an abstract rendition eternally poised to lash out its imaginary tongue from its mouthless face to snare an ethereal fly.

Minh dearly loved these figures. They took him far away from the real world where the most pretentious of men sought to bargain with the deepest of their secrets that they could remember or imagine for the favor of dying one moment sooner. For his art taught him not only how to kill but also how to prolong dying and agony indefinitely. The mute, folded paper figures never protested the manipulation and deformation that created them as did those spineless, vomiting cowards who inevitably soiled themselves before giving up the flesh.

After folding the third figure, a swan in flight, Minh's anger and frustration was fading. Still the witch annoyed him. *She and her friends must have cast a spell on us*, he thought. His North Vietnamese Ch'an Buddhist background believed in spells and sorcery.

After I have opened her flesh and released her life force, she will no longer be able to make fools of us. But they must

115

let me have her soon. Soon! he thought, the words of Major Xong echoing in his mind.

Minh decided to indulge himself with one more sculpture. He drew the final square before him and examined the hand-painted pattern.

"Chrysanthemums," he mused aloud. "H'mm." He began folding.

Sp. 4c., Douglas Laird had been trying for weeks to establish a contact who would introduce him to the nightlife of Tong Dushon. Tong Dushon is located on the demilitarized zone, the DMZ, between North and South Korea. Seoul, the capitol of South Korea, lies forty miles below it.

I've been here for a week, he thought. *I still haven't lined up a piece of ass.* Then one of the Koreans who sold black market goods at the base pointed out a Korean farm girl to him.

"You see Sue," he said. "Sue Park."

Doug was not one to be hesitant or shy in these matters, but he was very aware that he was dealing with a foreign culture. Therefore he waited until the farm girl was alone and then approached her.

When Doug was attending college in his home town of San Diego, he made frequent pleasure trips to Tijuana, which lay twenty miles to the south, in Mexico. He learned there, that it pays to be careful when you don't know what to expect of the local citizenry.

"Are you Sue Park?" he asked the young woman.

Sue eyed him with a guarded expression.

"I am Sue," she answered.

"I'm looking for a good time," Doug explained. "Kim sent me."

"Oh, Kim." Sue brightened up.

"You want a good time, you come see me tonight,

116

before dark," she told him.

Doug returned three hours later and followed the girl over the cold, hilly, desolate landscape.

Korea was a land of rosebushes without the roses. It seemed, at a glance, that nothing grew from the soil but thornbushes. Many previous generations of Koreans had served as slaves to the Japanese and Chinese. Neither governing country cared much what happened to the land as long as it produced more slaves. Hence, for a long period of time, there had been more Koreans than the land could support, and anything that remotely resembled a tree had been cut down to be used for firewood. Only thornbushes had resisted the depredations of the fuel-seeking Koreans.

It was winter. The river Doug and Sue approached was covered with ice. Sue skipped forward onto the surface of the river fearlessly. Doug wasn't sure that the ice would support his weight, but he didn't want to lose track of her. He tried stepping forward lightly in his combat boots. At first his progress was satisfactory. Then the ice began to crunch, and his feet sank further with each step.

Sue was now on the far shore, beckoning Doug forward. He ran after her, not knowing whether his next step would take him face down into the river. When he reached the shoreline he was running so fast that his feet were barely cracking the surface of the ice.

"Never stand still." Sue wagged her finger at him. "Those who hesitate are lost."

When they had walked a kilometer together Sue pointed and said in a tone of good-natured humor, "This is our good-time house."

To call the dwelling she indicated a hut would have been complimentary. Doug thought he had seen the poorest of the poor when he first saw the hovels perched on the hillsides around the Tijuana cemetery. But this structure made them look like first prize winners in an architectural contest.

"Come on GI," she said, grinning, as she tugged the sleeve of his combat jacket. "We will have a good time."

The walls of the house were alternating layers of chickenwire and wet cardboard with an occasional slab of scrap plywood, all mounted on a frame of salvaged lumber. The structure was, however, constructed on a foundation which raised it above the mud. Doug could make out a system of tile pipes running below the floor line. They were too large to be sewer lines.

"Are those pipes for heating?" he asked Sue.

"Yes, they carry the hot air under the house," she explained.

"Come inside with me. It's cold out here." She shivered and laughed.

Once inside, Sue spoke briefly to another Korean who was sitting on a futon-type mattress on the floor reading a magazine.

"I informed him we have a guest and asked him to put another log on the fire."

As they removed their coats and boots, the male Korean unwrapped a charcoal block from newspaper. The block was shaped like a cylinder ten inches in diameter and roughly as long. It appeared to have six thumb-sized holes in a hexagonal pattern through the round end with a seventh hole between them in the center. He bunched several sheets of newspaper individually and dropped them into a vertically positioned tile pipe that stood two feet above the floor. Then the man lighted a match and dropped it onto the newspapers, and after assuring himself that the newspapers had ignited, he lowered the form-fitting charcoal block into the fire. Then Sue addressed Doug.

"Okay, GI, these are the house rules. We party all night long for ten dollars." And still smiling cheerfully, she asked, "That okay with you?" Doug agreed and

118

handed her the money.

Sue was young enough to have lost her baby fat and otherwise showed no obvious signs of aging. She was cheerful but had no interest in sophistication. Her approach to their evening was matter of fact. She fed him a dinner of stir-fried rice and pork. Doug was grateful that the kimchi was offered on the side. He enjoyed the hot Szechwan peppers but the rotten vegetable smell of the kimchi never appealed to him.

What the booze supply lacked in class it made up for in quantity. She displayed some hash sticks. There was also an opium pipe, and the sickly sweet smell of opium began to fill the air.

"No opium," Doug said pointedly. Then he said in softer terms, "A man is no good in bed after smoking the pipe."

Sue giggled and put the apparatus aside. The young Korean girl proved an enthusiastic bedmate. She was eager to please and willing to experiment. After they had exhausted themselves, Doug decided to give the pipe a try.

Sue expected the opium to produce its characteristic symptoms of nausea, and when Doug began to show signs of queasiness she said, "Take a little hash with the opium. It helps the stomach."

Under the influence of the opium, Doug's mind drifted back in time. He felt like he was flying: like the time he and a companion tried out a Montgomery type, bi-wing, ultralightweight glider. The flying was great, even in the cumbersome bi-wing, but he had to run like hell when he landed, and the impact on his feet was almost as hard as a parachute jump. Then Sue's face, floating above him, brought back the image of another Oriental girl when he rafted the San Dieguito, that afternoon in March, two years past.

There are no true rivers in San Diego County. It is the

most southwestern county in the contiguous forty-eight states. There are a number of streams and dry riverbeds. The area receives only ten inches of rain in an average year and is termed semi-desert by geographers.

About once every thirty years, enough rain falls to turn the dry riverbeds into torrents of water. Doug joined his friends in taking the afternoon off from school. They rented a Zodiac, a French manufactured river raft, and set out for Rancho Santa Fe to find a path that they could use to carry the raft to the face of the Lake Hodges dam. The rafters traveled a side road the length of the river looking for the lay of the river and possible obstructions. It was an excellent first step toward being prepared but not good enough. A hillside had obscured that part of the river which contained the whirlpool. Hence, the party of rafters was unprepared as they rounded the bend in the river at forty miles an hour.

Doug vividly remembered the cataract that flowed over the top of the dam. One of his friend remarked, "The ranger said that the overflow is three thousand cubic feet per minute. Local news programs had warned enthusiastic novices away from the spot, but the authorities were not set up to deal with a situation that occurred so infrequently.

"It doesn't look so different from the Kern river we rafted up near Bakersfield last summer."

"No sweat," Doug replied.

Their confidence was not misplaced. They were as good as any crew who could have successfully rafted the river that day, but their luck almost deserted them. As they rounded the bend, the river took a dip and swirled in one corner like the bottom of a bathtub. The vortex spun them in a three hundred and sixty degree circle before it spewed them violently forth. The whiplash was tremendous. The Oriental girl was slapped in the side of the face with her own paddle. In calmer waters she assessed the damage.

"I think I've loosened a tooth," she remarked, pulling a white object from her mouth. It was a complete extraction with no fractures. She positioned the tooth properly and inserted it back into the socket and kept her mouth lightly closed until the end of the trip.

Doug heard later that the tooth had retaken.

"That was one tough woman," he remarked to his friends after the voyage.

The young man, dressed in army fatigues with Signal Corps black brass pinned to his collar, stood five feet, three inches and had blue eyes and brown hair.

"Sergeant Laird, reporting as ordered, sir!" he said as he saluted his commanding officer. The captain barked at him in reply: "Laird, I've been looking for a way to get rid of you since you joined this unit. The only reason you weren't thrown into the brig immediately after working over that Korean drug dealer was because the Korean authorities had less love for him than I have for you, if that's possible.

"I hadn't yet decided if it would be worth the two hundred dollars out of my own pocket that they wanted to complete the deal. But I have decided that you have been in Korea long enough.

"Fortunately for my wallet, I received an inquiry from Military Assistance Command, Vietnam, that appears to solve our problem. Someone in the Special Operations Group in Saigon is more aware of your sterling qualities than I am. They've sent us a briefing on the situation and a letter of inquiry asking if we will consider putting you on loan to them temporarily."

Sergeant Laird interjected, "Vietnam, sir?," in a decidedly unenthusiastic tone. Then the captain continued:

"I didn't ask you for your opinion, Laird. You are going to accept their offer and get the hell out of my hair or I'm going to use the transportation allowance that they sent me to pay for your flight to 'Nam, and bribe the Korean MPs to throw your trouble-making ass in jail. I'll get shed of you one way or the other. The flight leaves tomorrow at noon. It's all arranged. I have, here, an all points bulletin on you that I will activate at thirteen hundred hours tomorrow. Therefore, you had better hope I don't see you again. Get out!"

"Vietnam?" repeated Sue Park, plaintively. "Why do you have to leave, GI? I have enjoyed your visits at the good-time house."

South Korea maintained an active presence in South Vietnam, and Sue had personally known a number of young men who were inducted into the South Korean army and sent to Vietnam, never to return.

"Isn't it enough that we must fight to keep the Communists from conquering our own land? Why must we become involved in quarrels of other countries?"

But Sue quickly accepted the inevitable with Oriental fatalism and tried her best to make his last night in Tong Dushon a memorable one.

On his long flight to Saigon, Sgt. Doug Laird had occasion to remember the fight that caused him to leave South Korea.

Doug found that he was not partial to opium because of its tendency to cause vomiting without warning. His introduction to the drug during his first visit to the good-time house was to prove useful later in Tong Dushon when he was trying to score some hashish. His street connection, a wizened little middle-aged South Korean, deliberately misunderstood his request for the refined product of marijuana. The connection gave Doug a hand-rolled cigarette supposedly laced with hashish, but Doug immediately detected the bitter, alkaloid taste on his tongue and the sickly sweet smell. He thrust the cigarette back toward the dealer and motioned emphatically with his hands.

"No opium, no opium!" Doug declared.

The dealer concluded that his ruse had failed, and he would be left empty-handed. In order to prevent his evening from being a total waste he leaned forward as if to give Doug another cigarette and literally ripped off Doug's watch from his wrist, then fled down the street.

Doug didn't appear to be strong or fast for his size, but the Korean discovered, two blocks later, that he was overmatched. The swift-sprinting American struck the Korean between the shoulder blades, knocking him off balance onto his face. The Korean thug tried wrestling but never quite got his balance. Doug put him into a headlock and proceeded to ram the drug dealer's head into the side of a building several times. The would-be thief found himself on his back suffering rapid blows to his head from the GI's fists. Even at that, Laird found that he had to pry the semiconscious man's fingers from the watch. By this time a crowd had gathered, and Sergeant Laird could not break through them fast enough to avoid arrest by the South Korean Military Police.

It was raining when Sgt. Doug Laird arrived in Vietnam. The winter monsoon was in full swing. At least it was warmer than Korea, Doug thought, as he wiped the sweat from his brow.

There was something familiar about the Oriental woman in WAC officer's uniform, sporting "I" Corps insignia, who stood waiting for him. She reached up and grasped his hand as he started to salute, kissing him on the cheek as she embraced him.

"I'm so glad you volunteered to help my friends, the Black Eagles," said Linda Fong, who greeted him as he stepped off the Military Air Transport aircraft at Tan Son Nhut Air Base, north of Saigon. Doug hadn't seen Linda since his adventurous rafting trip on the San Dieguito River when she managed to salvage her tooth. He certainly didn't expect to see her in Saigon.

But, with the words of his commanding officer in Tong Dushon still ringing in his ears, Doug thought fast and replied, "I was happy to offer any help I could. However, I am a little confused by their request. I know that I couldn't possibly be the only soldier in the United States Army in the Asian Theater of Operations who has white water rafting experience."

"Of course not, but the next mission for the Black Eagles is right up your alley," Linda replied enthusiastically. "Naturally I wish I were going along," she continued, "but I am only an intelligence analyst, and don't have sufficient field training to qualify for the mission."

"Well, I wouldn't hesitate to go with you on any mission," Doug reassured her. "You are as tough as they come."

"I appreciate your confidence, Doug," said Linda, "but there are no more slots available for this mission."

Linda maneuvered the jeep skillfully over the wet runway approach lanes and drove them to the Special Operations Group company area through the Military Police checkpoint. Then Linda escorted Doug to Chuck Fagin's office.

"Welcome to Vietnam, Sergeant Laird," said Chuck Fagin. "I want you to meet your commanding officer on this mission, Maj. Robert Falconi."

Sergeant Laird shook the tall major's hand.

"We're grateful that you decided to join us. We need a man with your specific talents. Linda tells us that you

124

like to raft recently created rivers."

Sergeant Laird replied, "That opportunity did come up at one time. I didn't expect it to happen again so soon."

"Tell us, Sergeant Laird, what would you advise a team who were planning a trip similar to yours and Linda's experience on the San Dieguito River?" asked Major Falconi.

"Well, sir," began Doug slowly, "I'd advise them to scout the area thoroughly beforehand and take it very slowly."

"We can fulfill the former requirement from the air," commented Major Falconi as he fired up a cigarette with a battered old Zippo lighter. "But not the latter. We expect to be pressed for time. I will show you the barracks, and you can get settled in."

The stage was set. The isolation phase of mission preparation was shorter than usual, a scant twenty-four hours, compared to the usual seventy-two hours. But, it was an agonizing twenty-four hours for Robert Falconi.

There was no way of confirming whether or not the North Vietnamese army was buying the rumor that Falconi and Andrea Thuy were double agents, secretly in league with the Peking Black House, the trade name of the Chinese Communist Counter Intelligence. And, if the Reds bought the rumor—which had been supported by careful groundwork—there was no way of guessing how long the rumor would do its job of freezing Andrea's captors in their tracks.

There was a high probability that by this time the North Vietnamese army interrogation team had either beaten the information they wanted out of Andrea or had given up on the idea that she would give them anything.

In either case, the value of her life to them shrank, hour by hour.

Major Falconi stood, facing his men in the briefback room. "The purpose of this mission is no surprise to

125

anyone," he said. "We've located the site of Andrea's captivity. It is a former Buddhist temple in North Vietnam, converted to a prisoner of war camp. Our mission is to capture the temple and take Andrea back. Top Gordon will now outline the time elements of the mission."

The senior NCO of the Black Eagles took the podium.

"Please refer Operations Plan A," directed Sergeant Gordon. "Reveille will be at oh-one hundred hours."

"Why bother to hit the sack," grumbled Archie Dobbs.

"Chow will be served at oh-one thirty hours," continued Top Gordon, with hardly a pause. "We will suit up with conventional parachute harness, rigged for a static line jump at oh-two hundred hours, then board the jumpship, a C-one nineteen at oh-two thirty hours. Based on the meteorological report, containing, among other information, the winds aloft, our estimated time of arrival over the drop zone should be oh-five thirty hours."

Then Top Gordon picked up the wooden pointer and touched the map of North Vietnam.

"The grid coordinates of the DZ are: nineteen degrees, thirty-eight minutes latitude; one oh five degrees, thirty-six minutes longitude. This will be another rice paddie landing."

Blue Richards shivered and chattered his teeth audibly. "Another rice paddie landing at that time of the morning? If this game is played with leather balls, we'll all be well equipped."

Sergeant Gordon continued to ignore the interruptions. He had learned that they were part of a continual testing process by the professional warriors of the Black Eagles to assure themselves that their spit and polish senior NCO was completely absorbed into the unit.

"The rice paddie complex is of recent construction and

lies to the west and down the slope from the temple. After policing up the DZ, we will proceed east on the paved road toward the temple at oh-six hundred hours.

"Two men will break off from the main party and flank the anti-aircraft emplacement to the south of the temple. When we commence the assault on the temple, they will coordinate a diversionary attack on the ack-ack to keep those machine gunner's heads down and divert their fire from the main party. As soon as we secure the temple we will assist in neutralizing the AA battery. We expect at least a company of troops to be garrisoned at the temple and perhaps a battalion-sized unit of militiamen to be immediately available between the temple and the coast." Acknowledging the sober expressions and frank scowls on the faces of the team, Master Sergeant Gordon commented, "It is true that we appear to be taking the bull by the horns on this one, but we've faced heavier odds before and we are inclined to be prepared to pay heavily to successfully complete this mission. The word is that we cannot afford to let the Cong and the North Vietnamese army think that they can pick us off, one by one, by kidnapping and terrorism."

"Fuckin'—A!" drawled Blue Richards.

"Kick ass," another voice mumbled, in a subdued unenthusiastic tone.

Many eyes were cast down on their handout materials. At that moment Major Falconi imagined that he could feel every Black Eagle in the room restraining himself from looking backward at Lieutenant Loc, the man responsible for Andrea's absence.

For his part, Lieutenant Loc must have been convinced that no one else but Major Falconi and his henchman, Sergeant Dobbs, knew of Loc's part in the abduction of the Black Eagles' only female member. All he could sense for certain was the deadly commitment of the group to get the job done.

Sergeant Gordon continued: "We must neutralize the AA emplacement before the next step in the OP plan, which is to ex-filtrate everyone to the other side of the Song Yen Reservoir and join up together on the road to Dong Tau. At that point, we will link up with prearranged helicopter transport home, including a medivac chopper. We don't expect the prisoner or prisoners to be in good shape."

An overlay of the OP plan had been attached to the map of North Vietnam on the wall. The planned movement of the Black Eagles progressed in a sweeping arc that ran to the left and upward, over the temple and across the reservoir to the paved road.

Top Gordon then yielded the floor to the unit intelligence specialist.

Sfc. Ray Swift Elk took the podium.

"The North Vietnamese army detachment guarding the temple prisoner of war camp are garrison troops. But don't let that fool you," rang the rich baritone voice of the high-cheeked, plains warrior. "These boys are sharp. One platoon is always on guard at the temple. And while each of three platoons alternates the watch every eight hours, the fourth platoon is held in reserve. While not on duty, the troops are billeted in Xuan Hoa, only one half mile by paved road south of the temple. In addition there is a battalion of militia, National Guard-type troops, stationed in the surrounding area. However, even if they have been called up on alert, they will only be expected to perform traffic control duty and set up road blocks to prevent us from using the main roads for escape. The only other danger they represent lies in the fact that they have been trained in the technique of volley fire in group formations aimed at low altitude aircraft and could present a significant hazard to a heavily laden, slow flying helicopter."

Breath escaped pursed lips, and someone snapped a

pencil in the tense room.

"From our aerial survey, the anti-aircraft emplacement appears to consist of two Soviet twelve point seven millimeter DShK M one nine three eight-forty-six heavy machine guns on wheeled mounts converted to tripod for AA fire. These weapons are similar to our fifty caliber M two HBs. In fact some of the fifties we loaned to the French were captured by the Viet Minh at Dien Bien Phu in fifty-four and are often substituted on the DShK mount.

"We expect that the garrison troops will be equipped with Chinese Communist modified type-fifty, seven point six two millimeter or the seven six two modification of the MAT forty-nine, the French model forty-nine submachine gun modified to take the type fifty pistol cartridge.

"While it is true that much of the North Vietnamese equipment is scavenged and the local militia will be equipped with bolt action rifles, I would caution you not to treat this opponent as a second class army. They may be new to industrialization but their culture and society is accustomed to warfare. They have a history of conflict with the Chinese going back two thousand years. And some of that time they won clear victories. In fact they wore down the forces of Kublai Khan until he awarded them the status of an ally instead of a conquered nation. They are resolute, aggressive, and highly adaptable."

Top Gordon again took the podium and announced, "By now you have all met Sgt. Eddie Barthe, one of our new additions. Because he was a crew chief in the Air Cavalry, it's been decided that he should handle the supply requirements for this mission since we lost Charley Tripper when we set up the Pings.

"Our other addition, Sgt. Doug Laird, from Signal Corps in South Korea, will assume Sparks Martin's duties."

Sgt. Eddie Barthe addressed the group: "Since this is going to be an air drop, we will be limited to M-sixteens and M-seventy-nine grenade launchers in addition to the usual assortment of grenades. We will be totally dependent on the Evac choppers for machine gun support, and we will have to wait until rendezvous time to get it. No supply drops are planned unless we are delayed beyond our projected departure time, so you will be limited on food to the amount of C rations you can carry."

Sergeant Laird felt like he had been invited to a costume party. He was unaccustomed to the sharp-looking tiger-striped fatigues and the jaunty black beret on his head.

"Sergeant Laird," called out Top Gordon. "Henceforth we will follow the tradition of addressing you as 'Sparks'. Please give us a commo briefing."

"My information," Doug replied, "is that this team is most familiar with the ANPRC-six, hand-held AM unit, the Prick-six. So we will stay with what we know. The call signs will be: Falcon, for the Command Element; Alpha and Bravo for each team. The relief choppers will have ANRC-forty-ones. I was warned to pick out and field test the frequency determining crystals for each radio and that has been done."

Top Gordon didn't give Doug time to wind down before he announced, "Malpractice will give you the medical briefing."

Sergeant McCorckel addressed the two new additions, Sergeants Laird and Barthe. "Eddie, you've seen duty with the A teams so you are familiar with the serious consequences of untended insect bites as well as cuts and abrasions in this tropical climate. But Sparks has been spending his time up in the cold, northern climate of Korea. So let me emphasize to you, Sparks, and to remind everyone in the room that over fifty percent of the deaths

130

of American personnel in Vietnam to date have been due to insect bites, especially the local mosquitoes which transmit one of the more virulent forms of malaria. I know that it may seem that death is death, no matter which way you cut it, but, believe me, a bullet is a lot cleaner."

Top Gordon concluded the briefback session. "I will post the mission roster and team assignments. I know that you all have additional preparation to complete but try to get some sleep tonight. Reveille comes early at oh-one hundred."

Lt. Trung Uy Trang Loc went off shift from his duties as commander of Special Operations Group ARVN Security Detachment at Peterson Field at one-five thirty hours.

Chuck Fagin had issued a hand-held radio to one of his street operatives, with the following instructions: "Don't follow Loc too closely. We don't care where he goes or what he says, but don't lose him. Only let us know if he appears to be returning here."

After the operative left, Chuck Fagin thought to himself. *We don't care where he goes or what he says because our electronic eavesdropping section ferreted out the location and frequency of their transmitter a week ago, and we're going to be recording every word they send to North Vietnam.*

Then Fagin hurried toward that section of Peterson Field that housed the radio intercept apparatus and approached the door of a nondescript storage shed that was being surreptitiously guarded by a pair of men with binoculars. As he knocked on the door of the shed, unseen eyes recorded his entry. The two American MPs with field glasses and walkie-talkies were assigned to assure that no unauthorized personnel heard what was said at the gathering.

"How did you find this place, Chuck?" Major Falconi

131

asked inside the building as he pulled up a folding chair for the CIA case officer.

The flip-over blackboard, from which a second mission briefing map was hung, had seen better days. Baling wire had been substituted for one of its hinges. The sober expressions on the faces of the assembled Black Eagles confirmed that it would be very difficult to see the flip side of this briefback.

"The barracks are set up as planned?" Chuck Fagin's statement was voiced as a question.

"From the outside it looks like we're snoozing away peacefully, with all the lights out," replied Sgt. Ray Swift Elk.

Major Falconi once again faced the men he had addressed earlier that day.

"That was an excellent job of acting you guys did during the first briefback today. I'm certain that none of us agreed with Chuck at first when we heard about his decision to hold off nailing Loc after we learned that he was the one who gave Andrea to the Cong."

"Well, Robert," began Chuck Fagin, "in my end of this business you often learn the hard way that it never does any good to capture a double agent no matter how badly you want to. Unfortunately we often lose lives learning the lesson."

Robert Falconi said, "If we are to have any hope of getting Andrea back alive and returning the Black Eagles to Saigon intact, we must be able to mislead and outwit our opponent.

"At this moment Lieutenant Loc is undoubtedly on his way to relay every word of the first briefback to his Viet Cong contact who will transmit the information immediately to the North Vietnamese army who are holding Andrea. We knew from the beginning that the purpose of Andrea's abduction was to lure us into fighting the North Vietnamese on their territory, on their terms.

"Well gentlemen, we are going to take them up on that proposition, but not quite in the way they expect. I want you to let every word you heard during the first briefback sink in because nine-tenths of it is useful information. The difference between that plan and our plan is as follows."

Sgt. Archie Dobbs breathed an audible sigh of relief and kicked back his folding chair to lean against the wall.

"You don't know how relieved I am to hear you say that, Falc," Dobbs said. "You know I'd walk on razor blades to save Andrea or any other member of the Black Eagles, but that first plan you proposed was suicidal. It had enough holes in it to make a block of swiss cheese jealous. Only a totally disarmed man has nothing up his sleeve."

A "boo" issued forth from the back of the room, and a paper cup sailed close by Dobbs' head. Then the group settled into an attentive silence.

Major Falconi continued: "Now that we've misled them, we have to keep them off balance. The first plan was an attempt to do exactly what they would expect of us: Pick the most obvious DZ, make the most logical attack against their strong points, and ex-filtrate the rescued prisoner by the most conventional method."

Major Falconi pointed to the rice fields on the map west of the temple.

"Eleven parachutes will be dropped on the rice fields but nine of them will be dummy loads. Here's how it will go down. After dropping the dummy chutes the jumpship will turn left and fly past the temple, over the reservoir. It will make a climbing turn to the left where it will soon be obscured from the vision of the anti-aircraft emplacement by the shear-sided one thousand foot high hillocks which begin the coastal mountain range to the east. Both the first and second jumps will be static line rigged at eight hundred feet above ground level. The jumpship will level off behind the mountain under reduced power long enough for the remaining men in the second stick to jump comfortably. Then it will continue to climb into the line of sight of the North Vietnamese army, who, hopefully, will not even suspect the existence of the second group."

"No time for reserves," commented Sergeant Barthe.

"That's correct," said Major Falconi. "We can't afford the altitude that would give you the time to deploy your reserve chute in case of a Mae West. So it's even more important than usual that you double and triple check your rigging."

Major Falconi summed up the salient points of the mission.

"The North Vietnamese army must be convinced that they have us right where they want us. They know that they will have numerical superiority and that we have to come to them. We must take advantage of every opportunity to mislead them. The story we gave Lieutenant Loc was a good beginning. We lead them to believe that helicopters will be used for ex-filtration. In reality, helicopters will not be used in any phase of this mission. They will expect us to escape by air because it is the fastest method. We will not. In the event that we do not escape by air, they will assign their militia the task of setting of roadblocks on the paved roads in the area. We will not use any paved roads. They will expect us to attack the temple using an overland approach. We will perform an amphibious landing from the lake. They will expect us to use the most obvious drop zone, and we will do so, but only as a diversion."

Archie Dobbs had not forgotten the demonstration of magic put on by Eddie Barthe when the two Black Eagles first met one another in the barracks.

"It sounds to me, Falc," he commented, "like we're going to do what they don't expect us to do: be where they don't expect us to be and divert their attention elsewhere just to be sure they don't catch on too soon."

"And I thought I was a magician," Eddie Barthe added. "We should call this mission Operation Sleight of Hand."

"So be it," declared Major Falconi, and continued. "We have also led the North Vietnamese army to believe that there won't be any close air support except for the evacuation helicopters. Again, I'm afraid we've dealt them falsely. The Special Operations Wing has laid on four Skyraiders for this mission. They will be armed with rockets and machine guns as well as five hundred pound bombs. And if the North Vietnamese army thinks we cheated a little bit to accomplish our infiltration, they're going to be really upset at our method of ex-filtration."

Major Falconi turned and addressed the Black Eagles' Navy Seal, CPO3 Blue Richards. "Blue, I've seen you spent many an hour over a checker board. Tell me, what is your absolute, last ditch move when you can't afford to lose?"

"Well suh," drawled Richards, "not that I have personally used this technique. Yuh gotta remember, I only play checkers with mah friends. But if it was a situation where I couldn't afford to lose, I would be forced to accidently upset the checker board."

Sergeant Barthe folded his arms and looked askance at Richards. "I'd have never thought of that Blue," he said.

"That's the sneaky part of being in 'Sneaky Pete,'" contributed Ray Swift Elk, referring to the pet name often used for Special Forces.

"Thank you Petty Officer Richards," said Robert Falconi. "That is exactly what we intend to do."

"You got me curious, Falc," said Archie Dobbs. "So tell me, how are we going to tip over their checker board?"

"A fair question," replied Falconi. "Bear with me for a

moment. The first element of air support's mission is to take out the anti-aircraft emplacement. At that point we will have taken the high ground and established air superiority. Their next element is ground support fire against the garrison troops who will be called in from Xuan Hoa, leaving the temple guarded by *one platoon*."

"A piece of cake," said Sergeant Kim, sarcastically.

Major Falconi continued: "Once we've taken the temple and rescued Andrea and any other prisoners of interest, we will pick up the boats and make our way northwest, away from the temple, and for a moment, at least, we will appear to follow our false game plan while we hoof it a short way up the road toward Dong Tau.

"However, since we anticipate an ambush to be laid on for us by the North Vietnamese army from that direction, considering that it's the location where our evac choppers would have landed, we will leave the road and follow the dry riverbed to the west where we will rendezvous with Sergeants Kim and Barthe. It will then be time for the third element of air support's mission.

"After taking out the AA guns, they will loiter in the area, attacking enemy troop concentrations. Then, on my signal, they will skip-bomb the earthen dam that forms the reservoir with their five hundred pound bombs."

"Hold it, Falc," requested Sgt. Calvin Culpepper, one of the Black Eagles' demolition experts. "I've heard about those skip-bombing techniques. They work well against concrete dams along the Ruhr River in Germany in World War Two and did a hell of a job on the steel-hulled troop ships of the Japanese invasion fleet north of Australia in the Pacific Theater of the same war, but it seems to me that a skip-bomb might not work on an earthen dam, some of which are tens of feet thick at the base."

"Good thinking, Calvin," responded Major Falconi.

"To carry your logic one step further, it wouldn't be worth our while to blow out the dam all at once."

Falcon lit a cigarette and thoughtfully blew a smoke ring overhead. "Our technique must resemble one devised by Col. 'Pappy' Gunn against the Japanese. Each A-One Skyraider will make his bombing run at a carefully controlled speed and height above the water and, using the roadway that runs across the top of the dam as a measure of proximity, will release his bomb. The bomb will skip over the water like a stone and finally sink close to an ideal position for blowing out a portion of the dam and creating a controlled flow of water."

"Maybe." Blue Richards shrugged. "If'n the bombs blow at'll."

"Each bomb will have two fuses. The first is a depth fuse, set to detonate at ten feet in depth. In case the bomb fails to explode, the second fuse is timed to detonate the charge ten seconds after its release from the bomb rack.

"Even if the bomb does not reach the optimum depth," Falconi continued as he ground out the cigarette under a boot heel, "it will still detonate by the time fuse and be able to contribute to the final goal. By positioning the bombs at this specific location, we hope to blow a hole through the upper cross section of the dam."

"Are you sure you didn't recruit some science fiction writers for the planning team that thought this one up?" asked Malpractice McCorckel. "Has anyone ever done anything like this before?"

A grin began to curl the corners of Sgt. Doug Laird's mouth.

Malpractice continued: "Blowing out a dam so you can ride a raft down the flash flood sounds about like surfing a tidal wave."

"I can vouch for the skip-bombing techniques. It was worked out in every detail," volunteered Ray Swift Elk.

McCorckel's head was whip-sawed to the right and

then the left as he listened to Swift Elk's words and then turned as Sergeant Laird began to speak.

"And I can vouch for the river rafting."

"Sergeant Laird was recruited for this mission," explained Robert Falconi, "because he and his team rafted a flooding river under almost identical conditions. When I finish, he will have a few words for you. A second Skyraider will proceed two miles downriver where a tributary joins the old riverbed and drops twenty feet over a waterfall. The pilot will drop his bombs into the top of the waterfall with the object of reducing the slope of the falls to a series of negotiable rapids."

"Wouldn't it be safer to walk the rafts around the waterfall?" offered Sergeant Swift Elk.

"We will do that if we have to," replied Major Falconi. "But it is debatable whether it would be safer, because, in the final analysis, the success of this mission and the safety of our team depends on how fast we move. We cannot give the North Vietnamese army a chance to recover.

"Once beyond the falls, we still have to pass through the village of An Trach and proceed three miles beyond that to a point where the river is crossed by a railroad bridge. There we will be met by motor transport which will carry us seven miles to the coast. The flooding of the river at An Trach will temporarily distract the militia stationed there. We must follow soon after the crest of the flood to achieve maximum surprise and minimum resistance.

"Our motor transport is a World War Two United States Army halftrack, loaned to the French, and captured by the Viet Minh at Dien Bien Phu in 1954. These vehicles are still in use today in North Vietnam. When we meet the halftrack we will lash the rafts on top. The drive to the beach should take ten minutes under ideal conditions. Upon arrival at the beach we will un-limber the rafts and attach outboard motors. There will be a fast frigate waiting for us offshore which will eventually transfer us to a larger mother ship for a leisurely sea voyage home to Saigon.

"That's about it, men," concluded Major Falconi. "I will yield the floor to Sergeant Laird."

Sergeant Doug Laird spoke from his seat.

"I understand that the Black Eagles are familiar with the Underwater Demolition Team nine man rafts."

"Yeah, I'm so intimate with 'em 'cause I almost died in one," broke in Calvin Culpepper with disgust. "The Seals can have 'em."

"You ain't got your sea legs yet," retorted Blue Richards.

"Since I had a voice in selecting the equipment we'll use," Doug continued, "I picked a raft of French manufacture, a Zodiac. It's a favorite of many commercial river rafting outfitters. It's a six man raft, therefore lighter than the U.D.T., and has a double layer of skin impregnated with a fabric of touch plastic cloth. Nothing but a bullet or a sharp knife will puncture them. These rafts will take a wooden transom so we can mount the outboard motors."

"Not that any of us are strangers to hairy adventures," Blue Richards began, "but give us some idea what it's like shooting a river that's been dry for ten years."

"In my one and only experience of this kind we encountered undergrowth that had grown to be twelve foot high trees," Doug said. "We only saw the top four feet, so we simply rode over them. We also had to ride through a whirlpool."

"What about the waterfall?" asked Sergeant Dobbs.

"It's definitely worth a look-see before attempting it," replied Doug. "I've seen many heavy rapids on the Kern River, so I can judge quickly if it can be done. Our best bet is to concentrate on keeping the raft lined up straight through the rapids. It will be bumpy so hang on tight, but if you are bounced into the air try to fall toward the center of the raft. Here's another rafting survival technique worth knowing. If you fall into the river going through a rapid, take the rapid in a sitting position facing forward. Bounce your ass off the bottom and use your feet to ward off oncoming rocks.

"I feel funny reminding you guys, of all people, that there are no guarantees on any river trips, even under the best of conditions. But to be as safe as possible we will be wearing standard U.S. Navy life preservers."

"No more questions?" asked Major Falconi, looking around the room. "Okay, that's it men. Back to the barracks with a minimum of noise and light. Hit the sack. Oh-one hundred comes early in the morning."

Chapter Nine

Lt. Trung Uy Loc saluted smartly to the ARVN military police manning the gates of Tan Son Nhut Air Base outside of Saigon. An aura of mystery always surrounded the smartly dressed commander of ARVN security guarding the Special Operations Group detachment at Peterson Field. The SOG base was a world within a world, a base within a base.

All that was known of Lieutenant Loc was that he guarded the spooks. Lieutenant Loc did his best to maintain that mystery. He cast a short but penetrating glance at the uniforms of the two guards, then drove his car past their enclosure. It didn't hurt to gig them occasionally for uniform discrepancies.

Lieutenant Loc couldn't shake the burning sensation on the back of his neck as he left the briefing room. The inconsistencies and turmoil of his recent daily life prevented him from drawing the correct conclusion. Under the best of circumstances it was difficult for him to judge which day might be his last. He was a somewhat irresolute person with a flawed character, but a brave man, nonetheless. And his present course of action, once initiated, charted a predictable course forward. He was determined that he would finish what he had started. After one last rendezvous with the slimy Viet Cong subverters, he would quit their relationship permanently, even if it meant fleeing into Cambodia.

The field operative assigned to tail Loc knew the streets of Saigon exceedingly well. He could afford to lag far behind the ARVN security officer as he threaded his way skillfully through the narrow back streets. Had the tail been following Loc to uncover a secret location he would have been disappointed. The lieutenant's car stopped in front of a vacant lot. It was the phone booth Loc was interested in. The phone number of Loc's contact had been changed twice since the death of Gregor and Ngoc, the Vietnamese businessmen. Loc dialed the new phone number.

"Speak!" said the voice from the other end of the line. They exchanged passwords.

Loc continued: "As I reported to you earlier, the Black Eagles have discovered where you are holding their intelligence analyst, Lt. Andrea Thuy. They are, at this moment, preparing to depart early in the morning and make a parachute landing to the west of the temple onto the recently laid out rice fields overlooking the old river-bed. They have timed their jump to commence at first light."

"Again you have performed well comrade," said the voice. "Have no fear, your remuneration will be forthcoming. A meeting has been arranged for you with your new contact." He gave Loc the location of a warehouse in a little traveled district of Saigon.

"Do not forget the time, tomorrow night," reminded the voice. "Do not be late."

The open phone connection was replaced by a dial tone. Lieutenant Loc hung up the phone.

The information Lieutenant Loc had given to his contact was soon encoded into cipher groups of five letters each and transmitted by a directional antenna to Hanoi from the Viet Cong field radio station.

An SOG radio traffic monitoring detachment had

142

already narrowed the band of frequencies they would watch that night. A naval frigate off the coast of North Vietnam sampled the "skip," the differential propagation of radio frequencies at different wave lengths, through the same atmospheric path that would be used by the North Vietnamese. A computer-programmed high speed scanner found and locked in on the transmission and began recording it before the second letter of the first cipher group was sent. Because of the frequency and time of day of this transmission, it was identified as being of special interest and was earmarked for immediate processing.

"They've picked up a new Russian cryptologist in Hanoi," said the intelligence analyst to the radio operator. It took the computer one and one-half minutes to break their code.

Fagin received the confirmation of their transmission ten minutes after it was sent.

"They took the bait," he told Robert Falconi. "Let's hope for the sake of the two men in the diversionary jump that they still want to take the Black Eagles alive."

Then Chuck Fagin told Major Falconi, "Aerial recon over the area of operations has confirmed a number of military vehicles that appear to be World War Two army halftracks. They have been spotted more than once. Fortunately they are in regular use. We have an asset in the area who has access to the motorpool in Hoang Xa where the halftracks are stored. A U.S. Navy Seal team is on its way to secure one of the halftracks on the night before the mission.

"They will drive the halftrack to your rendezvous point where the unpaved trail that heads inland from the beach meets a railroad bridge that crosses the Song Yen River."

"Like the Marine Corps general said when he was surrounded, 'Now we've got them right where we want them,'" Robert Falconi replied, and laid his head down on the military cot to resume his catnap.

"Reveille!" bellowed Top Gordon as he strode from bunk to bunk in the Black Eagles' barracks. "Drop your cocks and grab your socks."

"Jesus Christ," muttered Archie Dobbs as he threaded the laces through the final eyelets of his jumpboots. "This reminds me of the fishing trips my uncle used to take us on. Not that I don't love fishing, mind you," he prattled to no one in particular, "but I was sure at the time that nothing was worth getting up that early for."

"Please endeavor to tie those shoelaces exceedingly well, Sergeant Dobbs," thundered the voice of Top Gordon in a sarcastic tone from the rear of the barracks. "We cannot haul you back aboard the jumpship if one of your boots falls off."

Buzz Martin recognized the career United States Marine Corps gunnery sergeant. Jackson White was in good shape for a forty-year-old man.

"Gunny, what are you doing here?" he said to the older man. "I thought you were babysitting the shave-tails at the M.C.R.D. Training Center in San Diego."

Gunny replied, "I was doing a stretch of sea duty when a query came down the pipe. They wanted to know if anyone had experience with halftracks. My God, that was World War Two for me."

"Did they ask you anything more than that?" asked Buzz Martin.

"No sir. But how can we get us a halftrack in Vietnam?" asked the sergeant.

"We're going to steal it," answered Martin.

"That's a tall order in more ways than one," commented Jackson White.

144

"I've been a hell of a scrounger in my time, but I can't think of any branch of the armed forces that would retain a piece of equipment that dated. Which salvage yard are we going to steal it from?"

"We're going to steal it from the North Vietnam militia," stated Lieutenant Martin matter-of-factly.

The gunnery sergeant's head canted to one side. His eyebrows knitted in consternation and he said, "I see."

"Tell me what you know about halftracks," requested Buzz. "I'm much too young to have seen any service in them."

"Well," began Gunny Brown, "it's a very large beast, only a smidge smaller than a deuce-and-a-half, with regular truck tires in the front that steer, and tank treads where you'd normally find the rear wheels. And it had more armor than any vehicle of its time except for a tank. Although not amphibious, it was the next best thing. I imagine a halftrack could outmaneuver a tank, but if I was driving, I'd rather outrun it. If well maintained, it would be a beautiful piece of equipment, that is, if you have a taste for hulking brutes."

"Sounds like fun," was Buzz Martin's final judgement. "I'd appreciate it if you would run me through the startup sequence and the electrical and fuel systems."

The two soldiers whiled away the remainder of the afternoon discussing the structure and capabilities of the World War Two war machine.

"Here's a copy of your mission briefing map," the skipper told him. "You and your assistant will be dropped off a mile down the coast from the village of Hoang Xa. A UDT raft with a crew of three will take the both of you in at oh-one hundred hours. Pay special attention to the landmarks. After securing the halftrack, you will be

145

looking for a trail bearing two hundred sixty degrees."

Later in the raft, Buzz Martin and Gunny shivered as the torrential rains fell ceaselessly despite the relative warmth of the ocean water in this latitude.

The rain and darkness rendered the outline of the shore indistinct.

"It's oh-two hundred," said one of the crew. "Be on the lookout for the signal light from shore."

The raft was floating silently, one hundred yards from the beach. Buzz had no idea how far north or south they had drifted in the past ten minutes. The rafters stayed outside the breaking ocean waves to avoid drifting in the strong, long-shore current, but there was still a southward eddy.

Finally one of the crew caught a flash of red from the beanch. He un-limbered his paddle and motioned them both to do the same.

"No motor this close to shore," he explained. "Even with the muffler, it's too noisy."

The five men paddled with deep, swift strokes, thrusting the paddles edge-on into the water at the beginning of the stroke and pulling it straight back toward the paddler to minimize splashes. As they spotted the signal light, they turned and stroked directly for the shore.

The skipper had previously explained that the mission would be dangerous. It would go very badly for him if he was caught. Of course, the mission was important enough to burn the contact if necessary, but it wasn't good practice to be wasteful of one's assets during a covert operation.

Wonderful lecture, Buzz thought at the time. *Tell me something I don't know already—like how much of this are the fuckin' Commies aware of? The other side runs covert operations too, and they pay less attention to the "rules" than we do.*

Besides, Buzz realized the U.S. Navy might want to come this way again, and the teams that followed him in the future would appreciate a friendly reception. He just hoped that's what he'd find that night.

The signaler was dressed in a North Vietnamese corporal's uniform. He had shut off the directional red flasher. This was a simple flashlight with a red lens that used a tube of opaque black paper to prevent side flash.

"I am Corporal Nguyen Phan," he introduced himself quickly. "We must hurry. It is too dangerous to stay here."

"I've kinda got that impression about Southeast Asia in general," Buzz answered. "Too dangerous to stay here. But, what the hell. That's what they say about New York, too."

Nguyen used the flashlight to illuminate three bicycles propped against a sand dune. Gunny asked how he carried the other two bikes to their position.

"I tied them to my back, of course," Nguyen answered matter-of-factly.

The three operatives peddled their bicycles inland on the jeep trail. After three quarters of a mile they intersected a paved highway running north and south. They rode north, single file, behind the corporal. At one point, a vehicle was heard approaching from behind them.

"Supply truck," commented Nguyen.

A fork in the road appeared less than a mile later.

"The motorpool where the halftrack is kept lies up this road," the corporal said.

"Ooh, whee! Don't be bashful, give me a good feel," said Sgt. Archie Dobbs to Sgt. Eddie Barthe, as Eddie traced the harness straps between Archie's legs, seeking unwanted twists in the straps that would bite into the flesh of the jumper upon deployment of the parachute, like thumbscrews.

"I did my best to make sure there were no kinks in those lines," said Archie. "If there are, I sure hope you find them, Blue. On one of our missions I found one the hard way, when the chute opened. Later they told me that I whispered soprano for two hours."

"We will jump in two sticks," Major Falconi had said. "Kim, you and Eddie will constitute the first stick, along with the eight French cargo chutes. The rest of us will be in the second stick, jumping in T-tens, using static lines for deployment.

"The first stick jumps at eight hundred feet above ground level. Because ground level rises rapidly after that, we will be in a climb as we pass over the dam and follow the line of the resevoir."

After he left the C-one nineteen, Robert Falconi glanced up to check his canopy, then oriented himself and searched the sky for the rest of the Black Eagles.

The steep walls of the surrounding hills loomed dangerously close. At daybreak, however, the uneven heating of the landsape by the sun had not progressed far enough to create thermal updrafts, and the temple was sufficiently distant from the coast to be, as yet, unaffected by the offshore breezes.

The ground appeared to be coming up fast. Robert Falconi had time to mark the position of the cargo chutes in his memory before positioning his body for a parachute landing fall.

Not being jump qualified, Sgt. Doug Laird was nervous about that part of the mission and had asked Sgt. Eddie Barthe for advice on how to land.

"You're supposed to roll," Eddie advised Doug. "Before your feet hit, you bend over, twist to one side, and try to touch your nose to your ass."

Doug had requested a few practice jumps but was turned down by Major Falconi.

"It has been our experience," answered the major, "that since the normal casualty rate for a parachute jump is above thirty percent, the odds are that you're equally safe if we shove you out of the jumpship and let you take your chances."

Doug decided, then, that his concern about leading his group of greenhorns on a white-water rafting trip was totally out of place.

"So far, this jump has gone very well," Top Gordon told Robert Falconi. "At first glance it appears that no one got sucked into the canyon walls, and the cargo chutes landed where they will be easily retrievable."

"Good!" Major Falconi said. "First I want you to find Sparks Laird and have him report to me. We need a commo check as soon as possible. Then organize a work party to police up the drop zone. Let's get this show on the road."

After consulting with Sergeant Laird, Major Falconi decided to inflate the rafts before transporting them.

"The chutes are buried, sir," reported Top Gordon.

"Very well," Major Falconi replied, then said, "Sparks, help me inflate this raft."

Together they attached the gas hose from the carbon dioxide cylinders to nipples on each of the six inflatable compartments that formed the structure of the raft.

Fifteen minutes had passed since the first Black Eagle's foot had touched the ground.

"Throw the cylinders in the raft. We will dump them in the lake," directed Major Falconi. "Contact our air support group on the radio, Sergeant Laird."

The recesses of the tropical canyon walls around them

were still dark, yet to be touched by the morning light. At this time of the morning the temperature of the air was almost comfortably cool.

The road showed signs of heavy usage. The constant monsoon rains only made it worse. As the road began to climb the final hill to the armory, they were forced to walk their bicycles.

"I can see the glow of the parking area lights from here," said Nguyen Phan, the militia corporal. "I can hear the noise, as well. There is more activity than normal. There should be only one guard on duty."

As they drew closer, Gunny remarked, "They're on alert, Lieutenant. We will have to assume that it was our boys, the team we've been sent to link up with, that shook them up. How about it, Phan," Gunny asked. "Is there another way inside?"

Nguyen Phan considered the question. "The cyclone fences were erected a short while ago, but the winter rains undercut the uprights quickly. In the section near the gully the concrete footing to one of the steel pipe uprights has been exposed. It's on the east side of the compound."

Phan attempted to draw a diagram in the feeble light cast by the distant camp floodlamps.

Gunny removed the waterproof pencil light from his fatigue jacket pocket and illuminated the ground in front of them.

Phan quickly sketched.

"Here is the corner of the compound and here is the floodlamp. Walk twenty paces and you will see the fence."

The rumble of a truck's exhaust was coming closer, and the three men could discern the whine of a transmission being geared down to ascend the hill.

150

Phan exclaimed, "It's a public transportation stake truck from the settlement where I live! I can recognize the face of my squad leader, the sergeant."

"This turn of events may be useful to us," Nguyen explained quickly to the two Americans. "I left word with the concierge of my rooming house that I was sick with the dysentery tonight in order to assure that I would not be disturbed. I can explain to them that I recovered sufficiently to answer the call-up. I could rejoin them without arousing undue suspicion.

"Now, listen! You can recognize the commander's halftrack by its whip antenna and red signal light." Then he pointed down the road from where they had come. "Down the hill, two-tenths of a kilometer is a hairpin turn. It will be necessary to reduce speed to negotiate the turn safely in this rain. I will explain to the commander that I must be his driver this evening in order to check out the repairs I have made to his vehicle. That will leave two out-riding guards. You must take them quickly. Do not worry about noise from gunfire. The halftracks backfire so frequently that only a report of a machine gun would attract attention."

"I remember these babies," said Gunny White. "Even when they are tuned perfectly they are noisy. One or two extra backfires will go totally unnoticed."

Cpl. Nguyen Phan pushed his bicycle out of the trees and rushed forward to the oncoming trucks.

"Hey!" he yelled, waving his arms. Buzz and Gunny listened carefully to the ensuing, animated discussion between Nguyen and the occupants of the cab of the truck. The militia corporal pointed to his mouth and then to his buttocks, and concluded by making two fists which he tapped, one on top of the other.

"The concierge of the boardinghouse where I live gave me some tablets that dried up the dysentery," said Nguyen. "I bicycled like hell to get here."

The sergeant's arm appeared from the window and pointed toward the rear of the truck. Following instructions, the corporal went to the rear of the truck where many hands were waiting to haul him aboard. The truck whined through first and second gear on its way up the hill.

"I don't like the idea of waiting in a location where I can't see what's going on," Buzz related to Gunny.

"I feel the same, Lieutenant, but sometimes patience is necessary. Phan was recommended by the company. All we can do is trust him," replied Gunny.

A soft rain began to patter the broadleaf vegetation surrounding them. When twenty minutes had passed they heard the rumble of many diesel motors warming up. Fifteen minutes later the rumble grew in intensity, and individual vehicles could be heard bouncing over the washboard road strewn with potholes.

"Get ready, Gunny," Lieutenant Martin called.

Gunny lifted the .45 before his eyes in the dim light. He moved back the slide and let it spring forward, catching the ejected cartridge in midair. He removed the clip from the base of the grips and reinserted the round. Then the clip was restored to its former position with a slap to insure the pistol would function.

"Never hurts to check," he commented to Martin, who imitated the procedure and moved across the road and waited in ambush.

A twenty-year-old, army jeep was the first vehicle in the column. Its transmission was shifted down into double aught granny to negotiate the hairpin turn. Lumps of mud could be heard slapping against its undercarriage with a machine gun cadence.

Every muscle in Buzz's body was tensed in preparation. He strained his eyes at the oncoming halftrack, trying to glimpse the key that would release him into action. Then he saw the banner flags and the red signal

152

light of the command vehicle and spotted the militia corporal behind the steering wheel. Mud from the spinning, slipping tracks stung his ankles as he leaped and grabbed metal.

The startled face of a North Vietnamese Armored Cavalry trooper loomed before Lieutenant Martin for only a moment, then dissolved into hamburger as the slug from Martin's .45 spattered his brains onto the side of the halftrack. Buzz balanced precariously in an effort to support the dead body and prevent it from falling into the middle of the road where it might alert the next halftrack in the column.

Buzz reached across the top of the vehicle and grabbed the corresponding victim of Gunny's deadly expertise. Then he helped the veteran marine sergeant climb aboard.

Corporal Nguyen was trying to coordinate the difficult task of keeping the halftrack on the road while he held a pistol to the head of the surprised North Vietnamese army captain. The captain shouted an oath in Vietnamese and appeared to prepare to jump from the slow-moving vehicle. Then he turned back toward Nguyen, revealing the 7.65 automatic in his hand. But the feisty little corporal wasn't having any that evening. He quickly shot the captain through the breastbone, brushed aside the automatic, and shouted to Buzz Martin for assistance.

"Too bad, we could have used that one alive!" shouted Lieutenant Martin over the rattling howl of the halftrack. One by one, Buzz and Gunny threw the bodies off the side of the halftrack facing the ravine, taking advantage of the centrifugal force created when they rounded each corner.

Temporarily winded, the two men rested against the quad-.50 caliber machine gun turret.

"These are the original fifty caliber barrels," commented Gunny to Buzz Martin. "And it's rigged for anti-aircraft use. With this baby I can turn this corner of North Vietnam into a Helicopter graveyard."

Buzz was happy to share the marine sergeant's sudden enthusiasm for their mission.

"It's still a good idea to make sure they don't see us first," he added. "Even this antique monster couldn't stand up to rocket fire."

Even under the illumination of the halftrack's headlights it was difficult to make out the lead jeep ahead of them in the rain. Lieutenant Martin looked carefully at his watch.

"It's oh-four hundred. We've got to be in position by daybreak. That gives us two hours to travel seven miles." He leaned forward and yelled in the corporal's ear. "Have you figured out a way to leave this parade undetected?"

The militiaman replied, "I've been over this area before, during maneuvers. This column was ordered to proceed south on the coastal highway to a junction where it meets a road from the east. They are to hold position and await further orders. That way they can be deployed in either direction at a moment's notice. It will be easy to leave the convoy. Bad visibility is not the only reason we are traveling so slowly. Each time we drive too fast in a column like this, the distance between vehicles gets so great that we lost sight of one another, and the lead jeep must halt until the rest catch up.

"Soon," he continued, "we will intersect the trail that leads to your rendezvous point. There it is, two hundred meters in front of us." Nguyen Phan reached above the steering wheel to the instrument panel and flipped a switch. All lights on the halftrack went out. Then he executed a smart right-hand turn, whipped through the overgrown roadside jungle growth and exited onto an unpaved trail. He slowed the big vehicle to a halt. He told Lieutenant Martin, "Many times my comrades and I have whiled away the hours during our weekly militia

154

meetings mocking our commanding officer's absurd orders. Some of us are so adept that we are indistinguishable from that fat slob you threw into the ravine. He has a high-pitched, nasal voice, and he swallows his words when he is excited. Listen carefully and you will see what I mean."

The militia corporal picked up the microphone and keyed the transmit button.

"This is Captain Thang to Lieutenant Ngo in the lead vehicle. This column is moving too slowly. You are ordered to proceed to our destination as fast as possible. Do not wait for the rest of the column to catch up. I will drop back and personally monitor the stragglers."

Lieutenant Ngo acknowledged the order and Corporal Phan replied, "Captain Thang, out," and released the transmit button.

"It will be half an hour before they regroup, discover that we are missing, and begin to look for us."

Gunny counted the remaining vehicles in the column as they roared by.

"That's four more halftracks and a jeep," he reported.

"Our unit is rarely up to full strength," Nguyen explained. "At any one time half our unit is down for maintenance."

"We're on schedule, so far," commented Lieutenant Martin. "Let's get to our destination before daybreak."

The militia corporal shifted the halftrack into gear and proceeded at a cautious forty kilometers per hour.

"Train that exotic-looking rifle of yours on the trail ahead," Nguyen directed Lieutenant Martin, indicating the sniper modified M-16 with a Starlight scope, capable of amplifying available light without the telltale infrared beam. "And warn me of any dangerous obstacles."

"I can't think of anything smaller than a tank trap that

would be dangerous to this monster!" yelled Gunnery Sergeant White over the din.

Getting in the spirit of the moment, Nguyen Phan purposefully broke the traction of the treads, a difficult feat in itself, and sashayed the rear of the halftrack to the left, dislodging a major portion of the trail in that direction.

"It's all good tank country!" he yelled back to Gunny.

"Its just that some is better than the rest!" retorted Sergeant White.

Lt. Buzz Martin experienced a momentary pang of loneliness, knowing that he could not fully share the bond of the passing of the years created between these two aging veterans by this antique, rumbling monster. But soon he was so caught up in the adventure of what was happening to them all that the feeling passed.

At several points in their journey the shifting of the earth had buried the trail. But the tracked vehicle created its own way with ease.

The first river was thirty feet wide and four feet deep at the center.

"She ain't amphibious," Gunny yelled as the halftrack launched itself into the river, wedging a spray of water to its sides like a snowplow and nearly burying the huge front tires. "But she's the next best thing."

They reached the Song Yen River ten minutes later.

Nguyen Phan pointed forward. "There's the bridge up ahead."

"Drive forward to the top of that knoll." Lieutenant Martin indicated a hillock to their right. "Let's get the lay of the land," he said to Gunny. "I don't want to sit out in the open, exposed, while waiting for our boys."

With the big diesel once again idling he asked Corporal Nguyen, "Where would you expect trouble to come from?"

"If they are being pursued," Phan began, thinking

156

outloud, "the shortest path from upriver would be the continuation of this trail on the opposite side of the railroad bridge."

"Sounds logical," commented Buzz. "Let's hide the halftrack in that stretch of jungle." He pointed to their left. "We have a clear field of fire toward the trail beyond the river. The sun will rise soon. We might get news of our boys from the radio traffic."

Sergeant Kim looked up to check the deployment of his canopy and had only enough time to catch a glimpse of Eddie Barthe before splashing into the rice paddie. Eddie met Kim halfway, fifty yards from the site of his splashdown.

"The only good thing," the magician commented, "about rice paddie landings is that you never have to worry about collapsing your chute." He squeezed water from his parachute as he rolled it up.

"Did you mark the location of the last dummy chute?" Kim asked him.

"Yes," Eddie answered. "It's the one with the orange stripe."

"Good," Kim continued. "We still have to retrieve some goodies from it."

Suddenly a two-foot high, elongated geyser of water shot up ten feet to their right, followed by a faint pop from the rice field on the next terrace to the south.

"That will be the militia," said Sergeant Kim. "I hope the rest of them can't shoot any better than that."

"Let's haul ass out of here," said Sergeant Barthe in agreement.

They waded for the dike that formed the border of the rice paddie. They were aware that a hundred-yard dash through knee-deep water to the edge of the paddie where it ended, falling off into the dry riverbed, was an exercise in futility.

Eddie looked back and saw the lone figure on the edge of the terrace above him, one hundred and fifty yards distant. The soldier had stopped firing momentarily and was beckoning to an unknown number of soldiers behind him. Eddie quickly stripped the clothtape from the plastic wrapped M-16 which he had so carefully waterproofed hours before the takeoff of the jumpship the day before. He worked the charging lever of the rifle and, putting the butt plate to his shoulder, he fired it, all in one smooth motion, so rapidly that it seemed like he had snapped off the shot.

But Sergeant Kim had worked long enough with Eddie, during their brief acquaintance, to realize that Eddie Barthe was a natural shot. Kim turned his head in time to see the figure on the horizon suddenly slump and collapse out of sight.

"That should keep their heads down momentarily," Eddie said.

"The plan calls for us to lay down a few booby traps on our way to the trees," reminded Sergeant Kim.

"There's precious little to use as a trigger for a booby trap," replied Eddie. He broke off what appeared to be a surveyer's stake. Walking forward with his rolled-up parachute beneath his armpit, he pushed the stake into the mud of the path before him at a shallow angle and wedged a hand grenade, spoon up, into the "V" formed where the stake went into the mud. Then he carefully stepped over the booby trap and followed Sergeant Kim toward the trees.

"Did you spot any of the dummy chutes?" Sergeant Kim asked.

"They are spread out in the trees on the other side of the riverbed," Eddie answered. "It should take time for the militia troops to check all of them."

"Next, we hike two hundred yards down the riverbed," Kim continued, "leaving plenty of sign, and go back and try to flank them as we work our way up the riverbed on the opposite bank."

Kim looked over his shoulder.

"Those militia troops are too quiet for my liking. Not knowing what they're up to makes me nervous."

"Let's make sure what they're up to," Eddie suggested. "Let's get their attention."

The two Black Eagles retraced their steps to the clearing bordering the rice fields. A squad of militia, reinforced with the prisoner-of-war camp garrison soldiers, had formed as skirmishers, facing them.

"The garrison soldiers are helping them," said Kim. "Those are Chinese type fifties talking."

The bolt action rifles of the militia constituted the bass notes, and the submachine guns of the garrison carried the melody. The hail of bullets shredded the jungle vegetation to the left of the two Black Eagles.

"I don't think they know where we are yet," commented Eddie.

"I've always wanted to play Ho Chi Minh, to be the one who enlightens," said Sergeant Kim, referring to the literal translation of the adopted name of the North Vietnam leader.

The two men crawled to the threshold of the rice paddie and took up firing positions. Sergeant Kim fired multiple bursts of three rounds each, aiming at the water in front of the soldiers. The ricochets resulting from the flat angle of fire quickly gained the attention of the advancing line of troops. One of the militia troops collapsed, face forward, into the muddy water. Spray from subsequent rounds spooked the remaining men.

Eddie was reminded of the time he had walked over a rise and surprised five ground squirrels sitting on a log. The challenge was to nail all five of them before they could flee from sight.

Eddie refrained from switching his M-16 to full automatic and began snapping off semiautomatic, individual rounds at the line of men from right to left.

At first the murderous firepower from the two Black Eagles only decimated the squad. Then suddenly half of the advancing soldiers discovered their wingmen were no longer walking beside them. When the decision came to retreat, two men survived of the original line.

"Do you think we got their attention?" asked Eddie.

"No!" replied Sergeant Kim. "I still don't think they know where we are."

Looking at the backs of the two retreating soldiers, Eddie added, "Hell, they don't even look interested."

Suddenly they heard the multiple *chunks* of a heavy weapons squad opening up with mortar fire.

"Hit the dirt," Kim shouted.

They barely had time to dive under an inviting-looking log before the shrapnel from the exploding shells shredded the treetops above them and splattered the ground around them with chunks of white-hot metal.

"That's close enough for me," yelled Eddie.

The two Black Eagles dashed down the trail as though pursued by hounds from hell.

"Sir, radio reports from the militia unit sent to the rice fields indicate that we have located the forces of the Yankee imperialist, pirate Black Eagles exactly where you predicted they would be, Comrade Major Xong. They were driven off by the courageous efforts of our patriotic militia, reinforced by elements of the garrison."

Major Xong carefully scrutinized the information given to him.

"Are you sure it was the main force?" asked Major Xong. "This could be a trick. How long were you engaged in battle with them? How many soldiers did you lose?"

"We lost one reinforced squad before they retreated under our mortar fire," answered the lieutenant. "In addition to that, we counted eight parachutes still hanging in the trees to the north of the riverbed. We pressed them so hard, they did not take time to retrieve their parachutes."

The apparent good news did little to cheer up Major Xong.

"According to the contingency orders of Colonel Truong in Hanoi I am assuming command of this installation until the present emergency is over. All of the garrison forces are to be activated immediately. One platoon will reinforce the militia and pursue the imperialist bandits who fled into the area of the riverbed. Another platoon will move across the reservoir and advance up the road toward Dong Tau and prepare to ambush the helicopters which are coming to evacuate the Americans. I will personally command this platoon. Notify the platoon that is off shift in Xong Hoa. Get them up and roust them out. Have them report to the temple as soon as possible and reinforce the garrison forces on duty now."

Major Xong left the temple-P.O.W. compound under the command of the captain of the garrison and hurriedly departed with his expeditionary force to prepare an ambush.

Chun Kim and Eddie Barthe reached the turnaround point two hundred yards downstream and crossed the dry riverbed to the opposite bank.

"We left enough sign back there," said Kim. "For at least ten men. Now is the time to turn silent, fast, and untraceable."

"Right," answered Eddie Barthe. "They will be investigating our trail as well as the parachutes."

"We'll have to unpack the cargo chute and move west, up the riverbed, outflanking them before their search sweeps detect us. Let's find a spot further up this bank to bury the chutes."

Kim and Eddie made their way stealthily up the riverbed, climbing higher and higher along the northern bank until they found a pocket of earth slump caused by the super saturation of the soil due to the rains. Excavation of the soft earth proceeded rapidly. The parachutes were buried, and they were shortly on their way.

As they approached the French cargo chute with the orange stripe Eddie exclaimed, "Ah! Our care package."

"Grab the bag and leave the chute," said Sergeant Kim.

The sounds of multiple voices and branches being snapped floated up to the two Black Eagles from the opposite riverbank below them as the reinforced militia pursued the ample sign the two men had left in their path.

Kim looped a logging knot around the heavy duffel bag with a length of parachute cord. They both slung arms and picked up either end of the load by the cord, then proceeded up the riverbed at the pace of a forced march.

Chapter Ten

"Captain Ngo!" the orderly called urgently. "There is a Colonel Kraschenko on the radio who is requesting to speak to Major Xong."

Captain Ngo's confusion was mounting rapidly. He was beginning to long for more normal times of the recent past when his daily routine consisted of maintaining security and secrecy for the interrogation teams which utilized his facility to debrief the VIP prisoners of war and recalcitrant party members who had fallen from grace. His company-size North Vietnamese army garrison force was usually more than adequate to handle the unwilling residents of the facility, who never numbered more than a dozen or so.

The current prisoner population of the facility, located on the site of a former Buddhist temple, had dwindled to one female, captured in the south of their temporarily divided but hotly contested country. How could one woman be worth so much trouble.

Captain Ngo strode down the veranda of the temple at a fast march, trying to maintain dignity and authority. The current situation had developed with such rapidity that it was threatening to run his mental feet out from under him.

Ngo grasped the microphone and pressed the transmit button, trying to maintain a polite but firm attitude.

While this Colonel Kraschenko was not in Ngo's direct line of command, his status as a Soviet advisor made the Russian officer potentially even more difficult to handle than a direct superior. Ngo had to constantly guess at the importance of an advisor's status.

"Colonel Kraschenko," Ngo began diplomatically. "This facility is under the threat of imminent attack. Major Xong has led a detachment of troops to the north to deal with the American helicopters. We have the Americans trapped in the old riverbed, downstream from the dam."

"I realize that," came the voice of Colonel Kraschenko. "I am the man responsible for alerting him that the attack was coming. In any event, we are currently ten minutes north of you in a Mil-four helicopter. In the absence of Major Xong I am directing you to consider my request to be the same as an order. You will deploy your perimeter defense between the heliport and the riverbed. Make certain that the heliport is secure. You will also locate Captain Sakharov and direct him to make himself available when I land."

The colonel's voice rang with authority. Captain Ngo was not about to equivocate or indicate in any other way that he did not have complete control of the situation.

"Your orders will be carried out immediately, Colonel Kraschenko. We shall be awaiting your arrival eagerly."

Captain Ngo was secretly relieved that he would soon be able to pass the situation on to a superior officer.

Forty-five minutes had passed since the Alpha team of the Black Eagles, commanded by Major Falconi, had touched ground. The two four-man teams carrying the rafts, with their cargo, were making excellent progress. The two teams of boat carriers were double-timing, one behind the other, down a gentle slope toward the lake when Robert Falconi sang out, "Alpha team, halt!"

His command was echoed by Top Gordon, who bellowed, "Lay it down!"

"I take back what I said about Hell Week," said Sergeant Blue Richards. "These rafts are so light I've hardly had a chance to work up a sweat."

His remark was obviously rhetorical. Twin rivers of sweat ran from beneath his arms, staining the sides of his tiger-striped camouflaged fatigues.

"Hell, I worked up a sweat while I was hanging in my jump harness," added Archie Dobbs.

"Sounds like time for salt tablets," commented Malpractice McCorckel, who started rummaging in his pack.

Dobbs squatted in the sandy soil and low-lying weeds which were a harbinger of the flora surrounding the lake not far from them. He addressed Robert Falconi: "If the aeronautical charts we are working from are correct," said the unit scout, "this next bend in the trail ahead is the only thing that is hiding us from the anti-aircraft emplacement."

"Right," answered Robert Falconi. "It's about time to move into the trees bordering the lake and make preparations for our amphibious invasion."

The ack-ack emplacement lay halfway up the slope of a rapidly rising one thousand hillock to the north of the temple. The temple was situated on elevated ground bordered to the west by a paved road leading south to Hoang Xa and north to Dong Tau. Two fingerlike projections of the lake embraced the northeast quadrant of the land surrounding the temple.

"Our plan," Robert Falconi reviewed, "calls for us to avoid the killing ground between the temple and the AA emplacement. From our present location we will move directly to the lake and put the boats in the water. Then we will row around the point and cross the southern projection. When we emerge from the trees bordering the shoreline on the other side, only one hundred yards

165

will lie between us and the temple. Unfortunately we will be in full view of the ack-ack for the entire distance."

Suddenly the ears of Sgt. Ray Swift Elk detected a familiar beat. He stood, trying to locate the source of the sound. The surrounding hillocks and the variability of the way sound is carried over open water added to the difficulty of his task.

"Sounds like choppers," Ray announced.

"Get the boats into the water!" Top yelled, already on the run.

"There are no helicopters in our OP plan," commented Major Falconi as he shouldered his share of the load. "So it can't be one of ours."

The group waited tensely as the sound seemed to come from everywhere. The shadow of the chopper passing overhead rushed swiftly over the open ground before them.

"Looks like a Sikorsky only bigger," said Sergeant Laird.

"It's a Soviet Mil-four," called out Sergeant Swift Elk, the intelligence specialist of the unit. "It's NATO designation is 'Hound.' From the multiple yagi antennas and the lack of underslung pods for stretchers or rockets, I'd say that it is a troop commander's aircraft."

"Maybe high-level visitors," Top Gordon commented.

"The more, the merrier," concluded Robert Falconi. "Management usually suffers when there are too many chiefs and not enough Indians." Then the squelch sounded off with a static burst from his Prick-6 walkie-talkie.

"Bravo to Alpha, do you read me?" came the call.

"Alpha to Bravo, acknowledged," answered Major Falconi.

Sergeant Kim's voice buzzed from the speaker. "We are within sight of the rendezvous point. The plan appears to be right on schedule. We have seen a platoon double-timing up the road to the north. I also thought I heard a chopper, but I haven't caught sight of it yet."

"Roger, that's confirmed," answered Major Falconi. "It's a Soviet Hound which may be carrying VIPs. But there is no heavy armament in the air as far as we can see. I am going to try to link up with our ground support. Over and out!"

"If the situation heats up according to the plan," Kim said, turning to Eddie, "the platoon of troops that passed by should be returning in a hurry. When they get over their initial confusion they will undoubtedly follow us down that game trail into the riverbed," he said, pointing to the north bank above them. "They're sure to bunch up at that switchback. It's a good place for a Claymore mine."

"And there is another good place for a Claymore where the same trail joins the road," Eddie added. "We can make them a North Vietnamese army sandwich for lunch."

The two Black Eagles set to work laying out their stage props in the amphitheater of death around them.

"Where's Sparks? Sergeant Laird!" called out Major Falconi. "Bring the ANPRC-forty-one." Robert Falconi lifted the rubber flap of the watertight cover for the bigger, longer-ranging version of the Prick-6 and switched to a second frequency.

"Odin, this is Valkyrie. Acknowledge!"

"Valkyrie, this is Odin," came the answering voice from the speaker. "We are at the orbiting point. Please advise. Over."

"Odin, this is Valkyrie. Do you have permission to fire? Over."

167

"Negative, Valkyrie. But I think one slow pass over the temple should provoke a visible response from the ground."

Any time an aircraft in the Special Operations Wing fired its weapons it needed clearance to fire. This often involved getting permission from the regional U.S. Army commander and every subsequent commander down the line. If one of those links was unavailable the aircraft would orbit overhead until that commander was found. Meanwhile the good guys got their tails shot off. The only time it was permissible to fire without clearance was when the aircraft was receiving fire from the target area. In this case the Intruder aircraft were going to sucker the North Vietnamese army into firing first.

"Roger, and out!" said Major Falconi, acknowledging and signing off.

Falc handed the radio back to Sergeant Laird and said abruptly, "Pack it up, Sparks."

"Sergeant Gordon," the major continued, "get the men into the boats."

He pulled Sergeant Dobbs aside. "Archie, I want you to work your way into a location within view of the anti-aircraft position but well clear of possible ricochets. When the target is neutralized by ground-support fire I want you to take it over if it is still operable or at least make certain it can't be used against us."

"Right, Falc!" acknowledged Archie Dobbs. The scout immediately stepped out toward the AA site, which was still obscured from view by the mangrove trees.

Colonel Kraschenko ordered the pilot of the Hound to make one circuit of the area around the temple in order to inspect how well his orders were being carried out. He noted, with satisfaction, the platoon of garrison soldiers deployed on the northwestern slope of the temple grounds, facing down over the riverbed. One look at the killing ground overlooked by the two DShK Mount 12.7 millimeter machine guns convinced Kraschenko that no attack would come from that direction.

As the Hound helicopter settled for its landing, the Russian KGB colonel could see Major Sakharov of the interrogation team waiting for him.

He exited the helicopter and approached the officer waiting for him.

"Good morning. Captain Ngo, I believe." Kraschenko returned the salute to the diminuative figure. The top of the little soldier's hat did not reach the shoulder line of the six foot two inch KGB officer.

When dealing with the North Vietnamese army, Kraschenko never could shake the feeling that he was supervising a military school contingent.

"Colonel Kraschenko, it is an honor to meet you," said Captain Ngo. "All has been prepared according to your orders. Your suite is ready, sir."

"Very well, Captain," said Colonel Kraschenko. "Please show me to my quarters."

Although it was 0630, Kraschenko could already feel a solitary rivulet of perspiration in the center of his back. He motioned Major Sakharov to join him. Yuri Sakharov matched the colonel's stride out of force of habit as the two officers moved up the gentle incline to the temple.

"You needn't worry," Colonel Kraschenko said to Major Sakharov, "about the status of our prisoner as an ally. The absurd story that she was an agent of the Comintern has been thoroughly debunked. Is the torture-master prepared to begin?"

"Yes, sir," replied Major Sakharov. "Our female Black Eagle has had the opportunity to watch the torture-master warm up on one of our Viet Cong agents, who we used to bloody the dog, so to speak."

"Ah, yes," the colonel said and smiled. "Her mind

should be in the proper state by now. But, I want to reassure you that if there appears to be a significant danger of rescue by her cohorts, we will evacuate her immediately to Hanoi."

Suddenly the canyon to the east echoed with the roar of four A-1 Intruder aircraft. The aircraft were divided into two teams. They made their initial approach on a heading of one-nine-five and began to pull out of their dive as they passed over the temple.

The roar of the huge piston engines reverberating through the canyon walls magnified the terror welling up inside the crew of the anti-aircraft emplacement. So great was their surprise and fear that they forgot to un-limber their weapons. "Omega One," called the flight leader of the second Intruder team to his flight commander. "You shook them up so badly that they didn't get off a shot."

The initial team of Intruders had broken off to the left and began their turn in preparation for another pass. The second team of aircraft was now descending over the dam.

"Get the prisoner!" yelled Colonel Kraschenko to Major Sakharov. "We must leave now."

The pilot of the Hound helicopter was trying to restart his main engine.

"It's too late!" yelled Major Sakharov to the colonel. "At this moment we should be more concerned about your safety. Come inside with me, quickly."

The AA crews had initiated firing, but their first shots were far off target as the tracer rounds could be seen floating up in the general direction of the Intruder Bravo team.

"Hip hip, hooray!" shouted Bravo flight leader over the radio. "We have hostile ground fire."

"It's a *go!*" echoed the flight commander.

"Take the ack-ack," ordered Bravo flight leader to his wingman. "I want that egg-sucking Hound," he continued, referring to the Soviet Mil-4 helicopter that was

170

beginning to develop lift from its main rotor blades.

Half inch bullets from the .350 machine guns on each wing of the second A-1H Intruder sped toward the two North Vietnamese army machine guns. Their momentum was aided by the forward speed of the aircraft and the force of gravity. The projectiles of purgatory plowed the earth and chewed the rock around the sandbagged emplacement, creating a cloud that obscured the fate of the occupants.

Archie Dobbs trained his field glasses on the site and waited for the dust to clear.

Lines of spouting dust and chunks of asphalt were caused by the bullets of the second Intruder as they raced toward the Soviet helicopter.

Colonel Kraschenko raised his hand in involuntary protest and shouted, "No! Not my helicopter!"

The pilot of the Mil-4 had turned his rotorcraft tail first to the approaching Intruder in hopes of minimizing his silhouette. But a single line of .50 slugs crawled up the spine of the Soviet chopper like the claws of an alley cat on a moonlight scrap. It was difficult to determine whether the control linkages were severed first in the rotorcraft or in the pilot.

The Mil-4 Hound went into a left bank that ended as it impacted onto the roof of a lower portion of the temple. The fuel tanks of the chopper ruptured and the fuel ignited, sending up a fireball which trailed clouds of dirty smoke.

Archie Dobbs could see no movement in the dissipating cloud of dust around the sandbagged emplacement. The shock value of the initial attack had reached its greatest level. Now was the time for his one hundred yard dash.

M-16 in hand, Archie raced up the incline to the silent revetment as fast as his combatboot-clad feet would carry him.

Kraschenko recoiled at the explosion of the Hound. He

sensed debris from the explosion flying in his direction. His mind had not recovered enough to discern the present from his memory of the immediate past. *I'd better go with Sakharov and seek shelter*, he thought.

Then Colonel Kraschenko turned and stumbled over Yuri Sakharov's body. The blond-haired, blue-eyed, Russian would never again charm any information from unwilling female dissidents. A piece of shrapnel from the explosion had caught him in the back, between the shoulder blades. He lay motionless on the ground, eyes wide open, staring at eternity.

Major Xong was one of the first combatants on either side of the conflict to hear the incoming flight of Intruders. At first he felt confused. There was no mention of fixed wing, ground-support aircraft in the report radioed to him from Colonel Kraschenko which was based on the information furnished by the double agent, Loc.

But it matters little, he thought, *how much damage those aircraft do to the temple, if the rest of their attack proceeds as we were told.*

His platoon was positioned off the sides of the road, out of sight.

We will surely annihilate the force of American helicopters that is going to land here with the purpose of evacuating the Black Eagles, he concluded.

Then Xong saw the fireball from the explosion of the Soviet helicopter, and his confidence waned.

As a professional soldier of Vietnam, he could look back on two thousand years of military history. The battles that had been fought to fend off the Chinese to the north and conquer the Khmers to the south were on a level with any western battle such as the Romans and the Carthaginians or Custer and the Sioux.

But now he felt indecision. His force was no match for the Intruders, and the only anti-aircraft weapons in the area had undoubtedly been neutralized by the surprise attack of the highly mobile American interceptors. He could no longer be of any assistance to the defenders of the temple, and the best information available led him to believe that he could still foil the ultimate objective of the Americans' attack.

The militia was deployed as planned to control all main roads to the south and west while the forces under his immediate command were in an ideal position to repulse and destroy an airborne attempt to evacuate the Black Eagles.

"Comrade Major Xong," said the young lieutenant who commanded the platoon. "Is it not our patriotic duty to abandon this position and go to the aid of our brothers defending the temple? I can see from here how they have bravely positioned themselves between the temple and the riverbed."

Insecurity created in Major Xong by recent events elicited within the officer humility and a sense of patience he did not normally display. Instead of upbraiding the less experienced officer in front of his men, Major Xong explained quietly:

"We are already divided in the face of an enemy force of unknown strength. Those parachutes in the riverbed could very well be a trick. We can far better display our patriotism by insuring that the lives of your brave brother soldiers, defending the temple, are not sacrificed in vain."

A pair of Intruders passed overhead, wing to wing, once again. With this pass, they strafed the roof of the temple, destroying the antennae of the radio installation.

"Look!" The lieutenant pointed at the southern dogleg of the lake.

The two Zodiac rafts, propelled by the Black Eagles'

Alpha team, had reached the shoreline of the lake.

"Bah!" exclaimed Major Xong. "They are too far away for effective rifle fire. And with the temple's antenna shot away we cannot warn out troops that they have been flanked. No one will be able to relay our message."

The two officers were forced to sit and watch the battle develop before them as spectators rather than participants.

Immediately after stepping ashore, Major Falconi shouted, "Sparks! Commo check." The major keyed the microphone and spoke, "Valkyrie to Odin, acknowledge!"

"Odin to Valkyrie, acknowledged. Do you have any more targets of interest?" replied the flight commander.

"Right now we need your eyes," said the major. "We need any intelligence you can provide on enemy troop positions and strengths."

"Odin to Valkyrie, Roger. On our last pass over Xuan Hoa we saw a concentration of platoon-size massing up into columns along the sides of the road. Once they decide to move, they'll be on you within ten minutes. By the way, you have the temple defense outflanked. They are deployed on the western slopes of the temple grounds overlooking the road. We will be in position for a strafing run on those forces momentarily. Be advised to avoid that area."

"Roger, I will comply," acknowledge Robert Falconi. "We will attack the temple now. Valkyrie to Odin, over and out."

"Sparks!" Falconi said. "Leave the big radio with the boats. We will be back."

Despite the strafing runs by the Intruders, the officers commanding the North Vietnamese army forces positioned on the west side of the temple still expected the main attack to come from the southern edge of the rice fields and the dry riverbed. The platoon of garrison-reinforced militia, sent out earlier, now appeared to have flanked the American airborne soldiers who had retreated into the thick jungle growth of the riverbed. The North Vietnamese soldiers on the hillside were eager to surprise the arrogant Yankee attackers and destroy them with mortar and submachine gun fire.

"Follow me!" instructed the flight commander to his wingman and steered his Intruder on a heading of three hundred degrees. He had only to wait a few seconds before his sights lined up on the temple defenders.

"Fire!" he instructed over his radio.

Twelve streams of tracer rounds marked the flight of the .50 missiles of death. The flight commander added a little right rudder as his bullets hit the lower slopes.

Whatever protective cover had partially hidden the enemy troops from his view was chopped into mulch and plowed under the soil. These were not .223 M-sixteen bullets that could be deflected by a tree branch, but rather high-velocity heavyweights that bored hot, straight, and true into their targets.

Over seven hundred rounds impacted into the hillside seeking less than fifty men. If any one of the soldiers could, by some stretch of luck, escape thirteen of the bullets intended for him, the fourteenth was sure to score a hit.

"Did you see any hits?" asked the flight commander over the radio.

"I couldn't be sure," replied his wingman. "But I know they'll need a new gardener down there."

"Maybe so," rejoined the flight commander. "But they won't need any fertilizer. Aside from their usual horseshit, there will be plenty of bone and blood meal."

*   *   *

Robert Falconi led the Black Eagles at a dead run beyond the mangrove trees that bordered the lake. A mere hundred yards separated them from the approaches to the temple. There was no more time for subterfuge or stealth or ambush. Their next moves looked to be a classical exercise in fire and manuever.

In terms of numbers the Black Eagles appeared to be evenly matched against the temple defenders who were being led by a KGB colonel in full dress uniform. But his soldiers were the cooks and clerks, the maintenance crew of the P.O.W. camp, who had been rousted out at the last second by Colonel Kraschenko.

The colonel had happened upon a Russian electronic technical advisor who had been summarily relieved of his job by the loss of the roof antenna. When queried, he replied that he understood and spoke Vietnamese.

"Tell these men," Colonel Kraschenko thundered, in the direction of the assembled Vietnamese house personnel, who stood with their mouths open, "that the next man I see, ten seconds from now, without a weapon in his hand, will be shot!"

Consequently the ragtag force that greeted the Black Eagles was comprised of old men, boys, and technicians, most of them, unwilling and unaccustomed to their assigned task.

The Chinese type-50, 7.65 submachine gun in the hands of Colonel Kraschenko was the first weapon to open up on the advancing Black Eagles. In his excitement, due to a long absence from the battlefield, the colonel was ignoring proper technique and firing long bursts on full automatic. Only the first round of the burst had any chance of striking on target. It bounced off the ground between two Black Eagles, inducing that side of the skirmisher line to hit the dirt and provide covering fire for the remainder of the attackers. The rest of the burst sailed harmlessly into the lake.

The colonel's action briefly put some starch into the remaining temple defenders.

Calvin Culpepper fired a well-placed round from his M-79 grenade launcher toward a trio of enemy soldiers who had been so careless as to bunch up together in a doorway.

The shrapnel-spewing shell separated the three instantly, shredding their flesh and leaving them dead or dying from shock. The remaining defenders had little inclination and precious little opportunity to bring their weapons to bear on the attacking force. With the precision of a championship football team, half of the Black Eagles would advance rapidly, firing well-aimed bursts of two or three rounds while the other half laid down covering fire of semi-automatic, well-placed individual shots.

Even with his superior training and greater experience, Colonel Kraschenko found it difficult to keep any of the attackers in his sights long enough to be sure of hitting them. Their coordinated fire and movement technique was simply too skillful to afford him the opportunity he needed.

Now Gregori Kraschenko understood, from firsthand experience, the reports of failure and frustration he had been receiving these many months from a cross section of Vietnamese and Laotians, line troops and guerrilla forces alike.

Kraschenko's notions of racial purity and superiority were also suffering a setback. The glimpse he caught of the attacking force convinced him unconsciously that members of at least three different racial extractions could work together as a team.

The stone dust from the ricochets of the continuous support fire off the surrounding walls was blinding him. One of the North Vietnamese army defenders, a cook pressed into service from the kitchen, stood up from his crouched position long enough to get off a shot. He paid dearly for his effort. An M-16 round caught him flush in the breastbone. The impact bounced him off the wall behind him. He sat down slowly and slumped forward.

These men are magicians, thought Kraschenko. *They never let us know their strategy long enough in advance to bring our superior quantity of forces to bear.* He had not received any further communications from Captain Ngo, who had departed five minutes past to direct the garrison soldiers assigned to defend the western slope. Kraschenko greatly feared that the prolonged burst of heavy machine gun fire from a flight of American ground-support aircraft, heard passing over minutes ago, had sealed the fate of those temple defenders.

The right flank of the Black Eagles' Alpha team was advancing ever closer. Kraschenko had not seen such coordination since his participation with a KGB team which was supervising a team of airborne shock troops suppressing an uprising in Czechoslovakia. As he ripped off a burst from his Chinese type-50 submachine gun, holding it around the corner of the wall to avoid exposing his body to counter fire, he saw Major Falconi directing the two horns of the American advance.

That must be Maj. Robert Mikhailovich Falconi, the commander of the Black Eagles, he thought.

A 5.56 round ricochetted off the stone wall and the spent round grazed Kraschenko's forearm.

"Keep their heads down!" he heard the tall American cry out in English as the tempo of the attacker's firing picked up.

A temple defender, who looked like a gardener from his clothing, broke from his position and began running toward the interior of the temple.

"Stop that man!" Kraschenko bellowed to the Russian radio technician. The advisor shifted position to bring his weapon to bear on the fleeing man. But as the brief burst of his submachine gun cut the man down in mid-flight, a trio of M-16 bullets hit the Russian in quick succession. The first clipped the heel off his boot, sending him tumbling while the second bullet spun his helmet, tipping it over his eyes and blinding him. The third round passed cleanly through his thigh as he tried to rise.

Gregori Kraschenko could no longer maintain a firm grip on his weapon. The slight wound he had received from the spent bullet had numbed his forearm. What his eyes were seeing did not immediately register in his brain. The Black Eagles were all around him, shaking down and lining up the few North Vietnamese army defenders who remained alive.

They simply overran us, Kraschenko thought. There was no protracted battle, no heroic defense.

Robert Falconi reached down to the KGB officer in dress uniform and hauled him rudely to his feet. Robert had no idea that this was the man assigned specifically to neutralize the Black Eagles. Falconi was simply operating from the premise that he still had not achieved the object of his mission.

Falconi grasped Kraschenko by the throat and propelled him backward against the wall.

"Slushait-ye, tovaresch!" (listen, comrade) Falconi growled to the Russian. "I want to know the location of your prisoner, the female ARVN lieutenant. There will be no delays and no bargaining. You can either help me or you can die."

Kraschenko doubted that the American failed to see the value of a KGB officer as a prisoner, but he was not about to point this out to the enraged American who was still fully in the possession of the battle lust of the recent struggle.

"I know nothing of the layout of this installation," the Russian replied in protest. "I, myself, recently arrived in the helicopter destroyed by your aircraft. But that man

179

can help you." He continued in a strangled voice, pointing at the Russian technician. "He is permanently stationed here and speaks the language." The technician gave his superior officer a look of shocked reproach. If he had time to dwell upon the matter, it would surely have occurred to him that secret police are never bound by the rules and codes of honor that they seek to enforce in others.

The two North Vietnamese army survivors were left where they lay, no longer posing a threat as long as the Black Eagles stuck to their schedule.

Malpractice McCorckel was assigned to stay and guard Colonel Kraschenko at the entrance of the temple while the rest of the Alpha team fanned out into the compound to mop up pockets of resistance and search for Andrea.

The Russian could not walk unassisted. Robert Falconi and Ray Swift Elk frog-marched him rapidly down the corridors.

"I do not know exactly where they are keeping her," said the Russian, "but I will guide you to the maximum security section."

Andrea Thuy had been allowed adequate sleep and food for the past day and a half due to the confusion about her status resulting from the scenario, the cover story planted by the Special Operations Group Counterintelligence Apparatus. She had used the time wisely, attempting to recover from her debilitating experience.

Andrea heard the staccato rhythm of the approaching gunfire and the occasional blast of a grenade. She hoped against hope the disturbance was the beginning of a rescue effort. There was still the very real possibility that her captors would seek to deprive her rescuers of victory by killing her.

The Black Eagles' intelligence analyst hugged the

stone wall out of view of the observation portal in the cell door when she heard a key rattle in the lock. The plucky member of the Black Eagles had no idea how she could resist her assassins as they came through the door, but she was determined to try.

As the door began to swing open, the North Vietnamese army guard with an automatic in his hand was propelled into the room by the explosion of a grenade.

Andrea had not prepared herself for the blast and was dazed momentarily. As the dust settled and no one followed up on the grenade attack, she concluded: *They still don't know where I am. I must get out of here or I might get left behind.*

She picked up the guard's pistol and a paring knife she found stuck into the wooden table outside the cell. She staggered along the corridor looking for a way out.

Andrea realized that at this very moment she was facing her greatest peril. If she did not escape this place successfully she might still be forced to submit to razor-sharp death at the hands of the torture-master. Her forward path seemed to carry her even deeper into the bowels of the ancient structure. But she did not want to change directions yet for fear of wandering aimlessly in circles.

Then Andrea saw the red-lacquered door and heard a faint nervous laugh from within. With pistol in one hand and knife in the other she eased cautiously into the room.

Horror seized her gut as she recognized the profile of the slender figure in the dressing robe gazing at several small pieces of square paper on the table in front of him.

Minh Khoa was terrified. Andrea's face was contorted with rage. Her eyes bulged from their sockets, which were dark and sunken from fatigue, pain, and starvation. The prisoner had never been in his presence when not in a totally helpless condition.

"Please," he whined, in a high-pitched screech, "I only do what I am ordered to do." He climbed backward onto his desk, clawing behind him for support. He couldn't take his eyes from the figure confronting him. Her flesh was wasted by ten days of forced starvation.

Andrea held the knife in her trembling hand and advanced resolutely toward him.

"You are less human than the poor, unfortunate creatures you have carved up so slowly," she rasped. "You are not a man. Therefore you have no need of your testicles. I will relieve you of them. I wish I had the time to do it. Centimeter by painful centimeter, for two days as you did to Mrs. Ky, but I am rushed for time."

Andrea feinted toward him with the knife, causing him to lunge further back on the desk. Then she quickly grasped his ankles, and in a move that required little strength, counterbalanced him over the back of the desk. He fell onto the back of his neck, his hands clawing upward.

Andrea sat on one of his feet and propped them apart with her knees. In a final gesture, before she left the room, Andrea slashed twice more, severing the motor nerve to his arms. Then, leaning backward against the desk, she pushed with her trembling legs and shoved the desk closer to the wall, pinning Minh Khoa upside down.

"Bon appetite," Andrea said, taunting him. "I sincerely hope you choke on them."

His only reply was a strangled rattle. He tried in vain to cough up the twin morsels she had forced down his throat.

Major Falconi was waiting for Andrea outside the door.

"I hear there's no cure for rape like revenge," he murmured consolingly.

"It will do for now," she replied, leaning on him for support.

"Who was that?" Falconi asked, indicating the twitching legs and the blood-stained claw of a hand, visible above the edge of the desk.

"That was the boogie man," she replied, and didn't offer any further explanation.

Robert Falconi went back into the room looking for clothing and spotted a fresh set of fatigues laid out across the back of a chair.

He offered them to Andrea who hesitated, then shrugged with acquiescence saying, "He certainly won't be needing them anymore."

The major keyed his walkie-talkie and announced, "Top! Blue! I've found Andrea. She's still in shape to move, and it's time to get out of here. Everybody rejoin Malpractice at the boats."

Once outside they could see the fire from the burning wreckage of the Soviet helicopter growing to involve more of the P.O.W. compound's structures. It was obvious that the blaze must ultimately claim the temple itself.

Falconi picked up the radio again. "Malpractice, contact air support and get an assessment of the situation."

Sergeant Malcomb McCorckel switched the frequency setting of the ANPRC-41 and addressed the flight of Intruders: "Odin, this is Valkyrie. Come in."

"Valkyrie, this is Odin flight leader. I hope you boys are almost through down there. We've impeded the progress of the column from Xuan Hoa, but my three wingmen tell me that they're Winchester, out of ammunition, that is. And we still have some demolition work to do."

"Odin, please hold the line," requested McCorckel as he relayed the information to Robert Falconi, who was leading the repatriated Lt. Andrea Thuy and the two Russian prisoners toward the waiting rafts.

Major Falconi replied, "Tell Odin to get on with the demolition. We can make our way to the riverbed from here."

But when the Alpha team and their unwilling guests had moved midway across the open ground, the air around them was filled with the buzzing of a hundred angry hornets. The column of the North Vietnamese army from Xuan Hoa had arrived.

The cry "Hit the dirt!" came seconds late for the Russian radio technician, who suddenly became dead weight in the arms of Ray Swift Elk and Doug Laird. The 7.65 steel-jacketed bullet that caught him between the shoulder blades was no less deadly for having traveled five hundred yards.

"I was afraid of this," Major Falconi yelled from his prone position to Top Gordon. "It's the column from Xuan Hoa."

"They're still at considerable range," replied Top Gordon, eyeing the rafts, not fifty yards ahead of them, longingly.

"But if they bring their mortars into play," yelled Blue Richards, "they can flush us out and finish us with area fire."

The temple detachment had finished the graveyard watch when called back into action. They had turned off the road before reaching the fortress and had moved out over the open area, the killing ground, between the heliport and the anti-aircraft emplacement.

Major Falconi attempted to establish radio contact with Sgt. Archibald Dobbs.

"Archie, what's your situation up there?"

Dobbs responded from his elevated vantage point, five hundred yards to the south.

"Nobody left alive here. Air support did a bang-up job. One of the twelve point seven Soviet heavy machine guns was blown off its mounts, but the second gun appears to be operable. I've altered the AA mount so I can depress the fire down onto the killing ground. Tell everyone there to stay down. As soon as the column advances past my position we will have them in a cross fire."

"Everyone keep your heads down," called out Falconi at the top of his lungs, relaying Archie's strategy as the air hummed death above their heads. "We have to suck them in closer before we counterattack."

The advancing enemy soldiers interpreted the American's lack of response as an indication of complete firepower superiority. They fanned out into a running skirmish line, yelling battle cries and hoisting their standard as they approached.

As the last elements of the platoon swept past Sergeant Dobbs, he opened up with his 12.7 messengers of mayhem. Slowly, back and forth, he mowed down the ranks of soldiers from behind.

The impact from the half-inch equivalent slugs knocked some men completely off their feet while it dismembered and decapitated others. Then Archie stopped the attack dead in its tracks by adjusting the elevation of his fire to sweep across the front of the enemy advance. Up, down, and across ranged the line of tracers, and the big gun chugged as the outsized slugs impacted into flesh and dirt.

When he sensed the charge was broken, Dobbs concentrated on the isolated mortar teams that were setting up to bombard the Black Eagles' position.

"We can't afford to waste a great deal of time getting Archie out of there," said Top Gordon.

"But it is worth a brief counterattack," stated Robert Falconi, and spoke once again into his radio.

"Archie, I hate to ask you to leave the party while you're having so much fun, but we've got to go. Ray and I will work our way out along the treeline to cover your retreat and pick you up. I'm sending everyone else to carry the rafts down to the riverbed. Time is growing short. Our air support has already left to implement the third element of their mission."

The heavy thud of the 12.7 stopped momentarily, and Archie's voice came over the radio.

"Will comply, Falc. I'll keep firing until I see you break away from the treeline."

"We're on our way." Major Falconi signed off.

Dobbs was blowing badly and near complete exhaustion when he joined up with Robert Falconi who covered their retreat to the treeline. Isolated rounds buzzed over their heads from the remaining elements of the North Vietnamese army.

"I think I'm finally warmed up, Falc," Archie panted.

Ray Swift Elk grinned at him and grabbed Archie's pack harness to help him along.

"Let's move it out, feather merchant," Ray said. "It would be a disgrace to be run down by a bunch of legs."

The three men double-timed through the treeline and soon caught up with the main party. As they drew near, Robert Falconi heard Top Gordon speaking into his radio.

"Alpha team to bravo team, come in. What is your status?"

"Alpha team, we are in position," came the voice of Sergeant Kim. "Be advised that a platoon from the temple garrison passed this point thirty minutes ago and appears to be lying low up the roadway."

Chapter Eleven

"Major Xong." The young lieutenant addressed his commanding officer, momentarily removing his eyes from the field glasses. "The relief colum from Xuan Hoa has been destroyed with our own anti-aircraft guns. The American gangsters have now wiped out half of the soldiers who were assigned to defend the temple. Our unit and our brothers in the riverbed are the only forces left in the area. How long must my platoon be held back from the real fighting by the fiendishly devised ruses of the Americans. It is time to bring to bear our superior numbers in order to trap and destroy the enemy."

Major Xong was a pragmatist. He could no longer cling to the illusion that the Americans expected to be rescued by a force of helicopters. He had no idea why they appeared to be headed into the riverbed where only death awaited them at the hands of the reinforced militia. But Xong was certainly willing to aid them in their lemminglike drive to oblivion.

"The time has come," the major announced to the young lieutenant, "to reexamine that option. I am placing you in charge of three light infantry squads. I will retain the heavy weapons squad here, in the open, where it might still be of some use. It will do you little good in the jungle.

"No doubt," Xong continued, "the Americans have

more bedevilment and trickery awaiting you. Should you fail to entrap them, we will pick up and coordinate the pursuit with the coastal militia forces."

The platoon leader did not bother to hide the look of disgust on his face as he directed the three squads to follow him south toward the Americans who were now visible, one mile distant, crossing the road and descending into the river canyon below the dam.

He concluded that Major Xong was a poor choice to put into command of the facility even though the major outranked Captain Ngo. Obviously the old man had spent too much time amongst the decadent Theravadan Buddhists to the south. He had become soft, too cautious for command.

The lieutenant sounded the call for double-time and commenced the chase.

When the Black Eagles' Alpha and Bravo teams linked up, they took the opportunity to crowd around Andrea and welcome her back. It was a very brief but significant moment. She was embarrassed but proud and pleased at the attention given to her.

Though still too weak to do more than stumble forward, holding on to Sergeant Ray Swift Elk, she said, "Give me an M-sixteen. I hope you left some North Vietnamese for me to kill."

"It is good to see you again, Major Falconi," Sergeant Kim said to the tall, green-eyed American. "We have found a good position located one hundred yards along this trail where it takes a wide swing to the left."

"Let's get there pronto," answered Major Falconi. "Have you set up a reception for the North Vietnamese behind us?" he asked as the assembled group shouldered the rubber rafts and moved out.

"Eddie set up a couple of Claymores on tripwires,"

Kim replied.

The rafts were light but cumbersome to manuever. As the group rounded the bend in the trail they could hear individual rifle fire from the approaching North Vietnamese army squads.

The ANPC-41 radio on Sergeant Laird's back crackled into life.

"Odin to Valkyrie," said the voice.

"Valkyrie acknowledging," replied Robert Falconi, taking the microphone. "What success have you had leveling the waterfall?"

"We've never been assigned to an earth-moving detail before," came back the reply. "When we return to base we're all going to ask for a transfer to the Seabees. We put six of our five-hundred-pound eggs into that hillside. It now looks more like a multistep ramp than a straight drop. I still have two eggs left."

"Then it's time to make like the Easter Bunny," said Falconi. "And don't take too much time blowing that dam. We're totally surrounded and to paraphrase a great general, we have them right where we want them."

"Roger and Wilco," came the parting comment from the lead Intruder.

The flight of A-H Intruders roared over the Black Eagles' position and began a graceful climbing arc to the left.

Then two explosions resounded close together from the direction of the trail behind them.

Maj. Robert Falconi un-limbered his M-16 and said to Top Gordon, "That sounds like Claymores. Bring along Kim and Eddie. We will try to slow their progress. Everyone else move the boats up this bank and load them up."

Sgt. Ray Swift Elk grabbed Colonel Kraschenko and propelled him up the incline.

Major Falconi and the three Black Eagles moved up the

trail and rounded the bend in time to see two squads of the North Vietnamese army over the remnants of their lieutenant and the first squad which were ripped to pieces by the Claymore mines. The mines were designed to project a cone-shaped blast of ball-bearing shot. The Black Eagles impeded their progress even more by firing on full automatic with their M-16s into the group of soldiers bunched up in front of their fallen comrades.

"Take cover," a North Vietnamese squadleader shouted before a 5.56 millimeter round shredded his vocal cords.

Then Major Falconi heard Blue Richards yelling from behind him.

"We're taking fire from the militia downstream, Major."

Top Gordon sounded off. "Time to retreat."

"I hope the Easter Bunny drops those eggs soon," Major Falconi shouted to him as they ran, full out, down the narrow game trail.

As his wingmen circled a thousand feet above him, the flight commander set up his approach and guided his A-lH Intruder on its final bombing run over the Yen Dam reservoir.

"There is no need for worry, Comrade Major Xong," reported the excited North Vietnamese infantryman. "The bombs from the western imperialist aircraft missed the dam. He flew too low and dropped his bombs too soon. I saw them skip over the water and sink immediately before they would have struck the dam."

"Oh, no!" exclaimed Xong, who was well trained in the use of explosives. "That is perfect positioning! At the right depth the pressure of the surrounding water will tamp the explosion—"

Before Major Xong could finish his explanation, the twin explosions of the two five-hundred-pound bombs blasted a furrow across the packed mud structure. As the geysers settled, a tube of rushing water projected over the top and commenced rapid erosion of the underlying soil.

"Eddie! Move your ass!" Major Falconi shouted after hearing the double whump of the underwater explosion.

The dedicated young sergeant was still snapping off bullets at the pursuing North Vietnamese army. Abruptly he stopped firing and lowered the rifle from his shoulder.

Eddie stared in open-mouthed amazement up the dry channel as the bodies of many enemy soldiers were catapulted upward by the onrushing torrent of water.

Robert Falconi almost yanked him off his feet as he dragged Eddie to the side and pointed him toward the waiting rafts.

"It's time to put on the life preservers, Major!" yelled Sergeant Laird.

"Put Andrea in the center of the lead raft and the Russian in the other," directed Major Falconi. He stepped into the crossing straps of his life preserver and lashed down the strap under his arms.

A brief chorus of screams was heard from down the river as the rising flood swept into the militia. Then only the water could be heard rumbling and hissing past the Black Eagles at forty miles per hour. The eddying current from the bend in the river crept ever closer to the rafts. The water that undermined the soil under the boats was moving much slower.

The look of terror on Colonel Kraschenko's face was matched by that of Archie Dobbs.

"Jesus Christ," he muttered as he paddled to maintain his balance. "And I thought you had to be crazy to jump out of an airplane."

The bodies of the drowned North Vietnamese began to surface around the rafters. Their sightless eyes stared accusingly before the current rolled them over.

Doug Laird addressed his fellow rafters: "Don't grab

191

onto any branches, even if they are holding us back."

Stretches of the river that held giant boulders now formed standing waves in the river's flow. The lead raft flew over a hummock of water formed by a standing wave and buried its nose deep in the following trough.

Although his hands were tied in front of him, Colonel Kraschenko gripped tightly, the rope attached to the top border of the raft. He shook the water from his eyes.

Robert Falconi grinned as he heard the words *Bosha moi* (my God) escape involuntarily from Kraschenko's lips.

The flight of Intruders made one last pass overhead, wagging their wings as a sign of farewell before heading home, but the Black Eagles were far too busy maintaining their balance, while fending off rocks and trees, to notice.

Blue Richards let off a rebel yell of exhilaration and paddled furiously.

Andrea quickly discovered that the center of the raft was the least padded and least gentle position from which to encounter the often rocky river bottom. She shifted forward and sat on the inflated thwart, grasping the life preserver straps of Malpractice on one side and Top Gordon on the other.

The next standing wave threatened to dislodge Malpractice from his perch. Only the fact that Andrea had a firm grasp on him prevented it.

Sergeant Laird balanced himself in a saddle position by stroking rapidly and thought ahead to the waterfall. Then he saw the second river fifty yards ahead of them. It was the tributary that joined the Song Yen from the north.

The OP plan map depicted the location of the falls shortly after the union of the two rivers.

"Falls ahead!" he screamed to the major. Doug signaled the raft behind him with his paddle to pull over.

The bodies of North Vietnamese were washed up along the banks of the river on either side of them. Many more were still being carried downstream as part of the burden of the river because there had not been sufficient time for biological degeneration to form gas from the rotting flesh and cause the bodies to float.

The rafters were taking a floating tour through a charnel house in which they earnestly hoped they would not soon become residents. Doug's sensation of foreboding was not a feeling that he could shake off quickly. It clawed at his gut as he joined Sergeant Kim and Major Falconi to hike the short distance toward the rapids ahead to inspect what was left of the falls.

The placement of the five-hundred-pound blockbusters had been excellent. The earth blown away from the top of the waterfall had created an excellent sloping ramp as it fell to the bottom of the incline. But the debris was being swiftly washed away at the very bottom, creating a final drop of six feet which was obviously growing every minute.

"What do you think, Sparks?" asked Major Falconi.

"It's as good as we could expect," responded Sergeant Laird. "And it isn't going to get any better. Now is the time to take it."

"You are certainly correct about that," commented Robert Falconi. "I received one final warning from the SOG planning team about this operation. Because we are dealing with a mud dam, the initial flow will only grow greater with time as it erodes the original spillway. If we don't complete our passage quickly we may not be able to handle the river at full flood."

"Time is wasting," said Sergeant Kim.

The trio of Black Eagles retraced their steps to the waiting rafts.

There is no point in dwelling on it, Doug thought. An image rose from his subconscious as they strode back to the boats, a memory from yet another rafting trip on the Kern River when a section of rope used to secure cargo had vibrated loose from a capsized raft and trapped him underwater. The sound of the rapids before him dispelled the memory from his mind.

Doug could sense the river rising and gaining speed. He helped push the raft into the current. The thunder of the approaching white water drowned out all other sounds save the occasional sharp clack of fist-sized rocks thrown up by the raging waters to bounce off the boulders in the path of the current.

The surface of the boulders, which hadn't seen water in ten years, had a wet, shiny newness of a newborn child.

Doug called out the stroke cadence and urged his team not to impede the progress of the raft in any way.

"Keep the raft pointed straight, maintain your balance, and row like hell!" he yelled.

Robert Falconi had never seen Archie Dobbs so petrified with fear. But everybody else was maintaining adequately. Andrea and the Russian colonel were holding their positions in the middle of their respective rafts. Blue Richards looked especially strong and confident.

The current swept them into the center of the cataract. It had taken the Black Eagles very little times to learn to work as a team to handle the bucking bronco twists of this river of death. They seemed to react as one when the lead raft leaped over the first standing wave of water.

The tough fabric of the raft enabled it to flow over the surface of an exposed rock contouring its shape automatically to follow the surface of the river. They neared the last of the rapids at the base of the incline, moving at fifty miles an hour. The river divided around a series of boulders. There was no time to pick one path over the other. Each raft took a different route by random chance.

Doug's raft took the last major drop in the river. At first the raft seemed to nose cleanly into the water after taking the six-foot drop. Everyone held onto the side ropes and leaned backward, touching their arching backs to the surface of the raft.

Like a bucking bronco that is almost played out, the river made one last attempt to shake them off its back. The crew of rafters could not recover quickly enough from the plunge to negotiate clearly the last boulder in their path.

Flowing over the boulder, the left side of the raft erupted into the air. Blue Richards adjusted expertly, but Archie Dobbs was caught off center and would have tumbled into the river if Doug had not reached out to steady him.

But even as the rippling motion of a cracking whip reaches its greatest intensity at the end of the rawhide, the end of the raft flowing over the rock snapped Doug off the transom. He reached for the rope that bordered the raft's edge and thought for a moment that he succeeded as he plunged into the river. Then Doug realized that it was merely a section of rope coiled in the rear of the boat.

Major Falconi directed the second raft to meet the first in the calmer waters beyond the rapids. A quick head count revealed to Falconi that someone was missing.

"Where's Sparks?" he called out.

Blue answered, "We lost him near the end of the white water."

Archie Dobbs squeezed the water from the corners of his eyes and added, "I felt him shove me back into the boat but then I lost sight of him."

The crews of the two rafts fought their way back into the strong current close to the final waterfall.

"I see a rope caught in a crack in that rock," reported Malpractice McCorckel.

A V-shaped trough formed at the surface ten feet beyond where the rope quivered tautly into the river.

"To hell with the blade," muttered Top Gordon and

slashed into the rope lying on the surface of the rock. Sergeant Kim secured the line below the cut and tied it to the raft.

They pulled in the body of the hapless veteran of many white-water rafting expeditions.

"Son of a bitch," commented Archie Dobbs about the situation. "One end of the rope got wrapped around his neck. When the other end snagged on the rock, it broke his neck before he had a chance to drown."

"Haul him aboard," directed Major Falconi to his crestfallen crew.

The magic charm has ended, thought Top Gordon. They were once again borne away by the main current of the river. Top Gordon reflected that on each mission the members of the Black Eagles were strong believers in luck until their collective cherry was busted by the first death in their ranks. Then the happy-go-lucky jovial group that began the mission was revealed to be a grim professional military team no longer convinced of their individual immortalities but resolved to complete the mission nonetheless.

Blue Richards's steady gaze bore into the eyes of Archie Dobbs to dispossess the unit tracker of the notion that Sparks had saved his life only to die in his place.

"Nobody said this job was going to be easy," Blue related to Archie in a level tone. "Let's get moving," he added.

"It looks like we got through the rapids none too soon," said Sgt. Ray Swift Elk, who had turned to look behind them. "The last of the dam must have given way all at once."

A two-foot-high ridge of water surged toward them from the base of the rapids. And remembering the instruction of their recently deceased mentor, the Black Eagles stroked vigorously with their paddles to keep the rafts straight and avoid capsizing. The crest of the flood carried them to the first bend in the river where it deposited them on the riverbank.

As they disembarked and paddled out into the main current once again, Robert Falconi said, "According to the map, the village of An Trach is the next inhabitation lying before us. I hope that surge disrupts their ability to react. We might be able to slip through without causing the militia to set up a hue and cry."

"It's a good time to rest," said Top Gordon to both float crews. "Two men in each raft will trade off every fifteen minutes and keep paddling slowly to prevent foundering on the riverbank. Everyone else take it easy and break out the C rations. I want us rested up so we can paddle full speed through An Trach if the situation warrants it."

Eddie Barthe remembered the words of Doug Laird during the last of the briefback when the dam-busting gambit was introduced. Doug had paraphrased the British philosopher, Lord Bertrand Russell: "White water rafting is characterized by long periods of boredom punctuated by moments of utter terror."

The moments of utter terror were over for the plucky signalman. He lay in repose beneath the vinyl canvas that covered his body.

Eddie Barthe looked around him, observing the crew members of the two boats secumbing to the gentle rhythm of the river as they drifted around the final bend before their passage through An Trach.

The shadows, cast by the jungle hanging over the river, became shorter with each passing minute although it was still an early 0800 hours.

Andrea had fallen into the sleep of the exhausted while her teammates kicked back and stared, sleepy-eyed, at the passing jungle. The peaceful rhythm of the river instilled such tranquility that only the occasional body of a North Vietnamese soldier, washed up on the bank, maintained their connection to reality.

"Heads up!" called out Major Falconi. "An Trach is coming up now. Remember, wave back to them and smile but don't fire unless they initiate it."

The flooding of the Song Yen had caught An Trach by surprise. One section of a pier had gone awash under the rising river and broke away from its foundation, trailing behind the section that was still sound with a plume of spray drifting away from it.

Two members of the local militia were discussing the fate of one of their fellow soldiers whose body was deposited on the bank by the flood. They saw the raft drifting down the river and followed it with suspicion, uncertain as to what to do.

The river picked up speed as its passage was restricted under the bridge ahead.

"Wake up Andrea," said Robert Falconi. "I have an acting assignment for her."

Falconi reasoned that because Andrea was Vietnamese and wore the uniform of a garrison soldier, she might confuse the patrolling soldier long enough for them to pass unscathed.

The militiaman motioned to two workmen who were pulling a handcart containing the bodies of drowned soldiers. They pulled their burden to the side of the road as the militiaman waved an ambulance forward, which was crossing the bridge and proceeding north.

Then they saw the two rafts passing under the bridge. The soldier ran across the bridge to follow them and scrutinized them closely as the Black Eagles drew away from him.

Andrea sat up straight and smiled at the guard. The soldier waved back, returning the smile reflexively. But the warmth faded from his face, being replaced by an anxious scowl. He yelled at Andrea and motioned with

198

his forearm, directing the two rafts to the southern riverbank.

Andrea smiled again and looked at him with a questioning expression, sensing the current bearing them swiftly away. She cupped her palm over her ear and called back weakly for clarification.

The man un-limbered the bolt-action rifle, and Top Gordon said softly, "Get ready Sergeant Barthe, we've got trouble."

The militiaman on top of the bridge cried out to the rafts again and raised his rifle.

"Take him now, Eddie," Major Falconi commanded.

Eddie twisted around from his saddle position on the raft, raised his M-16 and fired in one smooth motion. The soldier on the bridge toppled backward onto the roadway with a .223 bullet wound between his eyes.

"Break out the paddles," Major Falconi commanded. "Eddie, you keep their heads down."

The two laborers who had been hauling the cart rushed to the fallen soldier. Then one of them rose and ran to the village to spread the word.

The Soviet Mil-8, NATO designation, "HIP" troop-carrying helicopter had overflown Major Xong's position and was over the rapidly draining reservoir before he was aware of it.

The helicopter's North Vietnamese army markings were belied by the fact that it was flown by Soviet military advisors and the crack North Vietnamese army assault troops it carried, equivalent to the American Air Cavalry, and were commanded by KGB military advisors. This was Colonel Kraschenko's honor guard.

The Mil-8 was not a sissified command rotorcraft like the Mil-4 that had carried the colonel to the temple. It was not outfitted to transport the commander from headquarters to headquarters in semi-luxury. The HIP was a war bird throughout.

The Supreme Soviet Military Planning Staff had long ago committed themselves to a policy of initiating and prevailing in brushfire wars. The vertical takeoff and landing capability of the helicopter made it an ideal tool for this mission. Consequently the Soviet helicopter force, although not technologically superior to that of the U.S.A., often yielded machines of greater firepower and payload capability.

The HIP troopcopter, equipped with a 12.7 millimeter machine gun and 57 millimeter rockets, was designed for the head-on assault of enemy ground forces as well as air support of their own troops.

The pilot of the brute machine neither wavered nor hesitated when he spotted the burning wreckage of his commanding officer's helicopter on the ground. He headed straight for the action.

Major Xong and his remaining heavy-weapons support squad did their best to get the attention of the big helicopter. Because they no longer had the temple's base station radio to relay their communcation on the proper frequency, they were reduced to continuously transmitting their call sign and waiting for an answer.

Major Xong's radioman keyed the transmit button at thirty second intervals.

"North Vietnamese assault helicopter," he called. "Please acknowledge. This is the temple garrison ground forces commanded by Major Xong."

"There is no reply, sir," reported the radioman, belaboring the obvious.

"Keep trying until I tell you to stop," replied Major Xong in an exasperated tone.

The large Soviet troopcopter hovered for two minutes while it inspected the burning command copter. The radio next to Major Xong finally crackled in response.

The flat, emotionless voice stated, "You are Major Xong, otherwise known as Comrade Bua?"

"That is affirmative, this is Major Xong of North Vietnamese army counterintelligence. I assumed command of the garrison ground forces at the direction of Colonel Kraschenko."

The voice from the Mil-8 continued: "We can see the wreckage of Colonel Kraschenko's helicopter below us. Can you confirm whether he is alive or dead?"

Major Xong attempted to explain. "Two Soviet officers were seen being led away by the American raiding party. One was shot by the garrison relief force from Xuan Hoa."

The voice interrupted him. "This relief force—they are the bodies we see around the perimeter of the heliport?"

"That is affirmative," replied Major Xong.

"What was the size of the raiding force?" continued the merciless, implacable interrogator.

Major Xong felt a flush creep from his neck to his forehead. He hesitated and stammered, "There were eight men."

"*Eight men,*" repeated the voice in the same emotionless tone. "Can you give us their present location?"

Major Xong regained his composure and stated with authority, "They were seen entering the riverbed immediately before the dam was destroyed by the Yankee fighter bomber."

The voice stated with finality. "The men in this raiding party seem to have left nothing to chance. The least we can do is return the favor. You may consider the following a direct order from General Kuznetz of the KGB. You will gather together whatever forces you can locate and retrace the route taken by the raiding party known as the Black Eagles in order to confirm their disposition. Do not stop until you have checked every dead body. If the opportunity arises to coordinate your forces with those we contact down river, we will put you in communication with them. Over and Out!"

Major Xong could not bring himself to meet the eyes of his radio operator. He walked to the promontory overlooking the lake which was now spewing in a cataract through the steadily eroding orafice originally scratched out by the single American bomber.

He had been absolutely correct about the ARVN female operative. Andrea had been far from weak and had understood only one thing: force. She and her fellow Black Eagles had been in control of the situation from the very beginning. Every move he had made during the past week had been countered or used against him. How he ached to get his hands on her once again. But somehow he sensed that the outcome would not be any different.

The Soviet HIP helicopter executed a two hundred and twenty-five degree turn in a climbing right bank and began following the reborn Song Yen River.

The voice which had interrogated Major Xong so relentlessly belonged to Major Dubrovsky, a KGB military advisor. Major Dubrovsky addressed the navigator-radio operator: "Put me in contact with General Kuznetz."

When the contact was established he made his report.

"We have not confirmed the whereabouts of Colonel Kraschenko, although we have located the wreckage of his helicopter. The worst case scenario is that he is now in the hands of the Americans, and they have survived the disaster which they created. Their direction of travel would be taking them toward the coastal region. Their rafts are not outfitted for speed. I think we can run them down by following the river."

"Then do so!" replied General Kuznetz. "The loss of Colonel Kraschenko is nothing to us compared to the gain he represents to American intelligence. In the unlikely event that the American expeditionary force surrenders without a struggle, take Colonel Kraschenko into custody to face charges."

No explanation of the *charges* was offered by the general but none was asked for. The general continued: "However, if they make a fight of it, you are to utterly destroy all of them. I have had my fill of this Maj. Robert Mikhailovich Falconi and his Black Eagles, and I would consider his destruction a personal favor."

"I understand, General Kuznetz," came the sharp acknowledgement from Major Dubrovsky.

His voice now increased with vigor, and he postured himself pointedly toward the observation port of the helicopter.

"Your orders will be carried out," Dubrovsky finished and signed off.

Presently the radio operator reported, "We are in contact with the village of An Trach. I can't understand what he is saying."

"Then fetch one of our NCOs who speaks Vietnamese," retorted the major.

"The ranking Communist party member in the village reports that a member of their militia sighted two rafts passing under a bridge. A Vietnamese woman aboard one of the rafts wore a North Vietnamese army uniform. The rafts were directed to stop for inspection, but the cowardly Yankee imperialists shot the brave, generous militiaman who was trying to assist them."

"So they are despicable as well," commented Major Dubrovsky sarcastically. "Ask him how long ago this happened."

Dubrovsky harbored no illusions about the prowess of

this American force. They were undoubtedly men to be dealt with. He resolved not to make the same mistake as his predecessors and underestimate them.

"The village leader reports that twenty minutes has passed since the ruthless cowardly murderers escaped."

Dubrovsky sighed at the colorful rhetoric. "You have my permission to refrain from making a literal translation. Try to be brief."

Then Major Dubrovsky instructed his communications personnel.

"After you have obtained the pertinent frequencies of the local militia forces, you will coordinate the establishment of roadblocks on all major roads between here and the Gulf of Tonkin, especially on the coast. I don't care if it is being done already. We will get on top of this situation and stay there."

The Mil-8's two Isotov jet turbines, each with one thousand and seven hundred horsepower, could be heard howling from the ground as the helicopter passed over An Trach following the winding course of the swollen, flooded Song Yen.

"Lieutenant Martin, something's up!" said Jackson White.

Buzz Martin roused himself slowly from his uncomfortable sitting position and gazed at the railway bridge.

"It looks like a railroad inspection vehicle," he said.

The tires and hubs of the jeep had been replaced by metal railway wheels. It was manned by a driver, a machine gunner, and his assistant.

Buzz Martin evaluated the trio of North Vietnamese soldiers and their odd-looking improvisation for a moment.

"I can't see how they will cause us much trouble," he finally concluded, "unless more of them show up." He inspected his watch.

"Since it's about time anyway, let's attempt radio contact with our passengers. I think the call sign was Falcon."

He removed his Prick-6 walkie-talkie from its watertight case and checked its frequency crystal. As the radio warmed up he checked for proper antenna deployment and adjusted the squelch.

"Falcon, this is Buzzard," he repeated. "Do you read me?"

"Buzzard, this is Falcon," acknowledged Robert Falconi.

"Falcon, what is your position?" asked Buzz Martin.

"We are past the last tributary before the bridge. We calculate our estimated time of arrival at your position to be five minutes from now."

"Falcon, the North Vietnamese army has prepared a surprise party for you. There are three dogfaces with a twelve point seven millimeter machine gun mounted on a railway inspection jeep. They should be within sight of you soon. Sight in on the top dead center of the bridge."

Buzz Martin continued: "They constitute no problem for us, but I don't want to take them out until the last moment in order to avoid alerting any other forces in the area."

"I agree," replied Robert Falconi. "If we see any activity that constitutes a threat, we will fire before you do. That will be your signal to take them. Otherwise fire at your discretion. Over and out."

"Gunny! You and Nguyen make sure the quad fifty mount is operable," directed Lieutenant Martin.

"Yes, sir," replied Gunny. "Our buddy, here, ran me through the drill while you were asleep until I got it down pat. We had a hell of a good time."

"Well, un-limber them," Buzz directed.

Gunny and Nguyen carefully checked the lock and

205

load status of the four machine guns while Buzz kept an eye out for any precipitous movement from the bridge. Their plan of action called for Nguyen to make sure the engine of the halftrack was ready to start after the enemy soldiers were neutralized.

"There they are," whispered Lieutenant Martin. He could make out the first raft rounding the bend in the river.

"It is them. I think it is the Americans we were sent to stop," said the machine gunner, on the jeep, with excitement.

"I will make a report to headquarters at An Trach." The driver picked up the microphone and held it to his lips. Then he hesitated for the last time in his life.

"I think we should wait until we are sure. I don't want a false sighting to give this team a bad name."

Major Falconi was calling the paddle stroke cadence in the lead raft. The two rafts crept smoothly forward, helped along by the current of the river. Eddie Barthe lay prone in the front raft and drew a bead on the machine gunner with his M-16.

"Hell! That tears it. He's picking up his microphone," Buzz Martin muttered.

"*Hit him, Gunny!*" Buzz commanded.

Jackson White lined up his sights on the base of the jeep's machine gun mount in hopes that his first rounds would disable the weapon immediately.

Seventy-five yeards up the river, the Black Eagles watched the impact of the four streams of .50 slugs on the occupants of the jeep. The halftrack was hidden in the jungle, one hundred yards from the bridge. Because the four 50s were sighted in to converge on a target a thousand yards away, their bullets did not impact on one point. Keeping this in mind, Gunny had aimed midway between the gunner and the driver and minutely traversed the guns accordingly.

Everyone in the jeep died instantly, their flesh shredded and pulped by the impact of the big slugs and the exploding cloud of red-hot shrapnel created as the stream of bullets cut the body of the jeep into three pieces and tumbled them into the river. They steamed on impact. Bloody chunks of its former occupants were strewn in an oblong pattern on the tracks where they had fallen.

"How did I do, Lieutenant?" asked Gunny with a big grin on his face.

"Great job, Gunny," Buzz Martin commented with a straight face. Then he added, breaking into laughter, "But you used a little bit too much gun."

Shrill whistles and a rebel yell issued forth from the Black Eagles in the two rafts following the disintegration of the railway inspection jeep and the end of the threat posed by the machine gun mounted on it.

"All right, you crazy bastards!" yelled Top Gordon. "Row your asses off! This is not a picnic. That demonstration of fireworks is going to call everyone in the area down on our heads!"

Major Falconi called the cadence, and every back was bent paddling toward the halftrack. The prows of the two rafts lifted out of the water with each coordinated stroke of its six paddlers.

Nguyen initiated the start sequence, and the engine of the halftrack rumbled into life. Feeling the vibration of the big vehicle beneath his feet, Buzz Martin's attention was diverted from the carnage on the bridge.

"Move this beast out!" he yelled to Nguyen. "We've got passengers to pick up."

The treads spun off the mud they had been sinking into since before daybreak. The armored truck lumbered slowly toward the riverbank.

Buzz Martin leaped from the halftrack before it came to a complete halt and alighted on the ground in front of the Black Eagles who were lifting the rafts from the river.

"Lt. Randolph Martin, U.S. Navy," he said extending his hand to the tall major. "You must be Falcon."

Robert Falconi shook the lieutenant's hand and replied, "Maj. Robert Falconi, U.S. Army. And, you would be Buzzard?"

"You have a couple of prisoners," Buzz said in a questioning tone. "One of them appears to be a KGB colonel and the other is a North Vietnamese WAC?"

"He is a prisoner. She is the object of this mission," explained Robert Falconi. "She is one of our operatives who was kidnapped in Saigon by the Viet Cong."

Chapter Twelve

The rafts were soon lashed to the top of the halftrack, and the Black Eagles began climbing aboard.

Gregori Kraschenko appeared to be fascinated with the wreckage of the jeep still bubbling as the separate pieces were tumbled down river. His uniform was a mud-spattered, waterlogged shambles, but his voice still rang with authority.

"You will not succeed in this criminal abduction. I demand decent treatment. I am entitled to this as a prisoner of war by the Geneva Convention. I demand to speak with a representative of the Red Cross immediately!"

"Sir," Robert Falconi replied in mock deference to the KGB officer's rank. "I'd give you some dry clothes if we had any, and I will ring up the Red Cross as soon as I find a field telephone. Would you like a sample of our C rations?"

Top Gordon broke in: "Major Falconi, I have managed to find floor space on the halftrack for all of our men and equipment, but there is no room left over for the prisoner, not even with a shoehorn."

Robert Falconi was running out of time and was exasperated with the invective hurled at him by the prisoner, some in English, some in Russian, all of which he understood.

"Shove the bastard in an ammunition locker," he said. "And shut your mouth, Colonel. You're lucky we don't shoot you." Falconi turned to Master Sergeant Gordon. "Let's get the hell out of here."

Already bound with his arms behind his back, Colonel Kraschenko was picked up bodily and wedged into an ammunition locker in the side of the halftrack with two duffel bags for padding.

Before he slammed down the locker door, Blue Richards drawled, "Y'all have a comfortable ride, y'hear?"

Major Falconi added, "When I locate a samovar I will brew us up some *goryachyi chai,* comrade."

Robert Falconi swung up and sat behind Lieutenant Martin and asked, "What kind of speed can this relic make?"

Nguyen Phan replied, "This well-maintained North Vietnamese army transport can easily maintain one hundred kilometers per hour. As long as it doesn't bounce itself off the road," he added as the halftrack bounded over a bump, temporarily leaving the surface of the trail and jarring everyone's teeth upon impact.

Major Dubrovsky leaned forward to check his position once again with the navigator of the Mil-8 chopper.

"We should be coming up on it shortly, sir," replied the navigator.

The major had ordered the helicopter to be flown at one hundred feet over the water so they would not miss the rafts underneath the heavy jungle growth which overhung the banks.

"We are passing the northern tributary of the Song Yen. The bridge lies beyond the next bend," said the navigator.

The river was now in full flood due to the influence of

the draining reservoir. The wreckage of the jeep had been tumbled down the river by the fast moving water and was deposited high on the riverbank at the next bend in the river fifty yards to the west.

Major Dubrovsky could see sign on the ground that he did not fully understand.

"Those are armored vehicle tracks," his executive officer pointed out.

"Land the helicopter," Major Dubrovsky ordered. "We will gather whatever intelligence we can before resuming the pursuit!"

The twenty-eight man capacity troop-carrying helicopter landed in the clearing to the north of the bridge. The large rear clamshell doors opened. Twin columns of North Vietnamese shock troops disembarked and were exhorted to form up by their KGB military advisors.

Major Dubrovsky spoke to his XO: "We received a report that an armed railway inspection car was being dispatched to cut off the escape of the Americans."

"That's correct," said the XO, and handed the major his field glasses, pointing further down the river.

"At the bend in the river, see, high on the bank. The lump of twisted, perforated metal has no rust on it. In this climate that means the damage is minutes fresh."

The radioman cut in: "Sir, we have a report from the inspection party on the bridge. The officer states that there are scattered human remains and remnants of a machine gun on the tracks, including unfired twelve point seven millimeter ammunition."

"Human remains," said Major Dubrovsky to himself.

"We have been in communication with a motorized battalion of militia," continued the radioman, "who were dispatched, this morning before daybreak, to the intersection of the coastal highway with the next major road to the south. They have lost communication with their commanding officer, but state that his last orders were to rendezvous at their destination and await further orders."

"Ask them what type of vehicle was assigned to their commander," directed Major Dubrovsky.

The radio operator spoke briefly into his microphone and paused, listening carefully to the reply.

"They report that it was a World War Two American halftrack. It was the only vehicle in the battalion equipped with four fifty caliber machine guns rather than the standard issue single twelve point seven millimeter Soviet weapon. The guns are gang-mounted together in anti-aircraft fashion."

"The pieces to our puzzle are falling into place," Major Dubrovsky commented to his XO. "I think you are correct about the lump of metal on the riverbank. If my conclusions are as accurate as yours, we will be facing a vehicle not much less formidable than a tank and manned by a crew of maniacs that outwitted and destroyed a full company of North Vietnamese infantry, not to mention the local militia of two townships," he added disdainfully.

"He also captured our commanding officer and destroyed his flagship," added the XO.

"Now the job falls to us," stated Dubrovsky. "Recall our troops. I want us airborne immediately. Despite the heavy jungle growth obscuring the trail, we must locate these gangsters."

The executive officer jumped into action and grabbed the microphone from the radio operator.

"All advisors, recall your squads. We are departing immediately."

At a double-time pace the two columns of shock troops approached the Mil-8 and entered through the rear doors. The doors were secured, and the huge gas turbines surged, feeding power to the five-bladed main prop. The landing gear broke contact with the mud, and the heavy helicopter developed more lift as its forward motion increased.

The pilot held his forward speed to a fraction of its one hundred and sixty mile per hour capacity as the observers inside searched through the circular portholes for the halftrack on the trail below.

"Sir," the radio operator asked. "The motorized battalion of militia is asking if there are any new orders for them."

"Hold position as ordered," replied Major Dubrovsky. "We may need them for backup. In the meantime I want you to contact Sam Son, the next major coastal town north of us. The Americans must be planning an evacuation by sea. Ask if they have any coastal naval patrol forces. I want a boat dispatched to patrol offshore along the stretch of coast we are approaching. The new patrol torpedo boats with rocket firing capacity should be satisfactory."

The radio operator began leafing through his book of frequencies for the town of Sam Son.

"Something seems to be bothering you, Captain," said Dubrovsky to his XO. "What is it?"

"Shouldn't we have coordinated our efforts with the motorized battalion of coastal militia?" asked the captain. "In order to deprive the Americans access to the sea in case they manage to elude us?"

"I don't want it to be reported to General Kuznetz that I did anything to indicate I was anticipating failure in carrying out his orders," answered Major Dubrovsky. "Besides, I want these Black Eagles for myself."

Seeking to return to his commanding officer's good graces, the captain said, "I agree Major Dubrovsky. I was guilty of negative thinking. We now have the American raiders precisely where we want them. We have only to disembark two squads of our North Vietnamese army rangers in their pathway to cut them off."

"We don't *have* anyone *yet*," rejoined the more experienced, senior officer. "If we were to follow your plan, now, we might wound a few of them but the rest would scatter. I want all of them. Therefore, my plan is to proceed over this trail toward the coast. We will determine their position and try to stop them from the air. Even if that doesn't work we will have positively identified their position. We can then fly ahead of them, seeking out a site for an ambush where we can take advantage of the greater firepower in our rockets to disable the halftrack.

"The jungle overgrowth obscuring the trail from above makes this a difficult tactical situation. I refuse to play hide-and-seek with an armored vehicle on the ground. We cannot see them most of the time. They are not similarly disadvantaged.

"This reminds me of my youth in Siberia," reminisced the major as the Mil-8 skimmed over the jungle on its journey westward. "In one of my earliest missions in the army, my unit was loaned to the Ministry of the Interior to deal with a tiger that was terroriring a local village. Our orders were to capture the beast and transport it one hundred kilometers outside its hunting territory." '

The major paused in his story and turned to face his executive officer. "Tell me, Captain, how would you hunt a tiger?"

The captain's face briefly displayed uncertainty. Then he smiled and answered, "Very carefully, sir."

Major Dubrovsky chuckled in agreement. "Very good, Captain," he replied. "Now you begin to see the scope of our problem. It is commendable that you should have confidence in our abilities," the major continued, indicating the personnel and equipment around them. "For they are, by no means, insignificant. But, when you are hunting a highly mobile creature, well equipped to do battle, you must first seek to reduce its advantages.

214

Therefore, our first step will be to reduce the Black Eagles' mobility. Once they are crippled we can begin the final phase of our attack."

"What is our ETA at the coast, Lieutenant Martin?" yelled Major Falconi over the rolling thunder of the halftrack.

To the less experienced eye the enormous armored vehicle appeared to be hurtling, out of control, down the jungle pathway. Buzz Martin paused before answering. He searched for landmarks in the jungle, then answered, "We'd better ask our asset, Corporal Phan, of the militia."

Having overheard them, Nguyen Phan called back, "There is a clearing one kilometer ahead, where we cross the river. From there, it is another six kilometers to the coast."

Nguyen Phan shook his head. At first he thought something was wrong with the halftrack's engine when he heard and felt a surging, an increase in RPM even though he had not changed the position of his foot on the gas peddle.

Then he realized that what he was hearing was a beat-frequency oscillation. It often happened when one truck was overtaking another on the highway, and the two engines, revolving at almost identical speeds, caused the same surging sound. Corporal Phan listened more carefully and heard, over the growling of the revolving tracks, the familiar beat of high-speed helicopter blades. He immediately sought the attention of Buzz Martin.

"Helicopter overhead, very close!" he yelled.

Lieutenant Martin turned and relayed the information to Major Falconi.

"Gunny! Heads up!" Falconi bellowed, pointing to the sky.

The halftrack was approaching a clearing in the jungle around a meadow. Falconi instructed Corporal Phan, "Stay under the treeline."

Phan swerved the vehicle into the shadows, narrowly averting the emergence of the halftrack into the morning sunlight before them.

Then there were two explosions, close together, and the patch of green meadow lifted into a cloud of mud that showered the occupants of the halftrack.

Nguyen Phan quickly rotated the cantilevered soil-spattered windshield so that he could see and steered off the trail, further yet, into the jungle.

Archie Dobbs wiped off his face, spat, and looked back at Gunny sitting atop the mount.

"Gunny, you armored cavalry buffs are nuts. I agree with Willie and Joe, the two dogfaces in the *Stars and Stripes*. A moving foxhole attracts attention."

"Don't you worry, grunt," replied the older man from his elevated position. "If we can't see him, he can't see us. As soon as I do get a decent sight picture of him, he's going to look like a mallard that picked the wrong lake on opening day of duck season."

While the two men were talking, Top Gorden and Robert Falconi were waiting for the helicopter to return.

"What's he playing at, Falc?" asked the senior NCO. "I don't think he's coming back."

"He doesn't have to, Top. He's got the high ground," replied Major Falconi. "He knows where we're going, and right now he's picking his spot."

"It must be the river up ahead," said Buzz Martin. "We should be prepared for him when we get there. He doesn't have to make another pass here because he can accomplish his purpose by merely slowing us down. Every moment we waste here gives the North Vietnamese time to catch up with us."

Robert Falconi could feel the schedule outlined in the

OP plan weighing relentlessly on his shoulders.

"We've got to move," he said.

"Can you give us any intelligence on that chopper," Major Falconi asked Sergeant Swift Elk.

"It's a troop carrier," Ray answered. "It must be a Mil-eight, NATO designation HIP. The two large pods on the sides are fuel cells. Each of the smaller pods holds thirty-two of the fifty-seven millimeter rockets."

Major Falconi nodded his head, taking in Ray Swift Elk's briefing. He commented, "As long as they've got fuel they can stand off and blow us to hell. We can't allow them the opportunity to take potshots at us."

Sergeant Swift Elk continued: "The current models have a twelve point seven machine gun mounted in the nose, and she'll carry twenty-eight combat-equipped troops."

Major Falconi reviewed these facts and weighed them against their own capabilities.

"This halftrack is from an armored unit," he said, thinking aloud. Then he asked Corporal Phan, "What other weapons might be carried on one of those vehicles?"

"The other halftracks in our unit mount a single twelve point seven gun and usually carry a couple of mortars," answered the corporal. "Since this is the commanding officer's personal transport and mounts the quad fifty, most of its storage space is reserved for fifty caliber ammunition. But, let me think. If I remember correctly, we are carrying a Soviet hand-held rocket launcher."

"Rocket launcher?" Calvin Culpepper mused aloud with a lustful leer. "That's right up my alley."

"That's the standoff capability we've been looking for," commented Robert Falconi.

"But who is going to hang the bell on the cat?" asked Top Gordon.

"Or pin the tail on the donkey?" added Buzz Martin.

At the first mention of the Soviet bazooka, Sergeants Kim and Culpepper leaped off the halftrack and began an inventory of its ammunition lockers. Lifting the first hatch revealed an uncomfortable Gregori Kraschenko, kept company by two duffel bags.

"How are you doing, Colonel?" asked Sergeant Culpepper. Angry Russian invective issued forth from the colonel's mouth.

"S'all right." Calvin cut him off and slammed the door.

The third compartment was the charm. Sergeant Kim pulled out the rocket launcher and held it up. He looked at Calvin and asked, "Would you be willing to be my ammunition bearer?"

"Sure, Kim," said Calvin with a grin. "Somebody has got to keep you out of trouble."

The two Black Eagles, bearing launcher and rockets, walked around the vehicle and returned to the discussion looking, for all the world, like twelve-year-olds with a new toy.

"I think we've found our volunteers," said Major Falconi to Top Gordon.

"Fire up the beast, Nguyen, let's roll!" directed Lt. Buzz Martin.

"Here's the plan," said Robert Falconi to Kim and Calvin. "We will drop you two off at the river immediately before we leave the jungle growth that obscures this trail from the air. Buzz thinks that we can successfully play cat and mouse with the Soviet chopper in order to set him up for the rocket launcher. We'll have to play him loose and draw him in. If he suspects he is caught in a crossfire he may boogie and leave us to the North Vietnamese. We don't want that. We've got to finish him here before he can get more help. Get ready, your drop-off point will be coming up shortly," Major

Falconi said and turned to survey the landscape around the river.

Buzz Martin crawled over bodies to get to the AA mount. "Keep your eyes open, Gunny," he said. "That chopper is laying low somewhere out there. We're going to drop off a rocket launcher team and then lure the chopper into making a target of itself."

Gunny nodded his understanding and kept his grasp on the quad 50 pistol grips loose and ready.

"Kim! Calvin! Here's your spot," Major Falconi shouted.

The two Black Eagles leaped to the ground and double-timed toward the north end of the clearing. The tracked vehicle spun-mud and lumbered to the treeline.

Robert Falconi entered the probable climbing ability and rate of turn of the Soviet helicopter into the combat computer in his head. Then he instructed his driver, "After we leave the trees drive like hell for the river. But, after covering fifty meters, run back to the right."

"Oh, Lordie," panted Calvin Culpepper, trotting beside Chun Kim. "It's duck season in North Vietnam for sure. This reminds me of the time my pappy and I went after a thirty pound bass and found that we hooked a garfish instead."

"What was the problem?" asked Sergeant Kim, having no idea what a garfish was.

"Well," Calvin answered, "to begin with, our tackle was too small."

"What tackle would be big enough?" queried Kim, who sighted the rocket launcher on the horizon over the treeline at the south end of the clearing.

"A thirty-thirty deer rifle," replied Culpepper laconically as he rammed home one of the finned projectiles into the rear of the launcher. "Those are very mean fish."

"Are you hot?" asked Calvin, referring to the arming

system of the weapon.

"The red light is on," responded Sergeant Kim, and added, in a noticeable louder voice, *"Clear."*

Sergeant Culpepper moved well away from the exhaust path behind the bazooka.

"There goes Falc and the boys in the halftrack," reported Calvin. "Let's keep our eyes on the treeline."

"We should be approaching the clearing now," said Major Dubrovsky. "Begin your run!"

The oversized Soviet troopchopper had been loitering in an orbital flight pattern two hundred yards north of the meadow. It began its rocket-firing run at treetop level, maintaining the minimum forward speed necessary for its pilot to aim the rocket pods.

"We're right on time!" declared the executive officer in triumph. The halftrack emerged into view from the jungle cover.

"Fire when ready!" Major Dubrovsky ordered the pilot.

"I can't see the fuel tanks from this angle. Go for a head shot!" shouted Calvin Culpepper as he watched the Mil-8 approach them through his field glasses.

Corporal Phan began his turn at the same time the Soviet pilot fired his rockets. Because the pilot was leading his target, the rockets exploded in front of the halftrack, to its right.

The target in the sights of Kim's bazooka, although small in a frontal view, was coming straight for him with no lateral component to its velocity. Kim only needed to correct for the rise of the chopper in his sight picture.

The bazooka rocket impacted below the front windshield, spraying the legs of the pilot and copilot with shrapnel and slicing into the control linkages. The copilot screamed in agony, and the pilot, though terribly wounded, struggled to maintain control of the craft.

"Lead him, Gunny!" called Archie Dobbs, who was dry-firing the quad 50's in his imagination.

"Go teach your dog to suck eggs," rejoined the veteran marine who returned his concentration to the target.

Four streams of .50 tracer rounds could be seen reaching out and slicing into the wounded bird.

"We should find a place to land Major Dubrovsky!" suggested the captain emphatically and reached in front of him to assist the pilot.

Not wanting to admit that the situation had gotten away from him, the major retorted, "No! I will not report failure to General Kuznetz."

The argument became academic when the severed hydraulic system failed to respond to the commands of the dying pilot. The Mil-8 broached sideways in the air, giving Gunny a much larger and more vulnerable target.

The .50 tracer rounds, loaded alternately with armor-piercing rounds, tore into the fuel pods and converted the helicopter into a true, ethnic Molotov cocktail.

The exploding, burning skeleton of the dying warbird disintegrated as it impacted on the meadow one hundred yards south of the halftrack.

The expression on Robert Falconi's face portrayed a hardened heart. Although Andrea turned her head reflexively to avoid the penetrating heat, her mouth was set in a feral grin.

The occupants of the halftrack cheered the destruction of yet another obstacle in their path to safety. Major Falconi directed Corporal Phan to return and pick up the bazooka team.

"Kim! Calvin! Saddle up. We have a schedule to keep," he shouted.

The tracks of the armored beast resumed rotating after the two Black Eagles reached for handholds on the side of the truck and were hauled aboard.

The radio belched a burst of static, and a voice identified itself in Vietnamese. The officer in charge of Corporal Phan's armored battalion said, "We have received no further transmissions from Major Dubrovsky. What has happened? Do you require our assistance?"

Buzz Martin handed the microphone to Nguyen Phan who replied, imitating once more the high-pitched, nasal twang of his captain, "Can you not follow simple orders? Six hours ago you were instructed to hold position. I will ask the major if he needs you."

"Nyet, nyeh nam pomagai'tyeh," (No, don't help us) bellowed Robert Falconi.

"He does not need our help at this time," continued the corporal. "The raiding party was seen turning south onto the coastal highway. Hold your position and prepare to intercept them."

"Yes sir!" came the enthusiastic reply over the radio. "We are prepared to fulfill our patriotic duty."

Nguyen Phan turned off the radio, cutting them short in disgust.

"That should take care of them for a while," he told Major Falconi.

Chapter Thirteen

The location at which the Black Eagles were to rendezvous with the American naval vessel lay a scant four miles to the west. Even on an unpaved dirt trail the halftrack easily made forty-five miles an hour.

"Why don't you brief us on what's waiting for us on the beach, Lieutenant Martin?" said Major Falconi.

"The SEAL team that dropped off me and Gunny also left behind a couple of forty-five horsepower outboard motors buried in the sand with a small supply of fuel. Once we attach the motors to the transoms of the rafts our evacuation should proceed rapidly."

"I think it's time I contact the ship to pick us up. It should be holding position off shore."

Buzz reached for the ANPRC-41 and tried, without success, to put out of his mind the body of Sparks Laird which lay nearby. *There was always a price to pay on these missions,* he thought as he swayed to the rhythm of the bouncing, wallowing armored truck. Thus far, the price had been cheap in terms of numbers, but it was never cheap when weighed against friendships terminated and lives wasted.

The U.S.S. *Loweville,* a coastal patrol frigate, was making ten knots in the calm seas of the Gulf of Tonkin on a north by northeast heading, four miles off the coast of North Vietnam. She had been ordered to cruise from one hundred miles offshore to her present position at 0400 that morning. Her radio room maintained a twenty-four hour watch, expecting to be contacted by a U.S. Navy SEAL team on an ex-filtration mission.

Later that morning Buzz Martin's voice came in over the speaker. "Birddog, this is Buzzard. Acknowledge!"

The radioman notified the officer of the watch who was standing next to the hatchway. The lieutenant, JG, sent word to the captain and then took over the microphone. "Buzzard, this is Birddog acknowledging," he replied. "Give us an update of your situation."

"Birddog, we will be in kickoff position in ten minutes. We will contact you again when the ball is in the air."

"Birddog to Buzzard," came the reply, "message acknowledged. Over and out."

"That's it, Major," reported Lieutenant Martin. "The next time we call them we should be in the water in the two rafts making twenty-five knots straight out to sea. The ship will take us out of the water four miles offshore."

As Buzz Martin spoke these last words, the halftrack broke out of the jungle and entered the long meadow leading to the coastal highway.

"Sir, I have not been able to make contact on the frequency you gave me," reported the North Vietnamese Coast Guard torpedo boat captain over his radio.

The captain's superior officer replied, "Your orders were to patrol the coast immediately south of Hoang Xa. Perhaps the Soviet major commanding the helicopter assault force has a good reason for maintaining radio silence. In any event, you are to be on the alert for the Yankee raiders. We suspect that they may attempt to

224

escape by sea using some form of powered small craft. Look for anything unusual on the beach and report it immediately. We will arrange for shore units to confirm his identity."

"Yes sir," replied the captain. His torpedo boat could make thirty knots when all the engines were in proper tune. He had hoped for one of the newer, aluminum-hulled diesels, but as a naval officer he was grateful to be put in command of anything that floated.

The World War Two vintage craft had recently been retrofitted with Soviet, radar-guided, surface-to-surface missiles. The captain had wondered if he would ever have the opportunity to properly zero in the system under combat conditions.

He looked up from the radio and barked to his second in command: "Make for course two-zero-zero at ten knots!"

"Aye-aye, sir," came the response.

The captain slapped the oversized fiberglass pot onto his head and climbed topside. His second offered field glasses which the captain used to survey the beach.

"From the river estuary, southward, we will patrol a three-mile stretch of shoreline," he instructed.

The torpedo boat passed out of sight of the kickoff point as the halftrack slithered over the final sand dune before arriving at its destination.

"Hit the beach," commanded Top Gordon. "Line up the rafts to the rear of the halftrack." Then Sergeant Gordon joined the team of Seals to locate the package of buried equipment.

"Let's get those motors rigged and get the hell out of here," Top growled.

Robert Falconi addressed Ray Swift Elk: "You and Andrea help me prepare our KGB guest of honor for his departure."

Corporal Phan, late of the North Vietnamese militia,

sat idly behind the steering wheel of his impeccably maintained armored sweetheart and felt suddenly lonely. The realization hit him that his days with the battalion were now over. It was certainly not the military that he would miss. He had nothing left in him but contempt for their childish, albeit sometimes lethal attempts at intimidation and indoctrination. It was ten years since he had lost the two people who were most important to him. Even so, he would soon miss the camaraderie of the weekly drills. But, most of all, he would miss this one tangible object which he had spent so many hours maintaining.

Now he would travel south to join people who shared his hatreds, and he would fight a different kind of war. But he could not bring himself to picture the child of his labors used ever again to oppress the enslaved population of North Vietnam.

I would rather drive it into the sea, he thought, and cringed, instantly, at the image of its steel armor corrupted by the warm, salty water of the Gulf of Tonkin.

Perhaps the tall major will let me do it, he thought, *just before we leave.* With the elevated air intake for fjording rivers, she could plow far enough into the waves to put the driver's seat awash. The thought gave him a brief moment of wicked amusement.

A stiff, contorted Colonel Kraschenko was hauled from the ammunition locker and stood on his feet. He immediately collapsed to his knees because of the lack of circulation in his legs.

"Your desperate plan cannot succeed," Kraschenko said as he glowered at Robert Falconi. "If you agree to surrender your group to me at this moment with no further difficulties, I will arrange that you, personally, will be repatriated to the American Embassy in Moscow at the next exchange of diplomatic prisoners."

Gregori Kraschenko knew that there was no way

General Kuznetz would let him keep that promise.

"Naturally public opinion will force us to put the remainder of your group on trial in Hanoi."

"Check the knots around his wrists," Major Falconi said to Sergeant Swift Elk, disdainfully ignoring the KGB colonel's proposition.

"They are a mite picked at," commented the sergeant, "but they are still tight."

Andrea Thuy sat and watched while Swift Elk massaged the circulation back into Kraschenko's legs.

"Give me your other leg," he said.

Kraschenko made no move to comply.

"When those rafts are put into the water," added Lt. Andrea Thuy, "you can either walk out to them like the rest of us or you can be dragged through the surf by your feet, you Commie pig!"

For the tenth time since the sun rose that morning, Colonel Kraschenko regretted that he had not had the opportunity to personally interrogate the fiery female South Vietnamese patriot. He used his good leg to lever forward the leg that was still asleep to be massaged.

The Coast Guard torpedo boat out of Sam Son had completed the southern leg of its patrol circuit.

"This is far enough," said the captain. "Come about and proceed north!" he commanded. The four Packard V-8 engines growled softly, propelling the craft forward at ten knots. The torpedo boat banked to the left, keeping the shore in sight over its stern, and assumed its new heading.

As they crested the next wave the radar technician reported, "Captain, I think I have a positive radar contact on the beach bearing three-five-oh at four thousand meters."

Even with the field glasses the captain could not make

out the target, but he intended to be ready for any contingency.

"Battle stations," he spoke into the public address system. "Steady as she goes. Lock the target on radar. I want the stern twelve point seven battery ready to fire. If we launch a missile we will then give the target our stern for follow-up fire."

With its exhaust stacks pointed directly astern, the coastal patrol craft presented the smallest possible visual silhouette and noise profile to the beach. It drew closer to the radar contact with every passing second.

"Captain, it appears to be a halftrack from one of our armored militia units," reported the second.

The captain called back to the radio operator, "Raise the base at Sam Son. I want confirmation on the status of one of our halftracks with quad-mount anti-aircraft guns."

Sgt. Eddie Barthe was beginning to feel the effects of the noonday heat. He slogged back to the halftrack from the rafts.

"Major Falconi, the motors are mounted on the rafts, and the gas tanks are tied down," Eddie informed the leader of the Black Eagles. "Lieutenant Martin reports that we are ready to load them up."

Robert Falconi reached over and turned on the ANPRC-41, anticipating that Martin would soon be contacting their ship. He was surprised to hear a voice trying to get his attention from the speaker.

"Dog, Buzzard, this is Birddog, come in!"

"Martin! You are wanted on the radio," Falconi bellowed to the struggling navy lieutenant who was loading cargo into one of the rafts.

Then Robert Falconi picked up the microphone and depressed the transmit button.

"This is Birddog, go ahead."

"Buzzard, you have company, five hundred yards to your southwest."

"That halftrack is the command vehicle for a motorized battalion of the coastal militia," the torpedo boat's radio operator reported to his commanding officer. "Their C.O.'s body was found in a ravine not far from the motorpool."

Through his field glasses the captain could now discern figures around the armored, track-driven truck.

"Attention missile launching team," he growled through the P.A. system. "Target is confirmed. Commence firing sequence."

The technician manning the launch control console looked like a concert pianist as he began manipulating the buttons and switches in front of him.

"Missile away!" he called out. The surface-to-surface missile erupted from its tube and quickly leveled out in flight, homing in on the dot representing the halftrack on the radar CRT screen.

Robert Falconi turned and inspected the area, pointed out to him by the pick-up vessel, in time to see the puff of smoke that followed the launching of the missile. Its rocket trail rose above the horizon briefly, but long enough for him to confirm its nature in his mind.

"Outside," Major Falconi screamed, using the time-honored phrase from World War One that indicated incoming artillery rounds.

His battle-sharpened reflexes enabled him to dive behind a hump of sand quickly, but for Corporal Phan there was no sanctuary from the incoming missile except for the armored relic which was the missile's intended target.

The missile struck the halftrack square in the engine

compartment. The motor was blasted off of its mounts and attempted to follow the hood, which, being much lighter, sailed fifty feet into the air.

Corporal Phan died instantly from the rising cone of shrapnel.

"Gunny, check out the fifties," ordered Buzz Martin.

Gunny, U.S.M.C. managed to rise to a kneeling position before discovering that his left leg would not support him.

"I'm hit, Lieutenant!" he cried out.

Malpractice McCorckel immediately moved to his side.

"Surface-to-surface missile, probably radar guided," said Sergeant Swift Elk to Major Falconi. "The recycling time to fire the second round depends on the skill of the launch team."

Then the heavy thud of a machine gun could be heard from offshore.

"We're pinned down, sir," said Lieutenant Martin to Major Falconi. "The M-sixteens are no good to us at this range, and I think the bazooka went up with the halftrack. I don't think the frigate can help us because of our proximity to the enemy."

"In any event we can't afford to wait for them," Robert Falconi answered.

Sergeant Swift Elk dragged Andrea and Gregori Kraschenko to safety.

Sergeant Barthe ran toward the protection afforded to him by the rear of the blasted halftrack and climbed to the top of the vehicle which now had flames rising from the engine compartment. He inspected the quad 50s.

"They've been blown off their mount!" he exclaimed and searched the sand around him, finding the two detached machine guns.

The two remaining guns were still attached to their mount but were visibly out of alignment.

"You can still aim by tracer fire," said Buzz Martin

who had followed Eddie to the wreck.

Sergeant Barthe jacked back the charging levers of both guns and checked both belt feeds.

"I'll turn the carriage manually," directed Lieutenant Martin.

When the AA mount was pointed in the direction of the patrol craft offshore, Eddie fired. A twin stream of tracers floated away from him. He leaned forward on the grips, raising the barrels of the 50s, and walked the tracers steadily toward the stern of the torpedo boat. Due to the warped mount, one of the stream of tracers floated lazily to the left.

"Captain," reported the second in command. "I don't know how it is possible, but we are taking machine gun fire from the halftrack. And it's damned accurate," he had time to add before a .50 bullet pulped his head, spraying his brains all over the captain's uniform.

"Second missile ready to fire," the leader of the launch crew sounded off.

"Commence firing sequence," answered the captain. "Swing the boat into firing position."

Machine gun fire from both positions stopped momentarily. Sergeant Barthe addressed Lieutenant Martin. "The patrol boat is burning, sir," he said, "but I have a feed problem with the belts."

Together they quickly restored the functioning of the ammunition belt, and Eddie resumed his deadly accurate machine gun fire.

A torpedo boat crew member sprayed foam on the flames that threatened to spread to the gasoline tanks. He was lifted off his feet by two .50 bullets impacting on his chest.

Damned gasoline boats! the captain thought, and watched the second missile leave its tube. Then the growing flames reached the gasoline tanks.

The explosion of the patrol boat obscured the oncoming missile. Eddie and Buzz were deprived of what little warning they might have had. The striking missile obliterated the rear of the halftrack and detonated the fuel tanks, leaving a twisted hulk on the burning sands.

"Where did you get your medical training?" grumbled Jackson White to Malpractice who was sewing up the gash left by a piece of shrapnel that had ripped through the gunnery sergeant's calf muscle.

"I graduated from paramedic school at Fort Sam Houston, Texas," replied Sergeant McCorckel. "But before that I apprenticed with my uncle who was a veterinarian."

"A damned horse doctor. I knew it!" complained Gunny.

"And you're damned lucky to get one," replied McCorckel. "The surgical techniques taught by medical schools are great when you have a sterile operating room, an anesthesiologist, and lots of spare blood. The critters I worked on with my uncle are a lot like you: dirty, and stubborn as hell. I had to learn what's called bloodless surgery, the technique of sewing up the patient in such a way that they won't loose a lot of blood and get infected, even if they have a mind to."

Top Gordon saw to it that the loading of the raft was completed.

"I reckon we'll have no trouble finding room for anyone now," he commented balefully to Major Falconi. "There wasn't enough left of Lieutenant Martin or Sergeant Barthe to bring back."

"But I found their dogtags for graves registration," Robert Falconi consoled him.

The battle-weary, shell-shocked survivors dragged their rafts into the surf. Propelled by the forty-five horsepower outboard motors, they steered toward the waiting frigate, the U.S.S. *Loweville,* which was now in radio contact with Major Falconi.

232

As they drew abeam the burning remnants of the torpedo boat, Colonel Kraschenko finally concluded that he was not going to be rescued from abduction by the Black Eagles. The best he could look forward to was to be returned in disgrace during the next exchange of diplomatic prisoners. His superiors in the KGB would assume that he had been thoroughly debriefed by U.S. Intelligence. Kraschenko had no illusions what kind of unit he would subsequently be assigned to upon repatriation.

He watched the shoreline recede in the bubbling wake of the outboard motors and sat up, bracing himself with his bound hands behind him.

Colonel Kraschenko of the KGB addressed the man whose neutralization had been his military assignment.

"Major Falconi," he announced, "I wish to request political asylum."

When the expression of amazement had receded from his face, a weary laugh issued forth from Robert Falconi.

"You're a little late, Colonel," he responded.

Chapter Fourteen

Maybe I will meet my new contact tonight, thought Lt. Trung Uy Trang Loc, commanding officer of the ARVN Security Detachment at Peterson Field.

"This is the last time I will do business with the Viet Cong," he vowed.

He had sold many of his personal possessions and liquidated his savings. Adding this to the money he expected to receive tonight, he would be able to disappear from South Vietnam and resurface in Hong Kong, claiming to be a refugee.

Under an assumed name, Loc expected to find little difficulty providing security services for a rich patron.

Who knows what the future holds for me, he thought.

Then a dark vision rose from his subconscious, but he quickly brushed it aside. He rationalized that he needed the money too badly to attempt to flee without it.

The American, Major Falconi, seemed unconcerned about his involvement in the kidnapping of Andrea Thuy. The rest of the Black Eagles were apparently unaware of his role. If he had it to do over again, he wondered if his involvement with Comrade Bua could have been avoided.

Loc concluded that there was no way of knowing. Considering the turbulent events of his daily life, and his lack of family, he did not have the perspective to mourn the loss of potential personal ties, to regret the bridges he was burning behind him.

Lieutenant Loc drove carefully into the industrial quarter of Saigon. It was deserted at night. He didn't want to answer any detailed questions by the military police in search of curfew violations.

He arrived half an hour early, as planned, and walked three blocks to the contact position.

However, the hit man, an agent assigned by the North Vietnamese Counterintelligence, expected no less. He had been thoroughly briefed on Loc's background. He, too, had arrived early and had selected the most likely spot from which to detect, unseen, an approach of anyone entering the area.

When Loc backed into the dark recess beside the entrance of the warehouse, the agent shot him once, from behind, in the kidney with a silenced automatic.

Loc turned in surprise. The waves of pain coursed through his body. He sensed impending unconsciousness.

"Comrade Bua has a great deal of work on his hands straightening out the mess your lies caused us," explained Loc's assassin. "But the journey of a thousand miles begins with the first step. With your death we will take that first step."

Lies? Loc thought. He felt the same terror and fleeting confusion that he had experienced when Major Falconi had accused him of being involved with the black market. Loc slumped, unconscious, to the ground. The agent bent over his body, and taking careful aim, administered the *coup de grace*.

Epilogue

Trangville still suffered occasional harassment from the Viet Cong. Mei's brother arrived home after another day's work in the rice fields. After entering the house of his father and mother he ran his hand over the pelt of the tiger which was displayed on the wall opposite the front door. He felt that the tiger's skin had brought the family good luck after the death of his sister.

Mei's father disagreed.

"People who kill tigers make their own luck," he had said.

Tonight was a religious festival. Mei's brother was learning the art of the storyteller. When the daylight faded he would have a chance to display his training.

He was impatient for the sun to set so the evening portion of the festival could begin. In his mind he could still see the figure of Sgt. Eddie Barthe, in tiger-striped, camouflage fatigues, manipulating the swinging arms and legs of the sheet metal figurines from which the shadow show was cast. He could hear Eddie's voice uttering, in Vietnamese, the words of the story of the tiger hunt, with his strange, flat American intonation, and Eddie's

237

rendition of the tiger's fierce growl, as well as the cries of the dying Viet Cong.

The light was fading in the little village. He could sense the feeling of excitement and anticipation from the people he encountered. Perhaps his father was right. Perhaps men who kill tigers do make their own luck.

THE SAIGON COMMANDOS SERIES
by Jonathan Cain

#2: CODE ZERO: SHOTS FIRED   (1329, $2.50)

When a phantom chopper pounces on Sergeant Mark Stryker and his men of the 716th, bloody havoc follows. And the sight of the carnage nearly breaks Stryker's control. He will make the enemy pay; they will face his SAIGON COMMANDOS!

#4: CHERRY-BOY BODY BAG   (1407, $2.50)

Blood flows in the streets of Saigon when Sergeant Mark Stryker's MPs become targets for a deadly sniper. Surrounded by rookies, Stryker must somehow stop a Cong sympathizer from blowing up a commercial airliner—without being blown away by the crazed sniper!

#5: BOONIE-RAT BODY BURNING   (1441, $2.50)

Someone's torching GIs in a hellhole known as Fire Alley and Sergeant Stryker and his MPs are in on the manhunt. To top it all off, Stryker's got to keep the lid on the hustlers, deserters, and Cong sympathizers who make his beat the toughest in the world!

#6: DI DI MAU OR DIE   (1493, $2.50)

The slaughter of a U.S. payroll convoy means it's up to Sergeant Stryker and his men to take on the Vietnamese mercenaries the only way they know how: with no mercy and with M-16s on full automatic!

#7: SAC MAU, VICTOR CHARLIE   (1574, $2.50)

Stryker's war cops, ordered to provide security for a movie being shot on location in Saigon, are suddenly out in the open and easy targets. From that moment on it's Lights! Camera! Bloodshed!

Available wherever paperbacks are sold, or order direct from the Publisher. Send cover price plus 50¢ per copy for mailing and handling to Zebra Books, Dept. 1677, 475 Park Avenue South, New York, N.Y. 10016. DO NOT SEND CASH.

THE NEWEST ADVENTURES AND ESCAPADES OF BOLT
by Cort Martin